Santa Anna's Gold in a Pirate Sea

Jeffrey Roswell McCord

D1158603

Jeffrey R. McCord
5000 Estate Enighed, PMB 364
St. John,
United States Virgin Islands

Book cover design by Alice Gebura

ISBN:0989950824
ISBN-13: 978-0-9899508-2-4 (Jeffrey Roswell McCord)

"I like to think of space and time as analogous to the ocean, and changes in it as analogous to waves on the surface of the ocean; but those waves, of course, don't show up when one's miles above the ocean. It looks flat. Then as one gets down closer to the surface one sees the waves breaking and the foam. . . . [This] quantum foam [has tiny holes]."

— Physicist John Wheeler, in a 1999 PBS "Nova" interview. Wheeler was a contributor to the U.S. construction of the atom and hydrogen bombs during and after World War II.

"St. Thomas is the place that is on the way to every other place."

— Frederick W. Seward, son of William H. Seward, Secretary of State to Presidents Lincoln and Johnson, in his 1872 book "Seward at Washington," writing of transatlantic steamship days and the then Danish Caribbean island of St. Thomas.

CONTENTS

1 A REBEL CAPTAIN AND MEXICAN PRESIDENTE

"The very mention of my name had the same effect upon the Yankee Government as shaking a red flag before the bloodshot eyes of an infuriated bull."

— Captain Raphael Semmes, a raider in the Confederate States of America's Navy, October 3, 1864

"Though tortured before they were killed, these unfortunates [including Davy Crockett] died without complaining."

— an officer in Santa Anna's army who witnessed the murder of several Alamo fighters who were captured alive on March 6, 1836

Had I known that night would change my family's lives forever, would I have done anything differently? Would I have piled everyone into the pick-up truck and driven back up the mountain to our home? Doubtful.

It was a very hot, humid and still May night. I faced

tough odds. "Wagapalooza," the annual dog show benefiting the animal shelter on the Virgin Island of St. John, is one of the island's best attended annual events. Everyone on the island appeared to be present that sultry eve. Fifty or sixty dogs were being restrained.

My husky and I nervously awaited our turn to parade around the circle of grass in the only ball field with lights. Surrounding the "stage" was a colorful mélange of races and nationalities sitting in rows of fold-up chairs and milling about food and drink stalls. White continental transplants predominated. Middle-aged women wore mostly pink, turquoise and lime green accented shirts and white or beige shorts. Off-duty bartenders sported shirts emblazoned with the logos of the growing wide world of beers. Waitresses mostly wore as little as possible.

Afro-European islanders of all ages, too, attended in good numbers. They mostly wore sedate clothing in shades of tan and gray, though low cut calico dresses and sarongs wrapped many young women.

Everyone tried to cool themselves with hand-held fans made of woven palm fronds, folded over pieces of paper and anything else that moved still air around faces. Church women sported purple fans advertising funeral homes.

Waiting behind a rope line were the dogs. Many were a mix of pit bulls, Doberman pinschers and plain mutts familiar to islanders as animal shelter rescues. Training such victims of abandonment or fighting pit castoffs required patience and tenacity. Rescues, though, were often smarter than house dogs and often won "best trick" prizes.

Molly, our white husky, was lovable and mischievous, but didn't do tricks. Looks and congeniality were her strengths. Would she keep her ears erect when our time came? Would she display her full, furry tail in a curl or let it hang limp? She was not bred for hot Caribbean nights.

The officiating disc jockey had already warned folks as

a safety measure to keep dog water bowls filled and owners hydrated with rum or beer. It was water for Molly and beer for me. This was not the Westminster Dog Show.

Our dogs had moved with us from a Virginia farm where they had earned their keep by amusing the family and keeping pests under control. Currying human favor was their skill.

When our show time came, Molly naturally held her tail and ears erect. As we promenaded around the field before the liquored-up, boisterous crowd, Molly cunningly pulled us over to the first row of enthusiasts who petted and fussed over her. She pulled so hard, I spilled my beer.

The eight other entrants in our category had little chance against Molly's iconic husky profile. The "wagometer" measuring applause hit a perfect ten as we pranced around. She was crowned "Best Tail" on the island.

Walking back to our seats with our blue ribbon, St. John-born children surrounded us, tentatively approaching the exotic blue-eyed dog.

"Mister, mister, do he bite?"

"No, she loves children."

"But, is dat a wolf?"

"No, she's a West Indian sled dog," I replied.

I encouraged them to hug the ever tolerant Molly. Eventually, we made it back to our seats. My wife Mary, a petite blonde, and our son John, a tall 20-year-old, were off looking for snacks and water.

Earlier, Mary's standard poodle, Jack, had lost the "best costume" award, despite his indignity at being forced to wear water goggles, snorkel and an inflatable life vest with "Lionfish Killer" written on the side.

Because of his long, curly, black hair, the kids called Jack "Rasta dog." But, Rasta dog lost that night. And, Mary was in no mood to witness Molly winning her category simply by walking around in a circle.

Hard to believe that only one year earlier Naval Intelligence had hired me for the project of a lifetime: investigating the suspicious death of a retired Marine gunnery sergeant whose body washed ashore on St. John's remote Privateer Bay. Who would have guessed the death was related to UFOs? Who would have thought rivalry between national security agencies would place me in legal and physical jeopardy?

Well, that mind-bending assignment was finished. I was back in the comfortable groove of routine duties as maritime history professor at the Territorial College of the Virgin Islands. Still, the long arm of the bad guys had inflicted fiscal harm. Not long after my UFO adventure, my extra "overload" teaching duties — and pay — were sharply reduced. Since I had tenure, they couldn't fire me outright without legitimate cause.

Sure, my research made a huge contribution to what the Navy knows about unidentified flying and submersible objects. My work set in motion a joint National Geographic Institute and National Oceanic and Atmospheric Agency (NOAA) exploration of the five-mile-deep Puerto Rico Trench just offshore of our islands. The esteemed Institute and highly regarded NOAA had no idea their expedition was actually fronting for the Office of Naval Intelligence (ONI).

Certainly they were conducting groundbreaking research of an ocean canyon never fully explored. But, the real mission was to search for signs of unidentified submersible objects. Mapping the Trench floor, discovering new deep sea species, and studying gravity anomalies were all important. ONI operatives, though, were on board the exploration vessel, watching closely for signs of unexplainable objects or activity.

All that was deeply satisfying and I wished them well. Nevertheless, Mary and I were now wracking our brains on how to replace our lost income. Tonight's dog show was good family therapy.

As Molly and I sat enjoying our laurels and drinks, a tall, gray-haired Afro-European gentleman clad in khaki pants and flower print shirt came over.

"Are you Professor Thayer Harris?"

"At present," I replied, sizing him up. He had handsome West Indian features, but the accent of a mainlander.

"My name's Kwame Boateng," he said, extending his hand to shake. "A friend of yours, Commander Taft of ONI, suggested I contact you.

"Oh shit," I thought, "not again."

Taft had been my Navy Intelligence contact and "handler" during the investigation of the Marine's death. He was also part of a Navy cell secretly looking into UFOs.

"How do you know Lieutenant Taft?"

"He's now a Commander. And, he said you're partly responsible for the promotion. He even skipped a grade."

Great. At least somebody got some lasting benefit from our collaboration last year. I had already spent the consulting money I'd earned on repairs to my sailboat's diesel engine – not to mention filling in bullet holes in the mast and boom. The main sail had needed patching, as well. Now, scrambling to recover from my demotion, I found it hard to feel happy for Taft.

"So, how do you know him?" I asked.

"That will take some time to explain," he replied, "May I buy you a beer?"

He motioned to the temporary emergency bar made of a mahogany board set in a bamboo stall at the edge of the field. The beer-bellied, white barkeep stood behind the plank.

"Sure, Kwame, and water for Molly here."

The DJ was playing Toby Keith's country classic "Whisky for My Men and Beer for My Horses" as we walked to the bar.

I looked over the field and spotted Mary in animated

conversation with some island matriarchs. John was surrounded by female admirers. Kwame and I took stools and bellied up to the plank.

"You new to the island?" I asked to get the conversation moving.

"No. I was born right here – up the hill over in Estate Enighed. I joined the Navy after high school, left the island to see the world. First snow I ever saw was at the Great Lakes Naval Training Center in Michigan.

"I was young and excited; only came back a few times over the years. Still, Professor, I have deep roots here. I'm a fifth-generation Virgin Islander. My ancestors were brought as slaves from Guinea. And, we never forgot our roots."

He sipped his beer, looking over at a young West Indian woman in a tight, form-fitting sarong. Without question, she had a good figure.

"What about Commander Taft?" I asked to get his mind back on track, noticing he wore no wedding ring.

"First, you must know of my male ancestors. They brought a special gift from Africa. They'd been great shamans in their village. They could communicate with our ancestral spirits, drawing upon the ancients' strength and wisdom to cure the physically sick and mentally troubled in *this* world."

"What's that you say?" I wasn't sure I'd heard him correctly. How many beers had I downed thus far this hot night?

"I was saying that one male in each generation of my family has the gift to enter the spirit world to help heal those in need here and now. And, in my generation, I am that man – the last of my line."

Sipping my beer, I thought of our islands' Mocko Jumbie stilt walkers. They wore haunting masks and artfully ragged clothes, dancing and gyrating at carnival time as though their legs weren't strapped to wooden sticks six feet above ground. They did seem possessed, supposedly embodying spirits of the dead.

"Do you mean to tell me you communicate with ghosts?"

"Just what is a ghost, Professor?" he asked smiling, "I tell you I *can* reach out to some greater force — an intelligent force — when in a trance. My ancestors believed they were in communion with elders' spirits, believed it so strongly that when immediate family members died, they buried them right outside their doors or under front porches. They wanted them close at hand when needed."

Jeez, I thought to myself. Do I have a sign around my neck saying, "all ye of paranormal mind, come unto me"? First UFOs, now a ghost whisperer.

And, what about those dead relatives? How deep under the porch did they bury them? Wouldn't tree rats, land crabs and mongoose get at them? In this climate, what about odors?

"I see," I said. "So, how do you know Commander Taft?"

"Ah," he replied, "This is where it gets very interesting. After basic training and some fleet deployments, I wished to continue the family healing business. So, I became a Navy Corpsman. Over the years, my success with patients was graded above average — 'phenomenal' was the word used in fitness reports."

I wiped some sweat off my neck with a handkerchief, swatting away a mosquito. The crowd was thinning. Mary, John and the dogs would be ready to leave soon.

"So, where does Taft come in?" I asked.

"A captain in the Medical Service heard about me. He knew of a secret program — project Sun Streak, later called Stargate. Seemed our intelligence people had learned that Russia was recruiting and training people with psychic powers as spies. We were trying to catch up."

I almost choked on my beer.

"Are you kidding? The Defense Department had psychics?"

"Hard to believe, but yes. There was a psychic intelligence gap, you see. The Russians were way ahead of us. So, the Department funded research at Duke University, Princeton and Stanford to catch up."

I ordered another round as Kwame continued.

"I was assigned to a special unit. First, I was their guinea pig. I tested very high for extrasensory perception – probably my father's teachings as a child opened parts of my brain most modern humans don't use. After training, I became an active intelligence agent.

"We used something like astral-projection – out of body traveling, that is – to spy on foreign submarines and other targets. 'Remote viewing' we call it to make it sound more scientific.

"We've even helped locate terrorists and their bases."

Almost speechless, I eventually said, "That's amazing! Did you actually find people and things that way?"

"Let's just say our accuracy rate was way above 50 percent – high enough that the program survives to this day. In fact, not too long ago, the Defense Advanced Research Projects Agency hired a contractor to develop mental telepathy training so soldiers can communicate secretly. Project 'Silent Talk' they call it."[1]

Sipping my beer, I shook my head.

"You mean that all the time psychics, fortune tellers, shamans and others were being called nuts or frauds by the Establishment, our own government was hiring and training them?"

"Yes," Kwame answered, "This is where Commander Taft comes in. He's in charge of the Navy program. That's how he knew my record and Virgin Islands connection. Just before I retired, he called me into his office and suggested I get in touch with you."

I thought a few minutes, trying to remember a book I had read years earlier. Then it hit me: "Psychic Warrior" by a retired U.S. Army officer who claimed he did out-of-body spying in the 1990s.[2]

"That's all fascinating," I said to Kwame, "but, it's way out of my field."

Shit, I thought. If I go near this, the college might just have grounds to get rid of me.

"Why did Taft want you to contact me?"

He laughed as he ordered us both another beer.

"Not so much you, as your wife. You see, I'm a very good corpsman and remote viewer. Now, I want to use these abilities as my ancestors did to help people who are sick in body or mind. Commander Taft said you'd appreciate that; said your wife has a nonprofit group working here to help children with disabilities.

"So, here I am back on-island, a Navy pensioner who wants to volunteer."

Taken aback by the turn in conversation, I took a moment to think it through. This was a blessing. I could do a favor for Commander Taft without much effort. Kwame could then become Mary's problem – er, asset.

"You're right. Mary was appointed to the Territory Board for Persons with Disabilities and does have a group working with kids with special needs. Wait here, Kwame. I'll find her."

She didn't take long to locate and I brought her over for introductions. While Mary and Kwame got acquainted, John, the dogs and I walked to the side of the field. We watched the thinning crowd of revelers.

Almost immediately, Alma, the proprietress of "Miss Alma's," a popular West Indian restaurant, walked over to say hello.

"Why she talkin' to 'im?" she asked, nodding toward Kwame.

I explained his Navy medical training and wish to work with Mary.

"We have saying," she replied smugly, "'Big tree fall down, goat find he leaf.'"

Perplexed, I asked, "What do you mean?"

"I mean, he leave dis island for a hi' 'nd mighty job in

Navy many, many year ago. Now he back – a fallen man out of 'is head."

"You mean he's crazy? Isn't he a shaman?"

She laughed and walked away.

I looked over at Kwame and Mary in animated conversation and thought of Commander Taft. And, guessed I'd need to phone him about Mr. Kwame Boateng.

Meanwhile, with the summer academic break nearly upon us, I could escape into my current research: Confederate naval "raider" activity in the West Indies during the Civil War.

There's no doubt Raphael Semmes prowled these waters as captain of the notorious *C.S.S. Alabama*, a fully rigged sailing vessel and steam ship. She was 220 feet long with a 32-foot beam and a 15-foot draft. Her wooden hull was copper sheathed to reduce fouling. Under sail and with her 300-horsepower steam engine running, she could make 13 knots – faster than most ships of war in her era.[3]

Semmes, a former U.S. Naval officer and attorney, was as sentimental as any officer of his day and more valiant than most. Describing the *Alabama's* 24 officers after the war, he wrote:

> *"Virginia, the grand old mother of many of the States, who afterward died so nobly; South Carolina, Georgia, Alabama, and Louisiana were all represented in the persons of my officers; and, I had as fine specimens of the daring and adventurous seaman as any ship of war could boast."*

Virtually a one-ship navy, the *Alabama* captured and burned at sea 55 Union merchantmen valued at over four and one-half million dollars. She also sank the U.S. Navy's warship *U.S.S. Hatteras* in a battle off Galveston.

Semmes' strategy was simple. When spotting a ship on the horizon, he could tell from her masts and rigging whether she was Yankee or European. If Yankee, Semmes would use steam power as needed to overtake the target, then raise the British flag. When the relieved Union captain raised the stars and stripes in reply, Semmes quickly hauled down the Union Jack and ran up the Confederate ensign. The Yanks always surrendered.

Captain Semmes himself described what usually happened next. After her crew and valuables were taken off, the captured merchantman *S.S. Golden Rocket,* bound for Cuba out of Maine, met a sad fate:

> *"It was about ten o'clock at night when the first glare of light burst from her cabin-hatch. Few can forget the spectacle. A ship set fire at sea! It would seem that man was almost warring with his Maker. Her helpless condition, the red flames licking the rigging as they climbed aloft, the sparks and pieces of burning rope taken off by the wind and flying miles to leeward, the ghastly glare thrown upon the dark sea as far as the eye could reach, and then the death-like stillness of the scene – all these combined to place the Golden Rocket on the tablet of our memories forever."*[4]

At War's end, Semmes, by then a Confederate admiral, was arrested by U.S. forces and charged with piracy. His use of a false flag did seem somewhat unsporting.

My raider research was fun. I hoped a scholarly journal would publish my article, "Civil War in the Caribbean." It might even lead to a book and generate needed money.

Before too far along with my research, however, I stumbled upon a tantalizing fact. William Seward, President Lincoln's Secretary of State, had visited the then Danish island of St. Thomas.

While here, Seward actually met with former Mexican general and exiled dictator Antonio Lopez d' Santa Anna. That's right, Santa Anna – the villain of the Battle of the Alamo and executioner of Davy Crockett – that is, if one believes witnesses who say that hard-fighting frontiersman and ex-Congressman actually survived the epic battle only to be murdered upon capture. By two accounts, Crockett was among five or six Alamo survivors.

One Mexican witness says Santa Anna's soldiers found

Crockett and other Alamo men hidden under mattresses in a barracks room. Nevertheless, they died well:

"Though tortured before they were killed, these unfortunates died without complaining and without humiliating themselves before their torturers," wrote José Enrique de la Peña, a Mexican officer who claimed to have been present.[5]

Secretary of State William Seward, who at the time of the Alamo was a man in his mid-30s and active in New York politics, would certainly have read all about that battle. He would have known Santa Anna's dark reputation. Why, then, would Seward visit the old dictator 30 years later? And, why on St. Thomas?

These questions were tantalizing. It didn't take long to confirm Santa Anna did retire to St. Thomas. Parts of his mansion still stand as a tourist rental called "Villa Santa Anna."

What business did Seward have with His Excellency? I had a hunch the answer could break new ground in American history.

Before trying to track Santa Anna's Caribbean trail, though, I owed it to Mary to phone Commander Taft to check out our new shaman friend, Kwame Boateng. I was also curious about what was happening on the extraterrestrial front.

2 LAND CRABS LIKE COFFEE, CAPTAINS LIKE BITTERS

"The consequences for a person immobilized by illness or injury are too horrible to contemplate."

— British researcher Richard Gillespie commenting on one possible fate of the missing 1930s aviatrix Amelia Earhart – or her body – on a South Pacific island where the land crabs are carnivorous.

"I regret to inform you that twelve cases of [your most beneficial] Plantation Bitters found on board the Ariel, will not reach their destination, having been transferred to my vessel...Sirs, I trust you will not fail to freight each vessel likely to cross my path with Plantation Bitters and I will guarantee to place a case in the hands of [Confederate] President Davis."

— Excerpt from a taunting letter from Confederate Naval Captain Raphael Semmes to the New York manufacturers of an alcohol-laced patent medicine.

Over morning coffee, Mary and I talked about Wagapalooza and people we ran into. Naturally, the mysterious Kwame Boateng came up.

"Can you imagine a retired Navy medic volunteering for our group?" Mary enthused. "He's perfect – medical training, strong enough to help the kids in wheel chairs, and a handsome, tall, successful West Indian role model for the boys."

"Yes, a perfect volunteer," I replied, neglecting to mention his shamanic credentials. Mary had a heart big enough to embrace the homeless, people with special needs and others with challenges. But, she had been skeptical of my work with UFOs and had no great love for Lieutenant – now Commander – Taft or his boss, Admiral Turner. Her misgivings had proven correct – at least for us.

Mary had no need to know her newest volunteer was a psychic spy. All that was behind him, anyway. He deserved to be judged on his work today. Still, I needed to speak with Taft to set my mind at ease.

After breakfast, I took the ferry from St. John to Red Hook, the small St. Thomas port handling most St. John boat traffic. The 20-minute ride over aquamarine waters framed by smaller, thinly inhabited isles conjured thoughts of Sir Francis Drake, Blackbeard and all the other adventurers who had sailed this sea.

Taking the two dollar safari taxi from Red Hook to the college campus near the airport, I passed Charlotte Amalie harbor, still the biggest and best in the West Indies. Once it had been a major center of European-American commerce during the ages of sail and, later, coal-fueled steam ships. The trade routes led from Europe down the west coast of North Africa beyond the Cape Verde Islands and across the Atlantic to the West Indies.

Prior to the abolition of slavery in the British Empire in 1833 and Danish West Indies in 1848, this "triangle of trade" was formed by agricultural products such as sugar, tobacco and cotton carried from the Americas to Europe. Then, European manufactured items were shipped down the coast of Africa to be traded with African chieftains for slaves they kidnapped from interior villages.

Olaudah Equiano, who grew up in an inland Guinean village in the mid-1770s, described his traditional African upbringing in a culture of tribal slavery:

> *"Each master of a family has a large square piece of ground, surrounded with a moat or fence, or enclosed with a wall made of red earth tempered; which, when dry, is as hard as brick. Within this are his houses to accommodate his family and slaves; which, if numerous, frequently present the appearance of a village."*[2]

Mr. Equiano, who was kidnapped from his village by other Africans and sold to several masters in different villages, was eventually taken to the coast and bought by British traders. He and many others were packed in ghastly conditions on sailing vessels and shipped to West Indian ports. That unmerciful leg of the triangle, from Africa to the Caribbean, was the "middle passage." It followed the "trade" winds and Guinea current across the Atlantic – the route Columbus had pioneered.

I was reminded of this tragic history as the safari taxi passed flat land between Charlotte Amalie and what is now French Town. Slaves had once been landed, housed and prepared for sale there in what was then an empty flood plain. Ironically, today it's a container port.

Following the abolition of slavery, the same reliable trade winds and currents were used by mid-19th-century traders in general merchandise, agricultural produce and ore from mines throughout the Americas. With its big, protected harbor, state-of-the-art ship repair facilities, chandlery services, trained stevedores, warehouses for transshipment and fine eating and drinking establishments, St. Thomas became the first port of call for European ships coming to the Americas.

The age of steamships made St. Thomas even more important as a place to refuel with coal. U.S. colliers transported it to St. Thomas in a seemingly never-ending stream that fed mountains of coal stored mostly on Hassel Island in Charlotte Amalie harbor.

British, German and French lines carrying passengers, cargo and mail to the Americas were met in Charlotte Amalie by other ships going north or south. Vessels heading north from St. Thomas could readily pick up the Gulf Stream. Its current alone would carry ships up to the U.S. east coast at a speed of about five-miles an hour.

That rich circle of trade in the 1860s, much of it carried in unarmed U.S. merchant ships, attracted Confederate sea wolf, Raphael Semmes. Nothing in these waters could match the speed and firepower of his brand new British-built *Alabama*. She was a state-of-the-art steamer with full sailing rig and armed with rifled cannon. To increase speed under sail, her steam engine's propeller and shaft could be raised into a recess in the hull. This reduced water flow drag, increasing speed and maneuverability. When needed, her steam power ensured she'd catch any prey.

The exploits of Captain Semmes are well-documented. Now, I wanted to learn more about Santa Anna and Lincoln's Secretary of State, William Seward.

When I arrived at our hillside college campus, however, I went directly to my office, rather than the library. Seward and Santa Anna would have to wait.

Sitting behind the old gray, steel desk (part of the Navy's largess when it transferred barracks and officer housing to the Territory for use as a college), I stared at the 18th century map of the Danish West Indies on the green-painted plywood walls. It was that special shade of light, puke green that once graced many halls in U.S. government office buildings.

Looking at the ancient coffee maker sitting on a file cabinet, I felt an urge. Wrapping the three-day-old grinds in waste paper, I exited the building and walked over grass to the ghut (Danish for run-off stream). In a clatter, the hand-sized and bigger land crabs retreated to their holes as I approached.

I unfolded the paper and dumped the wad of coffee grinds in between a couple of holes. Several raced back out on pointy feet, snapping big fore claws, pushing each other away to get at the delicacy. I wondered if they'd really eat meat as people claimed.

Feeding old grinds to these ill-tempered crustaceans was part of my ritual of brewing coffee at the office. And, it was more fun than throwing lunch scraps out the door to the silently watching three-or four-foot-long iguanas. They could get a bit too aggressive, whipping their tails as weapons.

Back in the office, with a steaming mug of Puerto Rican mountain grown brew in hand, I quickly searched online on my desk-top for tid-bits about the government's use of psychics like Kwame.

A 1995 CNN news brief reported that former President Jimmy Carter publicly said the CIA had used a psychic woman to locate a "special plane" that had crashed in Africa. Satellites had been unable to find it.

Carter said the woman "went into a trance and gave some latitude and longitude figures. We focused our satellite cameras on that point and the plane was there."[3]

"Remarkable," I said to myself.

I then phoned Lieutenant, 'er, Commander, Taft on his secure line.

"Good morning, Professor. To what do I owe the honor of this call?"

"Just phoning to congratulate you on your promotion."

"Thanks. It was a long time coming, but still sweet."

"I'm sure. By the way, who's this witch doctor Kwame Boateng you sent us?"

"I didn't send him — merely suggested he contact my old friend on St. John."

"And, my wife. So, what's his story?"

"Kwame's an excellent corpsman who should have gone to medical school. He's very intelligent, honest and sincerely hopes to give something back to his people."

"What about this 'remote viewing' stuff you had him working on?"

"Well, you know, that's not for public consumption. Since I trust your discretion, I'll tell you that it really does work – not always 100 percent, but often enough for us to pay close attention to what they see and hear on their…travels. Kwame was one of our best."

"Why did he leave?"

"He'd put in thirty years and wanted to go home. It's that simple."

I suspected it might not be, but had to accept Taft's explanation at face value.

"What about our UFO friends? Any luck in the Trenches?"

"Nothing, yet. But, we're making some significant oceanographic and geological discoveries."

"Well, good luck. Feel free to call on me, if you need to."

"Of course we will, Harris. Take care and keep your flare gun handy."

He'd never let me live down the flare gun incident from last year's adventure. But, that investigation was over. And, I doubted he'd contact me again about any unidentified flying or submersible objects they might find. That was well and good.

We rang off with pleasantries and I headed for the library, feeling better about Kwame Boateng working with Mary. President Carter had said the CIA used such people and Taft confirmed the Navy still did. Kwame was legitimate, as far as I was concerned.

Now, I looked forward to escaping into pure historical research. As the Roman historian Livy said, "the best medicine for a sick mind is the study of history."

And, the more I learned about El Presidente Santa Anna and Secretary of State Seward, the less interested I was in my first target, Confederate Captain Semmes. It was obvious that Santa Anna and Seward's St. Thomas meeting was virgin (no pun intended) academic territory – untouched by modern historians.

What had they been up to?

I had ample resources to find out. Two hundred years of English-language West Indian newspapers were available on microfilm, some online. I could also access digitized books and papers in many continental U.S. university libraries from my St. Thomas office and college library.

I quickly traced Secretary of State Seward's interest in St. Thomas and the Caribbean to the final days of the Civil War. Among other duties, President Lincoln had Seward trying to clean-up the legal mess caused by our friend Captain Semmes and his British-built *Alabama*. Owners of private ships and cargoes sunk or seized by Semmes were pressing claims for reimbursement against the Federal government.

Semmes had even publicly taunted Union authorities and cargo owners with a letter he wrote from the Caribbean to the New York manufacturers of an alcohol-laced, popular patent medicine, Plantation Bitters. The addition of St. Croix rum was recommended to make the elixir even more effective.

In a fine example of Yankee ingenuity and marketing prowess, the Bitters' makers published Captain Semmes' letter as a product endorsement in a January 11, 1863 New York Times ad:

Messrs. P. H. Drake & Co, New York:
Gentlemen,
I regret to inform you that twelve cases of Plantation Bitters found on board the Ariel will not be able to reach their destination, having been transferred to my vessel. Having procured one case while at the Island of Martinique, its beneficial effects in my

hospital room and in curing the scurvy was such as to render it too desirable an acquisition to pass, particularly as it was evidently intended for the South from the name 'Plantation.' Rest assured, Sirs, I trust you will not fail to freight each vessel likely to cross my path with the Plantation Bitters, and I will guarantee to place a case in the hands of [Confederate] President Davis before the 1st of March.

I have the honor to remain, respectfully, yours,

RAPHAEL SEMMES [on board the C.S.S. Alabama, December 8, 1862].

In addition to using the letter, the manufacturers went further to capitalize on Semmes' endorsement:

The undersigned are exceedingly obliged to the gallant Captain for such a capital advertisement, and will assure him that, should he happen to visit Fort Lafayette [in New York harbor], we will endeavor to reciprocate his politeness with a case warranted to cure the ennui.

The above is but a sample of the miscellaneous and widespread fame of the Plantation Bitters. No [product] before ever performed so many cures, or gave such perfect satisfaction, 'they are just the thing for the weak, debilitated and careworn of all ages and conditions of life, acting as a gentle stimulant and thorough tonic.'

P. H. DRAKE AND CO.
No. 202 Broadway, New-York.

TRUTH vs. FICTION
HOW ARE YOU, CAPTAIN SEMMES?[4]

Though *Times'* readers must have found the ad humorous (by 19th-century standards), President Lincoln was likely not amused. With the Union Navy finding it impossible to capture Captain Semmes, Secretary of State Seward was pressured to resolve the mounting claims for property lost to Semmes' "piracy."

Seward, in turn, looked at Britain as the logical party to sue for damages. The steamship *Alabama* was, after all, constructed and outfitted with state-of-the-art artillery and fittings by Cammell Laird, one of Britain's finest shipbuilders. And, Cammell Laird had little difficulty completing the sale and delivery of the *Alabama* to the Confederate Navy – all under the nose of Her Majesty's Government, which had been warned by the United States against selling armaments to Confederates.

Eventually, an international arbitration panel decided Seward was correct. In 1871, Britain paid the U.S. $15 million for damage done by the *C.S.S. Alabama*. One observer said, "The defenselessness of Canada made it highly desirable for Britain to reach an amicable settlement with the United States."[5]

Beyond suing Britain, though, Seward had bigger plans. Captain Semmes and other rebel blockade runners had sold booty and re-provisioned at many West Indian islands. These included Danish St. Thomas, Dutch Curacao, French Martinique and British Antigua. Seward concluded and told Congress the U.S. needed a Caribbean island of its own for a Naval base.

Secretary Seward began corresponding with the officially neutral Danish government about purchasing its West Indian colony. The Danes were interested in selling for the right price. The haggling stretched on for months and years.

By April 1, 1865, the Union had virtually won the Civil War. The Confederate capital of Richmond, Virginia was abandoned by its government on April 2. To avoid its capture, the promoted Admiral Raphael Semmes, who was protecting the James River port of Richmond, burned his war fleet.

Victorious federal troops entered Richmond on April 3 and President Abraham Lincoln himself toured the city the next day. Freed slaves flocked to see and touch "Father Abraham." Some had fathers and grandfathers shipped from Africa to the West Indies where they'd been purchased and brought there by southern traders.

Ninety miles away, people in Washington were already celebrating victory and the end of the war. Among them was Secretary of State William Seward.

That month of April, 1865, however, marked a sharp downturn in Seward's personal life. On April 5th, while Lincoln was still in Virginia, Seward was riding downtown in an open carriage. Suddenly, his horses spooked, raced out of control and Seward was thrown out onto the cobblestone road. He broke an arm in two places and suffered a severely broken jaw, among other injuries. The 65-year-old would be bedridden for weeks as wounds and bones slowly healed. These were the days before antibiotics and effective orthopedic surgery.

To make matters much worse for Seward, less than two weeks later at about 10pm on Good Friday, April 14, Lewis Powell, a former Confederate cavalry man, talked his way into the Secretary's Washington home on quiet Lafayette Square. Seward's 35-year-old son, Frederick, met Powell at the top of the stairs leading to the bedrooms.

First telling a skeptical Frederick he was delivering medicine for his father, Powell next pulled a revolver from his overcoat, aimed at Frederick's head and pulled the trigger. The gun failed to fire. So, Powell repeatedly smashed the pistol on Frederick's head, fracturing his skull in two places and leaving serious contusions. He collapsed unconscious. Later, surgeons pulled two pieces of bone from his brain.[6]

Meanwhile, in a nearby bedroom, Secretary Seward's daughter Fanny was reading to her still bedridden father. Sitting with them was Sergeant George Robinson, a wounded invalid soldier serving as Seward's nurse. Hearing the fight on the landing, Sergeant Robinson opened the door. Powell burst in, thrusting a Bowie knife toward Robinson's chest. Robinson parried the blow with his arm, but the knife hit him in the forehead, knocking him down.

Powell then jumped onto the Secretary's bed, stabbing at Seward's head. The Secretary's right cheek was nearly cut off as Powell stabbed both sides of his throat searching for the jugular vein. Fortunately, Robinson got up off the floor and jumped on Powell. As they wrestled on the Secretary's sick bed, Seward rolled off on the other side.

Fanny's screams woke up Seward's other son, Augustus, a Union Army major, who ran into the room, joining Robinson in trying to subdue Powell, a large, powerful veteran. Augustus was stabbed twice in the head, the knife penetrating to his skull bone, and severely wounded in his hand. But, they got Powell out of the bedroom. Robinson, now deeply wounded in the right shoulder, looked for Secretary Seward as Augustus searched for his pistol.

Powell rushed down the stairs, stabbing an Army Department messenger named Hanzell who had been in a lower room and was coming up the steps to see about the commotion. Powell ran out of the house yelling, "I'm mad! I'm mad!"

Inside, Frederick, the most seriously wounded, Augustus and Hanzell were all bleeding. Fanny and Robinson, who was still on his feet despite his wounds, found Secretary Seward behind his bed in a pile of blankets and growing pool of blood. Seward, who was conscious and clear-headed, told them, "I am not dead. Send for the police and a surgeon and close-up the house."[7]

Neither Seward nor anyone in his house had any idea that Powell's attack had been ordered by John Wilkes Booth. Seward's murder was supposed to occur at the time President Lincoln was killed in Ford's Theater, a few blocks away. Vice President Andrew Johnson was also ordered murdered by Booth who aimed to behead the Yankee government.

Luckily for Johnson, the Vice President's would-be assassin, George Atzerodt, a German immigrant, lost his nerve, got drunk and rode out of the city into the Maryland countryside, leaving behind a revolver and Bowie knife in his hotel room. Tragically, Lincoln's luck ran out that terrible night.

Although Secretary Seward and his son Frederick survived their wounds, two months later Seward's wife Francis died of a heart attack. That very day, Lewis Powell, Atzerodt and three other Lincoln assassination conspirators were sentenced to death by hanging. The condemned included Mary Surratt, the first woman executed in the United States.

By odd coincidence, Admiral Semmes was incarcerated on piracy charges in the same "Old Capitol Prison" as Lincoln's assassins. Semmes must have heard the noise of their trial, held in a large prison common room. More ominously, he must have also heard the hammering and sawing of workers building the gallows outside the prison windows. And, the sounds of the crowd witnessing the multiple hanging would have been unmistakable.

Fortunately for Semmes, federal officials released him a few months later. He was permitted to return to his home in Mobile, Alabama.

Seward and his son Frederick took months to recover from their wounds. Like many a modern American, Seward decided a Caribbean cruise would help restore their health. Recovered, though with permanent facial scars, Secretary of State Seward (having kept his job under President Andrew Johnson, Lincoln's successor) commandeered a Navy steam ship and headed for the Caribbean in early January, 1866. Frederick and Fanny went with him.

Just three months earlier, in October, 1865 Santa Anna had written to President Johnson from St. Thomas, offering to help the U.S. rid Mexico of the French who were then occupying the Republic. This letter would later have unintended consequences for El Presidente Santa Anna.

Secretary Seward's first Caribbean stop was the Danish West Indies on January 9, 1866. Frederick described first seeing the archipelago on the horizon, "Out of the blue and tranquil sea were islands rising on every hand of varying size and form."[8]

The Sewards were charmed by St. Thomas, with its "high steep hills covered with verdure, and rows of square yellow houses and red roofs resembling a toy German village." Upon disembarking at Charlotte Amalie's King's Wharf, Frederick was pleasantly surprised by the mostly Afro-Europeans happily going about their business "laughing, talking and gesticulating."

They noticed the lack of carriages and wagons in the town's narrow streets and alleys. Instead, a variety of tropical fruits, vegetables and manufactured goods were carried by men riding donkeys, women balancing loads on their heads and carts pulled by donkeys or oxen. The Sewards loved the flowers and "luxuriant vines and creepers" in residential walled gardens. Inside homes, they enjoyed "cool rooms filled with easy chairs, fans, shades and screens."

Lavish state dinners were held in Secretary Seward's honor and meetings with leading citizens were arranged. He and the family also toured local attractions, including Blackbeard's and Bluebeard's Castles that capped two of the three hills commanding the harbor. Both "castles" had been Danish military observation towers built in the late 1600s. Tourists were told they had been used by pirates.

On Charlotte Amalie's third hill below the Danish vice governor's home, ex-Mexican President Santa Anna lived in an airy villa with spacious grounds overlooking the bay. He warmly invited Secretary Seward to visit. Seward agreed.

Frederick described their meeting with Santa Anna:

"In response to [General Santa Anna's] message of welcome and good wishes, Seward called to visit him. [The General] rose from a table covered with papers to bid the American Secretary welcome with Castilian courtesy, and then sat down to chat awhile on the past, present, and future of Mexico. He was a large, fine-looking man of Spanish features and complexion, dark, keen eyes, and dark hair, and showed no signs of bodily infirmity save a slight limp. One would have pronounced him between fifty and sixty instead of being, as he really was, nearly seventy.

"Briefly recapitulating his position [on] Mexican national politics, he said he was a Republican; that his countrymen had failed in maintaining their independence [against the French] because they lacked organization and a head; that partisan dissensions had opened the way to the French invasion, but that French domination was repugnant to Mexicans.

"[Santa Anna said he was anxious to help rid Mexico of the French], that he was impatient for the coming of that time; that he once sacrificed one leg fighting for his country, and was now ready, if need be, to sacrifice the other; that in the coming contest he looked and hoped for American sympathy and aid."[9]

Santa Anna also told Seward that Benito Juarez, the leader of the Mexican opposition, was not competent to unite the nation and throw out the French. Only he, Santa Anna, could do so.

Unfortunately for him, Santa Anna did not mention his belief that Seward's visit was in response to the General's letter to President Johnson offering his services. Certainly, Seward did want the French out of Mexico. He wanted teeth put in the Monroe Doctrine. All Europeans must leave their American colonies, in his view.

Santa Anna was more than willing to make deals with his former American enemies. While still in power back in 1853, El Presidente Santa Anna sold about 30,000 square miles of what is now southern Arizona and New Mexico to the Americans for $10 million. The U.S. likely used its brand new $3 gold coins to settle what is known as the Gadsden Purchase.

Santa Anna personally pocketed about $6 million of Gadsden money, adding to his already ponderous wealth. Today, his Gadsden skim alone would be worth more than $200 million.

During the 1850s, Santa Anna was also an unsavory slave trader. He kidnapped thousands of Mayan Indians in the Yucatan peninsula and sold them to Cuban sugar planters.

No wonder locals reported seeing many trunks of gold and silver unloaded at the King's Wharf when Santa Anna arrived in St. Thomas in the spring of 1858. He brought so many Mexican silver dollars that some said they caused inflation in Charlotte Amalie's economy. Local historians call it the "Mexican silver crisis."

In addition to a treasure in specie, Santa Anna also brought a retinue of relatives, retainers and supporters.

"I stopped here to continue my tranquil life," he said upon arrival. "The door to discord has been closed forever."

He had a very comfortable life in St. Thomas. He purchased a villa and several adjacent properties, forming a compound on fashionable Denmark Hill. Villa Santa Anna was just below the mansion Catherineberg, then home of the Danish vice governor. Today it's the official residence of the governor of the United States Virgin Islands. As an editorial in the local newspaper urged him to do, El Presidente did "feel pleasure" living in Charlotte Amalie.[10]

Ironically, in 1862, with Santa Anna living the life of a celebrity on shore, a U.S. Navy steamer (the *USS San Jacinto*) visited St. Thomas harbor in search of Captain Semmes or other Confederate "pirates" who had reportedly stopped there to do business. The federal ship was named after the Battle of San Jacinto, the final engagement of the Texas war of independence.

During that 1836 battle on the banks of the San Jacinto river, the fleeing General Santa Anna was captured dressed as a common soldier. Texan General Sam Houston's soldiers caught Santa Anna hiding in high grass. His true identity was given away when another prisoner addressed him as "El Presidente."

Always a ladies' man and dandy, the night before the San Jacinto battle, Santa Anna is rumored to have had sex with a beautiful 20-year-old, local, indentured servant woman until daybreak. An editor in 1842 described what happened, according to a witness (who may have been Sam Houston, himself):

> *"The Battle of San Jacinto was probably lost by the Mexicans owing to the influence of a mulatto girl [Emily] belonging to Colonel Morgan. Emily was closeted in the tent with General Santa Anna [all night and] at the time the [sun rose]and Mexican soldiers raised the cry `the enemy! they come! they come!' [she] detained Santa Anna so long that order could not be restored.'* [11]

Folk legend benighted young Emily as the "Yellow Rose of Texas," immortalized in a then popular, but racist song:

> *There's a yellow girl in Texas*
> *That I'm going down to see;*
> *No other darkies know her,*
> *No darkey, only me;*
> *She cried so when I left her*
> *That it like to broke my heart,*
> *And if I only find her,*
> *We never more will part.*

Chorus:

> *She's the sweetest girl of color*
> *That this darkey ever knew;*
> *Her eyes are bright as diamonds,*
> *And sparkle like the dew.*
> *You may talk about your Dearest Mae,*
> *And sing of Rosa Lee,*
> *But the yellow Rose of Texas*
> *Beats the belles of Tennessee.*[12]

Although he lost Texas and opponents eventually forced him out of Mexico, Santa Anna enjoyed life as a West Indian grandee. Women were plentiful for a wealthy, active man in his 60s. St. Thomas "ladies – many of them young and beautiful – are seemingly fresh at every entertainment," observed a 19th-century Charlotte Amalie physician.[13]

Beyond dalliances, it's possible Santa Anna, who was married, kept a 19-year-old mistress and child living in a rented Charlotte Amalie house next to a town house he owned. Señorita Emilia Trabuc, unmarried and with no job, had arrived from Cartagena, Columbia. Catagena had been Santa Anna's last port of call before moving to St. Thomas. Emilia had an infant daughter born on the island and was attended by three servants.[14]

Santa Anna was an avid gambler on local horse and donkey races. He also raised and fought game cocks. To satisfy all his appetites, gold and silver coins were always at hand.[15]

Just what happened to all that gold and silver? From available records, it sure looked as though Santa Anna had brought a lot more to St. Thomas than he spent during his eight years there. Like other piratical gents in these parts, he may not have trusted banks.

The questions were many.

Did Santa Anna bury or hide trunks of gold? And, if he had, who would know about it? Few people today even know he lived in Charlotte Amalie. His stay there is at best an historical footnote.

I thought about the possibilities on the ferry ride back to St. John.

3 THE SEA IS A HARSH MISTRESS

"There is nothing more enticing, disenchanting and enslaving than a life at sea."

— Joseph Conrad, "Lord Jim," 1900

"Hang the expense," I proclaimed to the men lounging amid the machinery, engine parts and beer bottles filling most of the shack under the sea grape trees. "The Yacht Club lounge," I called that open-sided, tin-roofed hut, replete with broken-down beach chairs, moldering paperback books and an old wooden desk.

Presided over by Albert, the sea chandler, the building was the nerve center of the Coral Bay boat yard. It's where ship wrights picked up work, and wisdom and justice were dispensed in Coral Harbor – the favored anchorage and mooring site within the vast, pristine Coral Bay comprising much of St. John's eastern quarters.

"I tell you, I won't give up *Perseverance* unless she sinks or my wife sells her out from under me!"

One must stand firm in front of the men. No sign of fear can be shown.

"Well-said, Harris," Albert offered, standing up from

his desk chair. "A toast to the Professor!"

Heinekens were raised, clinked and gulped down by several weathered seamen hanging out in the shade. One young man wore a cap under his long, blonde hair proclaiming his boat's name: *Buxom*. She was a forty-five foot wooden schooner built right there. Named after his mother, Albert says.

We were discussing chronic problems with the in-board diesel engine and the propeller shaft's stuffing box on my family's thirty-year-old, cutter-rigged sailboat. The stuffing box encases the shaft where it goes through the hull of the stern. The box is filled with packing – oiled oakum in the old days, now mostly teflon strips – to cushion the propeller shaft so it doesn't chaff the fiberglass or wooden hull as it revolves. The box also keeps water from pouring in.

Unfortunately, this critical box is inconveniently located, requiring acrobatics to crawl over the entire engine in a small hot compartment to adjust a bolt controlling the aperture of the hole where the shaft enters the box. If the bolt is too loose, water will rush in. If too tight, the shaft can't turn properly.

Although a good sailor, I knew nothing about engines. And, my six-foot-two frame didn't fit easily into the engine compartment. Relying on helpers had been my solution. I had already paid to have the stuffing box issues taken care of. Could the shaft and engine be out of alignment? Had my helpers proven unhelpful?

It was shaping up as another lesson in the ABC's of modern seamanship. Boat stands for "break out another thousand."

Sadly, my accounts were running dry, even as water rose in the bilge. Naturally, the automatic bilge pump was also malfunctioning. This was an example of why most boats sink at their mooring or dock, rather than in a dramatic storm at sea as depicted in the movies.

Perseverance would not meet that fate. I could hand

pump the water out and finagle the bilge pump to keep the leak under control until I thought of a solution.

"Captain Semmes had engineers aboard the *Alabama*," I thought to myself, as I considered my next move. Should I hire local talent to solve the problem or go to a marina? Nanny Cay on nearby Tortola is a marina where every part imaginable is available, as are skilled artisans and mechanics. It also has a Caribbean beach and tiki bar to keep Mary and John happy while boat work progresses.

Undecided, but eager to get back to my real job, I said to the crew in the shack, "Catch you later, gentlemen." Head erect, shoulders back, I walked out from under the shanty roof and overhanging tree limbs, up the dirt lane to my aging Toyota pick-up truck. It, at least, was a sound vessel.

I'd often thought that, whether modern Mexican revolutionary, Middle Eastern guerilla or Caribbean sailor, Toyota pick-ups were the vehicle of choice for men of action. Just watch CNN and see what the latest batch of gunmen are driving across the desert.

Before I could reach the truck, however, Harry Elliott came up behind me and put a hand on my shoulder. A thin six-footer with a long, angular face, Harry always wore a faded, red Mount Gay Rum cap atop his short, graying blonde hair. The cap messaged that he'd raced around Barbados in one of the Caribbean's leading sailing regattas. His blue, short-sleeved shirt and pink shorts were also classic, old-salt attire.

Harry was an expert seaman and mechanic. He ran a salvage business and had come to the rescue of many boaters run aground. He'd also saved more than a few from sinking at their moorings.

Not bashful about racing to an abandoned wreck on the rocks – or on the bottom – to claim salvage rights, Harry was an expert diver and commanded a good crew. Proudly calling themselves "pirates," they actually worked (mostly) within applicable U.S. and international maritime laws and codes.

"Don't lose heart, Harris," Harry said. "I've made every sailing mistake in the book and my boat's still afloat. We'll get that engine fixed. It's probably something simple. We can handle it right here."

As he spoke, he hesitated as a shapely, young brunette with a canvas boat bag walked closely by us and down the path to the dinghy dock.

"She's out of our league – even if we weren't taken," Harry observed, shaking his head.

To change the subject, I asked about business at his Square Rigger Trading Company. In addition to salvage operations, he was one of the few T- shirt makers anywhere who was a master of the dying art of real screen printing to emboss real cotton shirts. He also owned and operated an historic 110-foot, steel schooner, *The Black Knight,* rumored to have been used as a rum runner out of Florida during Prohibition days by Joe Kennedy, father of President Kennedy.

"How's business?" I asked, genuinely concerned.

"Been busy all season, but slowing down a bit now," he said, referring to the Caribbean high season of winter months now behind us. "It seems all the rich people are hiding."

"Yes, most have gone back to the real world."

" I can't complain too much," he continued. "Been a hard winter, though, for the sailing charters."

True enough. For two or three months, the Trade Winds had blown between 20 and 30 mph with three- to six-foot swells virtually every day. For those who lived aboard in Coral Harbor, it was weeks of boats rocking and bucking at their moorings. Hard to sleep. And, harder still to take tourists out for day sails.

"Well, the wind has calmed; let's hope it's clear sailing for a few weeks," I said. "Now, I must be on my merry way back up the road."

I climbed into the truck and headed back up Bordeaux

Mountain to cross the ridge line road leading to our house above Cruz Bay on the other end of the island. To take my mind off the boat, I thought about Santa Anna's gold. Could it be buried somewhere on St. Thomas or St. John?

I was shaken from my reverie by a half-dozen feral donkeys standing in the road. Getting out to pet the tamer ones and move them all off the road, I looked at the rocky cliffs and verdant hillsides. Treasure could be hidden anywhere.

Santa Anna wouldn't have stashed it on St. Croix, 60 miles away and much more populous back then. And, St. Thomas was too busy a place. St. John, though, was a likely spot to hide something in the 1860s. In those days, it had only a couple hundred residents – mostly old ex-slaves freed by the Danes in 1848 and youngsters born freemen thereafter.

One of them must have been the male ancestor of Kwame Boateng. Probably the island medicine man, I thought.

After reporting in to Mary about the boat, we sipped drinks on the porch and watched the splendid sunset. I asked about Kwame and his work with special needs kids.

"He's doing great," she said, motioning for a refill of her bourbon glass. "He's gentle and knows as much about medicine as many doctors. He also knows how to manage children – guess that goes with being a Navy petty officer, or whatever he was."

"That's great," I replied, avoiding mention of his peculiar specialty or, for that matter, the details of the latest boat dilemma.

Later that night, I went back online to try to find more about Santa Anna's movements in the Caribbean. I had ordered the definitive biography of the "Napoleon of the West," as Santa Anna styled himself, and thought it should have arrived in the mail by now.

Next morning, I was at the white concrete U.S. Postal Service building across the street from the old Danish fort and former island administrator's home. Waiting my turn in a long line, I eventually got to the window.

"Good morning," I said brightly to the postmaster who was a woman resplendent in corn-rowed hair and sea-shell necklace.

"Good morning, Professor. What can I do for you this fine day?"

"I'm waiting for a book that was mailed from the mainland over two weeks ago. It's not in my box."

"No worries. Soon come."

I thought to myself, "not 'soon come'." That was the favored response of islanders whenever a work deadline was missed or a shipment was overdue.

"Excuse me, ma'am," I said sweetly. "I didn't quite hear you."

"I said, dooo not worry; it will come soooon," she said loudly; then, sternly called, "Next."

Wondering whether a female postmaster should really be called a postmistress, I departed and walked down the sidewalk near the customs dock. Self-absorbed, I almost bumped into none other than Sir Keithley. He claimed to be the bastard son and only blood heir of Lord Claymore, but had no way to prove it. But, we still called him Sir Keithley or Lord Claymore, depending upon the occasion.

He was heading toward "Caps Place," a loud bar some called shady – and not because it shields patrons from the sun.

"My goodness, Keith," I said with genuine surprise. "Who let you out of Coral Bay?"

He looked me over with blood shot eyes and straightened his oil and salt stained Royal Navy captain's hat. Its gold crown atop an anchor was thread bare, though still visible above the cap's visor.

"Why, they let me out for good behavior now and then, matey," he replied with a laugh that bobbed the graying, black pony tail emerging from his cap. "Came over to do err'nds; but first, need a drop to set me straight," he said, pointing at Caps.

Here in Cruz Bay, he was a fish out of water. His closely cropped salt and pepper beard and moustache clothed a thin, red face. Skinny, sun mottled legs emerged from weathered, baggy Gurkha shorts. The sleeves had been cut off his grimy, khaki tropical officer's shirt, open halfway to his navel, revealing a thin silver chain from which hung three Spanish pieces of eight.

He'd be fashionable in an isolated village in Kenya or at Skinny Legs bar in Coral Bay. Here, with a few upscale tourists off small, luxury cruise ships still milling about, he was a tad out of place. He did provide local color, though.

"Well, it's good to see you here in the big city," I said as we both entered the bar's open archway. "What are you drinking?"

I needn't have asked. It was common knowledge throughout the Lesser Antilles that Sir Keithley only drank Pusser's rum of Royal Navy fame. Hearing his stories was worth the extra cost of springing for a Pusser's or two.

"Pusser's, straight up now, no ice, no bullshit," he cautioned the bartender. It was ginger beer for me, it being too early in my day for alcohol. But, for Sir Keithley, an "eye opener" was in order every morning. Just like many an aristo back in Merry Olde.

"So, how did you get over from Coral Bay, my lord?"

He had no transport other than his aging 48-foot Brigantine, the *Bonne Chance*. She was as genuine a 19th-century sailing vessel as one could build in the 20th-century. As a point of pride, he had no radar, but did have running lights and a radio, as required by the Coast Guard.

"Why, I sailed over, don't you know. What'd you think?" he said with a note of shock. "I anchored 'er in Frank Bay and walked to town. Came over for some supplies."

"You know, Keithley, you're just the man I wanted to talk to. You've been in these islands as long as anybody I know. Have you ever hunted treasure?"

He cocked his head, downed his rum and looked me in the eye. Fingering his three pieces of eight, he asked: "How'd you think I got these? In a f'ckin' shop?"

As he looked at his empty glass, I waited in vain for him to continue.

"Another Pusser's for his lordship," I yelled.

It came quickly since it was still early morning and the bar was fairly empty. With glass in hand, Sir Keithley continued, "See, laddie, about the time I was working with the crews dredging the 'arbor of Road Town over in Tortola – must 'ave been thirty years ago – I 'eard all them stories of ol' Black Sam Bellamy. The Prince of Pirates 'e was called back in the time of Blackbeard."

He paused for a sip.

"Well, sir, Black Sam 'ad a small fleet and made 'imself real comfortable-like in Trellis Bay over on Beef Island where the Tortola airport is now. He captured many a rich ship out Anegada way and 'ad a cozy arrangement with an old mate of 'is from Port Royal who was the Brit Guv'nor.[1]

"And, the Danish Guv'nor also made merry with old Black Sam and even Blackbeard in those days. Why, they knew Charlotte Amalie by its original, better name – Tapphus, meaning beer hall. It was a bigger port and had more trade in all goods – legal and otherwise – than Road Town. And, ol' Black Sam gave the Dane Guv a nice cut of any booty 'e sold there."

Sir Keith downed his remaining rum and cleared his throat.

"Damn," he said, pointing to his Adam's apple. "Got this little tickle 'ere."

"Another round for Lord Claymore," I yelled.

"Well, sir, Black Sam was real comfy in these islands; plenty of easy merchant ships to take; friendly authorities; good, safe harbors where 'e could 'ide a fleet, if necessary."

"So, what happened?" I asked, growing impatient.

"What usually brings down a man? You needn't

answer. I'm a'gonna tell you."

He looked me in the eye and slapped the bar.

"A woman! Why 'e could 'ave had his pick of any squeeze from Jamaica to St. Kitts – could 'ave 'ad a bloody 'arem, if he wanted. But, 'e 'ad to 'ave just one and she was up Cape Cod way."

He paused for another sip.

"Maria Hallet was 'is first love, see. Today, she's known as the Witch of Wellfleet. But, she must 'ave been very sweet, indeed. So, Black Sam leaves 'is piece of paradise and sails north with his fully rigged three-masted ship, the *Whydah,* filled with four or five tons of gold, silver, jewelry and what not.

"But, 'e runs right into a fierce nor'easter off the Atlantic Coast of the Cape in 1717. And, don't you know it, now. He wrecked just off that coast a few miles from the port of Wellfleet – right across the dunes was 'is sweet 'eart in that nice, safe Cape Cod Bay port."

"So, what happened?"

"Black Sam and most of the crew were lost. The few survivors were taken to Boston, tried and 'ung."

"Where do you come in?"

"See, I already knew the story of Black Sam – who doesn't? But, it must 'ave been in the mid-80s that news reached Tortola that treasure 'unters thought they'd found the *Whydah* and were forming a team to salvage 'er.

"Now, that there struck my fancy. By then, I was a diver – even explored wrecks right 'ere. So, I hopped on as a crewman on a yawl sailing up to Marblehead and made my way out the Cape. Got myself hired on the *Whydah* salvage vessel."

"An incredible story," I said sincerely. "So then what happened?"

"I dove on 'er for about a year – earning top wages, mind you, and a few souvenirs," he explained, fingering his pieces of eight. For an instant, he looked vacantly at the wall, lost in time's (and Pusser's) mists. Then he continued.

"Six million dollars was raised from investors to salvage 'er. And, they recovered more than $300 million in treasure by the end. But, me, I got bored – tired of diving in cold, rough water and the stand-offish, New 'ngland ladies on shore. Made enough to come back to these islands and build my *Bonne Chance,* though. And, a bit more than that, I should say."

Quite a story, indeed. I had a couple more questions.

"So, the salvagers . . . er, salvors, I guess it is . . . They got to keep the treasure? I mean, was there any other claim?"

"Well now, the f'ckin' Commonwealth of Massachusetts tried to seize it because it was in Commonwealth waters, don't you know. But, they lost in a court battle! Seems the ancient law of the sea still rules, by God. An abandoned boat belongs to the finder, as it bloody well should."

He looked down into his glass again. I bought him another, but vowed to myself that was the last on my tab.

"So, Keithley, have you ever hunted for treasure on land?"

"Can't say I 'ave. But, that'd be tricky what with land owners and such. Very tricky. You may know that an early resort owner found relics – a cannon, musket remains and such – out on the shore of Tortola's Trellis Bay. Bet it belonged to old Black Sam 'imself back in the day.

"But, t'was on the finder's property, see. So, no problem. Now, if you don't own the land, you'd 'ave to make yourself a deal with the owner or go in on the sly, if you know what I'm saying."

"Yes, I see." I was already thinking along those lines. Keith leaned over, clasped my arm and squeezed.

"Now, look 'ere lad," he said in earnest. "I'm game to join any sport – land or sea. Just let me know 'ow I can 'elp."

With that, I left him relaxing at the bar. By then it was

near noon and Cap's Place was coming alive – bar and tables filling up and a mix of salsa and calypso music blared into the street.

That evening, while John played with our two dogs in the yard, Mary and I had drinks on the deck. I told her Sir Keithley's story.

"Why, that old fool!" she said. "He's a drunk and a pirate himself. And, he's certainly no aristocrat."

"That may be true," I said. "but, nobody knows these waters better than him."

"Speaking of water," she said. "Can Sir Keithley fix our leak and bilge pump?"

I admitted he could not.

"Don't worry, she's pumped out and the leak is slow. I got the bilge pump reconnected to the battery; should be fine for a couple of days."

"We'll see," she replied.

4 A LEGACY OF CHICLETS

"Thomas Adams attempted to make toys, masks, rain boots, and bicycle tires out of the chicle from Mexican sapodilla trees, but every experiment failed. One day in 1869, he popped a piece of surplus stock into his mouth and liked the taste."

— About.com[1]

"[Y]ou are a sneaking puppy, and so are all those who will submit to be governed by laws which rich men have made for their own security; for the cowardly whelps have not the courage otherwise to defend what they get by knavery; but damn ye altogether: damn them for a pack of crafty rascals, and you, who serve them, for a parcel of hen-hearted numbskulls. They vilify us, the scoundrels do, when there is only this difference, they rob the poor under the cover of law, forsooth, and we plunder the rich under the protection of our own courage."

— Pirate Black Sam Bellamy speaking in 1700 to the captain of a captured British merchant ship somewhere in the Lesser Antilles[2]

Having dispensed with the boat for a couple of days I felt comfortable returning to Santa Anna.

I'd determined the Napoleon of the West had brought a vast fortune in gold and silver to St. Thomas. Unfortunately for him, he'd ultimately be swindled out of part of his booty by clever con artists, lawyers and Washington lobbyists.

Santa Anna had convinced himself that Secretary Seward's visit with him on St. Thomas had been a watershed event. Seward's polite questions about his health and views on Mexico must have greater significance than small talk, El Presidente was certain:

"From the diplomat's mysterious conduct, I understood his intentions." [3]

Santa Anna believed Seward's visit was a secret signal that U.S. President Andrew Johnson supported his return to Mexican power. So, Santa Anna hired a representative in Washington. Meanwhile, on St. Thomas, watching all this were two of his South American business associates. Well aware of El Presidente's immense vanity and self-delusional prowess, they hatched a plan.

They prepared and showed His Excellancy forged documents they claimed had come to them from Seward's staff. The papers proved the Americans supported Santa Anna's return to Mexico. All he needed to do was buy a boat, arms and supplies and the U.S. would back him. These were to be procured in New York. His business associates would handle it all for El Presidente.

Santa Anna gave deeds to certain properties to the schemers. They took the next steamer to New York where they promptly sold the deeds to bankers, pocketed the money and disappeared. Meanwhile, the unknowing Santa Anna worked on a proclamation to Mexican citizens announcing his imminent return. He took a steamer to New York a few days later.

Upon landing there in the Spring of 1866, El Presidente learned from his Washington representative that Secretary Seward did not support his return to Mexico. In fact, the

U.S. was backing the young populist reformer Benito Juarez as leader of its southern neighbor.

Establishing himself in a rented house on Staten Island, Santa Anna hired Thomas Adams, a business man and former U.S. army photographer during the Civil War, as his interpreter and secretary. The General pursued lawsuits at great cost against the con men, banks and others in a hopeless battle. His legal bill alone was $30,000, an immense sum in those days.

Although his suits failed, Santa Anna did win a measure of positive fame with Americans:

> *"During the many hours they spent together, Thomas Adams often noted the General's habit of cutting and chewing thin slices from an unfamiliar, exotic plant—not exactly palatable, yet elastic enough to tire the most persistent jaws. The General called this plant chicle. Adams experimented with it, blending it with various sweeteners and flavorings. The results were wildly popular: it has never left the American mouth. The Hero's enduring legacy is chewing gum."*[4]

I recalled the old Chiclets sign in Long Island City, Queens. Visible from the 59th Street Bridge, the sign sat atop the American Chiclet Company factory, delighting generations of New Yorkers. Through much of the 20th century, they were still tapping trees for chicle syrup in Mexico's Yucatan peninsula.

I decided to ask our oldest son, Sam, whether the Chiclet factory was still there. Sam, a young New York lawyer would get a kick out of the Chiclet and Santa Anna stories.

Later that day, I phoned him and learned that the old factory was saved from demolition and now houses the New York City Department of Design and Construction.

Sam offered to help with any Santa Anna research in New York. I made a note to myself that his legal prowess might become very useful down the line.

Meanwhile, though, I needed to get back to basics. I

learned that, although the aging Santa Anna never returned to St. Thomas, his son and other relatives and associates continued living there. I was certain a generous amount of gold and silver remained with them. Now, I had to discover what became of it.

Sadly, however, the 150-year-old trail had grown very cold. Conventional historic research offered nothing new.

I wrestled with what to do next. Then, it hit me. Could Kwame Boateng use his special talents to intuit what happened to the gold? I thought of President Carter's tale of the psychic discovering a plane wreck.

Police also use psychics. There was the famous work of an extra-sensitive British woman, Nella Jones, who had helped Scotland Yard recover a priceless, stolen Vermeer painting. She worked on more serious crimes as well.

"Nella gave invaluable assistance on a number of murders," explained Detective Chief Inspector Arnie Cooke in a British newspaper interview. "Her evidence was not the type you can put before a jury. But, senior investigating officers have got to take people like her on board and accept what they are saying."[5]

If Scotland Yard used such people, that was good enough for me. I phoned Kwame and we agreed to meet for lunch at the "Pickles in Paradise" deli in Coral Bay the next day.

That morning, I rowed out to *Perseverance* in the harbor mooring field to check on her leaky stuffing box. I started her engine to recharge the batteries, then got out the big wrench, opened the engine room door and tightened the stuffing box bolt a turn or two – just enough to slow down the leak to a slow drip. Perversely, a constant slow leak was needed to keep the stuffing wet.

I then worked the "automatic" bilge pump manually. It was hard, sweaty work with little elbow room.

Satisfied she'd be safe for a few more days, I climbed up the companion way and sat in the breezy cockpit to cool down. Suddenly, fish were jumping all around the boat. A fresh easterly sea breeze and three to four foot swells had brought a school of small shiny fish into the inner harbor. And, to my delight, two small dolphins – probably youngsters – were rolling through the school, eating and playing.

After locking the hatch, I climbed down to the dinghy and shoved off amid hundreds of jumping, splashing, silvery speckles. The dolphins were close. Like me, they were heading toward the shallows where wind and current were forcing the fish into a trap.

Rowing toward the old stone Danish pier that juts out of the mangroves and serves as the boaters' dinghy dock, I heard sea birds before I saw them. Circling and plunging pelicans, watchful white egrets and blue herons standing in shallows between mangrove roots together with pterodactyl-looking frigate birds floating a few hundred feet above the water all suddenly joined the dolphins at this fishy smorgasbord. The curious flopping splashes of pelicans dive bombing their prey and the sounds of otherwise statuesque egrets and herons stabbing fish in the shallows made a delightful symphony as I rowed through the melee.

One pelican missed my oar by inches, splashing water on me as he snagged a snack. Two fish jumped into the dinghy. I took the cut-off bleach bottle used as a bailer to catch and throw them back.

Then, the head of a sea turtle popped up, several yards away. He'd been feeding on sea grasses growing on the harbor bottom and came up to breathe. No doubt wary of the surface turmoil, he quickly dove back down.

I tied up the dinghy and looked out in the harbor at the ballet of boats swinging gently to their moorings. The view had changed little from the 1900 photograph of a West Indian school teacher and children dressed in Sunday best lined up on that same pier awaiting the arrival of the Danish Crown Prince. To the left a few hundred yards off the dock and up on a ridge above the mangroves, the now rusting tin roof of the old stone Danish custom house still rises amid sea grape trees.

Satisfied that all was well with our boat, I drove over to Pickles in Paradise. Kwame sat at a table on the roofed porch admiring the feeding sea birds in the harbor just visible through the mangroves across the shoreline road. Atop his salt and pepper hair he wore a "Born to Rhumb" charter boat cap. I chuckled at the playful use of rhumb, as in the nautical term "rhumb lines," i.e., a steady course or line on a chart that appears straight, but actually curves with the Earth.

"Great to see you."

"And you, Professor."

"Mary tells me you're doing very well with the kids."

He smiled as we watched a teenager walking by toward the Coral Bay crossroad where he'd likely hitch a ride up Centerline Road over the mountains to Cruz Bay.

"The children are a delight to work with," he nodded. "Your son, John, has impressed me with his empathy. He has a way with the younger children. I gather he is a special young man himself."

Not wanting to get into detail, I replied, "Yes, he's had an intractable seizure disorder since an infant. Based on our experiences, Mary founded her group and eventually became an expert."

"Well," Kwame continued. "She certainly is. I do enjoy working with the children. I only wish I could do more than one Saturday a week."

"Unfortunately, Mary's funding and availability of volunteers limits the program. But, that could change."

Beverly, the restaurant owner, said good morning and took our orders of sandwiches and iced tea. A middle-aged man with longish hair sat at a table next to us, eyes glued to his handheld device. His tie-dyed T-shirt said "Legalize Marinara." The name and phone number of a pizzeria in Hoboken appeared in small print below.

The interruption enabled me to shift the conversation.

"What do you do with yourself when not working with Mary?"

"I fish on a boat owned by a friend. When needed, I crew on a charter out of Cruz Bay. I'm also volunteering for the St. John Rescue squad."

"Such great stuff!"

I leaned forward to get to my point.

"Have you ever thought about your remote viewing days and possibly using your skills on private projects?"

"Funny thing you should ask," he said with a smile. "A few of us who worked in that program have lingering effects – both good and bad. I sometimes have very, very vivid dreams – other worldly dreams – some, even while awake. The Navy psychiatrist who worked with our team said, 'it happens.'"

I recalled old Alma's warning that night at Wagapalooza. He's a crazy fallen tree, she'd said.

"What did the psychiatrist recommend?"

"Well, he offered tranquilizers," Kwame said, frowning. "He thought I should stop remote viewing, but stay in the program as a trainer. Commander Taft agreed and made a good case that I should stay."

So, I thought, there was more to his retirement than Taft revealed.

"But, you left," I said tentatively.

And then, leaning forward, Kwame blinked his eyes and briefly smiled as he continued.

"Here's what can happen. Once your brain is trained in astral projection – remote viewing, if you will – it seems to crave more. Sort of like when you first make love, you want more."

"Interesting," I offered. "You know, I bet your village shaman ancestors never stopped their work."

"Quite correct. It was a life-long calling and they never lacked patients."

Seeing an opening, I jumped in.

"Kwame, I'm working on some historical research and

you may be able to help. But, first you must tell me of the limitations of remote viewing. Can you see things in the past?"

He laughed.

"Yes, it's been done. I once visited a plane crash moments after it happened. But, the crash actually occurred five years *earlier* in North Korea. It was a carrier-based Navy F-14 Tomcat. I happened to know the pilot …only slightly, though."

His eyes teared up.

"You see, I watched him die in the cockpit and heard his thoughts…"

"Wow," was all I could say.

"Yes. My mission, of course, had been to locate the wreckage and determine how the plane crashed; what happened to the pilot. See, it was in the mountains below a rock ridge – out of easy sight of our satellites. The Navy needed closure on this old, secret MIA."

"Incredible. You mean your mind traveled back five years?

"Exactly," he replied. "Hard to believe. Hard for *me* to believe."

He sat back, drank some tea, and continued, "But, it can be done. I knew a man who, as a training exercise, traveled to a Civil War hospital *during the war*. It was in a church that still stands not too many miles west of our Ft. Meade, Maryland offices.

"The church is in the village of Sharpsburg, close to the Potomac River. The wounded from the terrible Battle of Antietam were treated there. My friend – the remote viewer – found the trip too painful to remain more than a few minutes…you see, he saw and felt the butchery of the surgeons…Observing his physical reaction – respiration, blood pressure and so forth – his control brought him back quickly."

"Sounds grim," I said. "Why go back to such a place?"

"It was training, my friend. Training for what we'd see

on military missions – such as my visit with the dying pilot. They wanted us conditioned – hardened, if you will – so we could handle it."

"You mentioned a 'control.' What's that?"

"'Who's that,' is the correct question. Remote viewers have a partner – a controller. Here's how it works. A viewer is given the target. But, on military spy missions he's not told anything about it other than basic information. We needed to be able to get to the targets with very little information because our client intelligence officers didn't have much; that's why they needed us.

"Each mission begins with a viewer in a 'quiet room' resting on a very comfortable couch or easy chair, listening to carefully selected music – all this helps him fall into a trance-like state. At the same time, certain background musical notes and tones stimulate neuronal activity.

"The operative is hooked up to brain and heart monitors and the controller sits beside him, keeping track of the viewer's physical state. He also helps guide him to the target by asking questions and giving direction. When the target is acquired, your partner asks what you are seeing and feeling. As needed, the controller provides reassurances that all is okay. A tape recording of the 'trip' is made.

"And, if the viewer gets into trouble psychologically or physically, the control calls him back, telling him the mission was accomplished."

"And, who would a controller be? A shrink?"

"Controllers are usually former viewers; but, might be a psychologist, or anybody else trained for the program. Commander Taft wanted me to continue with the unit as a trainer and controller, rather than retire."

"Kwame, this incredibly exciting," I said. "I'm going to do some research on all this, so I can better understand what you're talking about."

Kwame looked at me intensely, staring into my eyes.

"Professor, we went much further and were far more

successful than anyone outside the program knows," he said in a hushed tone. "Under pressure from a Freedom of Information Act lawsuit during Bill Clinton's Administration, the CIA and Stanford Research Institute publicly released thousands of documents. I'm sure you'll find them and media reports. They only scratch the surface, however. No one outside the program knows what we are achieving."

He took a sip of ice tea, glancing at five donkeys walking toward the deck where we sat. They stopped a few feet away to nibble at Beverly's flower garden. I chuckled.

"As you search reports and books available online, think about it like this," he continued, "Think of the Wright Brothers' technology and flight history that anyone can access. That's the equivalent of what you can find on remote viewing. Now, think about a space shuttle and *its* technology and flight history. That's what's still secret."

We'd finished lunch and I'd heard about as much as I could handle. I told Kwame I'd see what I could learn. We'd meet again when I was more up to speed.

Returning home, I found Mary and John were out working on crafts projects with an elementary school special ed class. I went immediately to the computer. First stop was mainstream physicists. I wanted to learn current thinking on time travel. I hit pay dirt with a transcript from an old PBS television "Nova" show.

Princeton University professor John Wheeler, who'd worked on the secret atom and hydrogen bomb projects and was an expert on Einstein's theory of relativity, offered an explanation of "space-time" that I could grasp:

"I like to think of space and time as analogous to the ocean, and changes in it as analogous to waves on the surface of the ocean, but those waves, of course, don't show up when one's miles above the ocean. It looks flat. Then as one gets down closer to the

surface one sees the waves breaking and the foam. I see no way to escape the conclusion that a similar foam-like structure is developing in space and time."[6]

Like foam, Wheeler added, space-time is filled with tiny holes.

Einstein, of course, said that if an object traveled faster than the speed of light, it would travel back in time. But, he also proved that would be impossible – at least impossible for conventional physical objects moving in a world governed by conventional physics.

In Dr. Wheeler's space-time foam, however, there are tiny holes. Couldn't tiny objects like sub atomic particles go through those holes? Go back in time?

Tiny particles, such as photons of light, can take on both physical and non-physical forms in the bizarre world of quantum physics. University of California physicist Raymond Chiao, who worked under then Princeton professor John Wheeler, believes "objects" can travel faster than the speed of light – back in time, in other words. Neutrinos and tachyons are among the still hypothetical, but predicted "particles" some physicists believe break the light and time barriers.

So, subatomic particles – such as those some believe are the building blocks of human consciousness – may be able to travel faster than the speed of light. They may also be able to travel back in time.

Moreover, if Professor Wheeler is correct about space-time being like the surface of a foamy ocean, the particles might also be able to travel through holes in the foam and go back in time without needing to travel faster than light.

In short, there were two possible avenues for the mind to travel back in time. But, can consciousness comprised of such subatomic particles actually travel out of the body?

Back in the late 19th century, Russian psychiatrist Y. L. Ohotrovich, a pioneer in hypnotism and founder of the first international society of psychologists in Paris, scientifically studied a famous "medium." He concluded that her psychic abilities were real and "manifestations of an organic energy." Later, in the 1930s, the Soviet Academy of Sciences found that such "biological emissions" can transfer information.

By 1963, the Russians had proven telepathic communication between a person in St. Petersburg on the Baltic Sea and one in Sevastopol on the Black Sea, a distance of more than one thousand miles.[7]

These and other Russian successes were discovered by U.S. intelligence agencies, which feared we could be spied upon by Soviet psychics with no defense against them. They also feared Soviet soldiers could communicate telepathically with no need for radio transmission; communicating in a way we could not intercept and monitor.

So, the American government funded research by Stanford University physicist Harold Puthoff, a U.S. pioneer in scientifically studying psychic abilities. Based on his research in the 1960s and 70s, Dr. Puthoff , like the Russians, concluded that certain "paranormal" abilities such as remote viewing involved a form of biological emissions. He believed the answer may be found in the subatomic world of quantum physics.

Many years later, research by two University of Ottawa professors, funded by the Natural Sciences and Engineering Council of Canada, focused on a 24-year-old female college student who can self induce out of body experiences. Using the less loaded phrase "extra-corporeal experience" (ECE) to describe what the student achieved, the professors found her ECE to be a mixture of visual and kinesthetic perceptions. For instance, during one ECE she spun herself in circles and felt dizzy, even though her corporeal body was resting in bed.[8]

Using MRIs and other monitoring devices, the Canadian study of the student was the first conducted on a healthy, non-pathological person able to elicit ECEs on demand. Her case raises the possibility that this extrasensory ability is more widespread among people than is known. The student believed her ECE's were nothing special – that anybody could do it.

Although mystery still surrounds the science behind such abilities, the abilities themselves are real. And, every human likely has "ESP" potential. In Britain, University of Northampton professor Chris Roe, Ph.D found that up to 85 per cent of normal people possessed "some form of clairvoyance – the ability to 'remote view'." And, with a "modicum" of training, Dr. Roe says anyone can sharpen these innate skills.[9]

Amazingly, Dr. Roe also concluded that "time does not seem to be a barrier to remote viewing." Even Stephen Hawking, the most famous physicist on Earth today, admits time travel is possible.[10]

So, there we have it. Science has found a mind can probe or travel out of body to any geographic place and at any previous time.

Next, I asked myself a simple question. How can a historian use this extraordinary tool?

Eyewitness views of any historical event seem possible. But, realistically, would any major university or scholarly journal accept stories brought back by remote viewers or extra corporeal experiencers? There's a reason Scotland Yard can't use the evidence of clairvoyants in court – even though accurate and key to solving serious crimes.

As in so many other areas of science and sociology (not to mention religion), willful ignorance is blissfully non-controversial. Recalling my own UFO adventure and subsequent drop in income and academic standing, I reached a fateful conclusion. I would harness these powers to aid my family. I would find Santa Anna's gold.

To bring Kwame into my project, though, would require a conversation with Mary. That would be a toughie. Nevertheless, it was time she learned of his special abilities.

That night, after dinner, we were admiring yet another

beautiful sunset. Mary was comfortably seated as I began.

"I was reading an article by a retired Army Captain who says he was a psychic spy. They used ESP to spy on Russians and others. And, the Russians have been using ESP to spy on us. Isn't that incredible?"

"All the stuff about ESP, mediums and psychic powers is hard to get a handle on," she replied. "It's hard to know what to believe."

"Well, you always say you have a 'mom's intuition' about people and the future."

"Yes," she replied immediately. "Like when I said no good would come from your UFO work."

"And, you were correct. At least, for us. The Navy and government, though, did learn a great deal from my research."

"Yes, and we're poorer because of it," she shot back.

"Speaking of the Navy, what's new with Kwame?"

"Still doing well. The kids love him."

"I had a telephone conversation with Taft to check him out."

"So, tell me what he said. Wait, my 'mother's intuition' tells me I'm going to need a drink first."

When she returned with a bourbon for her and a beer for me, I continued.

"Taft's a Commander now. That's a pretty big deal. Anyway, he told me more about Kwame's medical talents. He has unusually high and proven ESP that helped diagnose patients. He had an exceptionally high performance rating as a Corpsman. He also did some intelligence research for the Navy. In fact, his experience might help me with Santa Anna."

"What do you mean by ESP?"

"I mean, his father and male ancestors were considered medicine men in their African and slave villages. They had special powers – the ability to perceive the heart of people's problems and gain guidance from their ancestors. They also, of course, knew the medicinal trees and herbs to treat physical illness."

"That makes sense," Mary said. "We've certainly seen plenty of natural medicine here; like that neem tree over there."

She pointed to our big, old neem tree. Among other applications, neem leaves and oil are used to treat gum disease. Toothpaste is made from it. Also, neem tea is good for stomach ailments.

"Right," I continued. "The Navy, CIA and major universities researched ESP and human consciousness. Taft was in charge of the Navy's work. He says Kwame's a genuine mystic."

"How does all that relate to your work?" she asked in a skeptical tone.

"The same ESP abilities that help make him a great medic and diagnostician also make him very good at assessing information. My Santa Anna research has hit a road block and I think Kwame can help."

"Would you need to pay him?" She asked, hitting one nail on the head.

"I don't think so. I bet he'd work as a volunteer or intern – the way people work with the Virgin Islands National Park archaeologist."

"In that case, I don't see why you shouldn't ask him," she said.

"Good. I'll speak with him."

And, I did. The next morning he and I met for coffee at the benches outside the National Park headquarters across the cove from the Cruz Bay customs and BVI ferry docks. A delightful breeze flapped the palm fronds. Wavelets slapped against docks as we talked.

"Kwame, I've done some reading and think I understand a bit more about remote viewing. Now, I want to explain my historical research project."

After thoroughly briefing him on Santa Anna and my conclusion that a significant amount of gold is missing, I got to the point.

"Could you go back and view events involving Santa Anna and what he did with assets he may have left behind on St. Thomas?"

"That's possible," he said. "But, I don't speak Spanish or Danish."

"I've thought about that," I replied. "It shouldn't be a problem. British and American shipping and trade were critical. English became the language of business in Charlotte Amalie. And, by the 1860s, all Danish and church schools on St. Thomas taught English."

"So, you think Santa Anna would have conducted his business meetings in English?"

"Well, I believe his accountants and bankers would have kept his accounts in English and probably spoke that language in their offices," I explained. "And, the largest bank in St. Thomas at that time was the West Indies Colonial Bank, a British business."

He thought about it.

"That would certainly make things easier," he allowed.

"Now, Kwame, this could end up taking more time and effort than either of us can foresee.

"And, if our collaboration leads to discovery of gold or silver, I would do the honorable thing and compensate you and any others we might need to bring in."

He asked the obvious question.

"What kind of compensation ?"

"I've thought long and hard," I said sincerely. "The old seamen who came to these waters before any of us – even before your ancestors – had a good system."

I finished my coffee and pulled down my hat for shade from the morning sun now reflecting off the water in front of us.

"Yes," I continued. "In the 1500s, British buccaneer Henry Morgan set the precedent for several generations of seamen. They had a code.

"The Captain received two shares of any prize; the first mate received one-and-a-half shares; the lower class of officers received one-and-one-quarter shares and the common seamen one share each."

He looked at me skeptically.

"Buccaneers? Prizes? Are we pirates?"

He *was* perceptive. I laughed and slapped his shoulder.

"No, but we are on a treasure hunt. As we proceed, I'm certain we'll need to bring in more people. And, since I can't pay anyone up front, we need a fair way to share what we recover."

"Now I see where you're going," he said.

"Because of your importance to this project, you should get the first mate's share of one-and-a-half."

"But," he asked. "One-and-a-half of what?"

"Let's say there are ten of us and we find ten dollars. As Captain, I'd get two dollars; you'd get $1.50; another lower ranked officer would get $1.25. That would leave $5.25 to be divided equally among the remaining seven people – seventy-five cents each."

He looked perplexed.

"Doesn't sound like much, I know. But what if we find $10 million or $100 million?"

Chuckling, I added, "You might well ask, 'Why follow Henry Morgan's share system?'"

He smiled, and said, "Ok, why use Morgan's system?"

"Good question. Sir Henry Morgan is ranked number eight on Forbes magazine's list of top-earning pirates. He lived to a ripe old age, was knighted and got away with $13 million in today's dollars. Not the most money of any pirate, but he was one of the few who lived to enjoy it."[11]

Kwame thought about that.

"Do you mean Forbes, that financial magazine for the wealthy?"

"That's the one," I said. "Some writer got the strange idea that today's Wall Streeters are akin to old pirates. So, they did a ranking of them by wealth, just like they do with modern financiers."

"That's funny."

"It is funny, until you think about it," I said. "Then, you realize it's insulting for men like Sir Francis Drake and Sir Henry Morgan to be compared to today's bankers. They were men of honor – sea captains who took real risks with their own lives and ships; not, like these bankers who risk other people's money to make their fortunes."

Kwame shook his head in wonder. Then, he frowned.

"You know, Professor, depending upon where that treasure we're looking for might be, we could run into legal and other hurdles trying to get it like your pirates did."

"Quite true," I replied. "But, first we have to find Santa Anna's gold. Then, we'll need to think like a scheming investment banker and act boldly like a pirate."

I thought of Lord Claymore and his comment about how tricky it is to extract treasure on land.

Kwame sat there thinking.

"That all sounds about right," he said to my surprise and delight.

So, we shook hands on our agreement.

In a great mood, I returned to my home office and made a shocking discovery.

5 FIRST SPACE (TIME) SHOT

"I never felt such a strange sensation as when the machine first left the ground and started her flight...I was soaring up above my fellow beings in a thing my own brain evolved. It was a sweet experience. It made me think I was far ahead of my brothers for they must still walk and I could fly."

— Gustave Whitehead describing his alleged first powered flight in Fairfield, Connecticut on August 18, 1901, reported in the Bridgeport Sunday Herald. This apparent witnessed flight took place two years before the Wright Brothers' first flight in Kitty Hawk, North Carolina.[1]

"I saw the other day a map, 'The United States as they now are, and in the future,' and it included all these places – Mexico, Central America, Cuba, Santo Domingo and even poor Jamaica. It may be that the man who made the map understood the destiny of his country. At any rate, he understood the tastes of his countrymen."

— English novelist Anthony Trollope writing in 1859 of his time in St. Thomas in his book "The West Indies and the Spanish Main."[2]

It's common knowledge that Secretary Seward wanted to buy the Danish West Indies in the 1860s to establish a U.S. Navy base. But, the plan got much further than preliminary negotiations. A treaty had actually been signed by the President of the United States and King of Denmark on October 26, 1867. It would have transfered the islands of St. Thomas and St. John to the U.S. in return for $7.5 million.

The King was so confident the deal was done that he "sorrowfully" made a public announcement to his West Indian subjects (and the world) the day after the treaty was signed:

> *"Royal Proclamation to the Inhabitants of St. Thomas and St. John, 27 October, 1867*
>
> *"We, Christian the Ninth, King of Denmark, the Vandals and the Goths, Duke of Sleswig, Holstein, Stornmarn, Ditmarsh, Lauenborg, and Oldenborg ...send to our beloved and faithful subjects in the Islands of St. Thomas and St. John our Royal Greeting.*
>
> *"We have resolved to cede our Islands of St. Thomas and St. John to the United States of America ...and have concluded a convention with the President of the United States ...With sorrow do we look forward to severing those ties which for many years have united You to Us."*

Considering that Secretary Seward had that same year orchestrated the purchase of all of Alaska for $7.2 million, Denmark was getting a very good deal – $300,000 more than Russia got for Alaska. Seward really wanted the "Stars and Stripes flown from the North Pole to the Caribbean."

Newspapers in the United States reported the acquisition of the islands as all but accomplished. I wondered what Santa Anna thought as he sat in New York reading about it; feeling betrayed by Seward and robbed by conniving bankers. Did he welcome the Yankees buying his neutral Danish island sanctuary out from under him?

Would U.S. creditors and Mexican opponents stake claims on his fortune stashed on soon to become American soil?

Even if he had buried trunks of gold and silver on St. Thomas or St. John, as I had naively supposed, he wouldn't leave them there. Instead, he'd be looking for a new safe haven. Where might that be?

Pondering these questions, I decided it was time to report on my progress to the family. We were sitting around the weathered teak table on our deck admiring hummingbirds feasting on Mary's birdfeeders. This was part family meeting and part teachable moment for John.

I explained all my research; that it had taken me to the point where Santa Anna had been swindled in New York, abandoned by Washington officials and was sitting in a rented house on Staten Island.

"The sale of the islands to the Americans would only be completed if Congress ratified Seward's treaty. We now know that after years of argument the treaty was rejected," I explained. "But, Santa Anna in New York, and the businessmen and ruling class on St. Thomas had every reason to believe it was going to happen. Once signed by the king and president, newspapers reported it as a done deal. The U.S. would buy the two Danish islands."

Mary thought about that as we sipped her freshly brewed tea – homegrown sorrel, lemon grass, hibiscus flowers and peppermint.

"Let me guess," she interjected. "Like many powerful men, I'm sure Santa Anna was vainglorious. He'd just been humiliated again by Americans. I bet he didn't want his St. Thomas palace and wealth to fall under American rule."

"Did Santa Anna really have mistresses?" John asked, revealing the part of the story any young man would note. "Did he really capture Davy Crocket alive at the Alamo? In the movies, Davy always went down fighting."

"Well John," I replied, "even though he was married,

Santa Anna did seem to have girlfriends, and young ones at that. And, there are witnesses who say the Mexicans did capture Crocket alive and then killed him."

Mary quickly jumped in to deliver the story's lessons.

"Today, John, married men shouldn't have girlfriends without their wives' permission," Mary explained solemnly. "And, civilized people don't murder prisoners."

"What about the death penalty?" John shot back. His cognitive differences meant he took everything literally – that is, truthfully. There were no shades of gray for him. State killing was state murder.

"Ok, we're getting way off track now," I said. "Let's not talk about murders, executions or mistresses. The question is what did Santa Anna do next?"

"He probably wanted to move from St. Thomas before it became American," Mary responded.

"Correct," I said. "During his lifetime, he'd seen the United States take half of Mexico by war or treaty. I'm sure he'd had enough."

Mary leaned toward me, asking the million dollar question.

"What about all that gold and silver you've been going on and on about?"

"That's the question, Mary, that we need to answer."

"Despite his failings as a man, Santa Anna was no dummy," she continued. "Wouldn't he have deposited the money in a bank vault?"

She was probably correct, of course.

"At first, I thought he might have followed the lead of other Caribbean villains and buried it. But, even if he had, he would have retrieved it and stored it in a bank vault; that would be the first step toward transporting it somewhere safer."

I continued, "A bank could arrange safe shipment of the treasure off island and out of impending American control. There were only two banks in Charlotte Amalie in the 1860s – the local Bank of St. Thomas, and a branch of the London-based British West Indies Colonial Bank."

Mary thought about it a few moments.

"If I were Santa Anna, I'd go with the big British bank tied to London," she said. "Wasn't London the world's largest financial center back then?"

"Yes, it was. And, the BWI Colonial Bank could also obtain priority space on Royal Mail Steamers. St. Thomas was the Royal Mail Steamship Company's Caribbean headquarters back then. That's why the BWI bank was there."

"What's a steam ship?" John asked.

"Google it!" Mary told him. Then, she looked at me.

"Well, it should be simple to look at the Colonial Bank records to see if he was a customer."

"Not so simple. The St. Thomas branch closed early in the 20th century and the whole company was bought by a larger London bank. It eventually became part of giant Barclays Bank. Any surviving records would be at their London headquarters or in British government archives. I can't afford to go to London to find out."

"Guess you've reached a dead end," Mary said. She knew that statement would make me work harder.

As we talked, I thought of an alternative way to explore the Colonial Bank branch. Why not remote view it? First, we'd need to learn what to look for and when.

"Yes, well, I might be able to find something in the Charlotte Amalie library's antiquities section," I replied to Mary. "They do have old letters and newspaper articles. A lot of information can be gleaned from the gossip that was reported as news in the 1800s."

"It still is," Mary said.

The next morning found me in the colonnaded stone court yard of the Enid M. Baa Public Library, once the stately mansion of Frederik Emil Baron Von de Bretton whose ancestors arrived in St. Thomas in 1690. Built in 1818, the mansion's top two floors were the Von Bretton's living quarters. Today, they house the library's historical collection, reached by climbing the same curved exterior stone stair case used by the Von Brettons. It was odd to think that Santa Anna and Secretary Seward were both likely entertained in this very house by the well-connected Baron. Both walked up the stairs I used.

On the top floor, I found the antiquities section housed in a wooden partitioned room cooled by ceiling fans. A dozing docent was in charge. Waving a hand fan advertising Cruzan rum, she directed me to the microfilm files.

I first explored the St. Thomas Tidende, the newspaper of record for the island's governing and merchant classes. I chose October, 1867 as the most likely month in which to find possible news of Santa Anna and his reaction to impending American rule.

After three hours, I found something useful; very useful. On October 27th, El Presidente's son, Angel Lopez de Santa Anna, then in his late twenties, had dined with Sir Fitzroy Grannum, Managing Director of St. Thomas' BWI Colonial Bank branch. The cabled announcement of the U.S. purchase had just arrived on island.

Their dinner venue was the Commercial Hotel and Coffee House overlooking Emancipation Garden and the harbor. Constructed about 1839, the Commercial Hotel and dining room were among the most fashionable meeting places in town. Renamed the Grand Hotel, it remained open into the 1970s and 80s.

I wondered what they talked about? There was only one way to be certain.

The next day, I met Kwame and explained he now had a remote viewing target. But, he changed personnel on me in midstream. I should be the remote viewer, he said.

"I'm the medic and experienced viewer, Professor," he argued. "It's safer, if I train you and stay with your physical body to monitor its condition. At the same time, I'll vocally guide your consciousness on its journey. I can read the messages your body will signal about your mental state as you travel. I know when to pull the plug and how to do it. It's the only safe way to do this."

It was, of course, the chance of a lifetime. It didn't take long to convince myself that I'd be safe in Kwame's hands. After all, Commander Taft had wanted him to be a trainer and controller.

"You may be on to something, Kwame. I'm familiar with the history of the town and harbor. And, we may be able to do better than your military colleagues by concentrating intensely on the precise target and date."

"That might work," he admitted. "Our operatives were purposely kept in the dark about their intelligence targets. Almost all were in current real time. In most cases we knew very little about them."

"Yes. We'll be focusing only on 'back time' targets. My hunch is that the more historical research I do in advance, the more easily my mind can reach back to those days."

That settled, we next needed to agree on the target. Naturally, I wanted to go right to the hotel dining room. We needed to know what Santa Anna's son said to the British banker.

Kwame, though, suggested a smaller, easier test target within the same neighborhood and time period.

"Let's do a test run with a target that is not so crucial; a target that would not have so much stress placed upon you the first time out."

Looking at period maps, I located the British West Indies Colonial Bank at 8B Dronningens Gade (Charlotte Amalie's Main Street). Almost directly across the street was a general goods store popular with ship pursers: Haardemael and Andersen, Provisioners. A perfect trial target.

We started planning the launch. First order of business, Kwame said, was securing an electroencephalogram device to display patterns and intensity of the brain's electrical activity. And, I would need to wear a simple, digital blood pressure monitor on my wrist.

"I must be able to assess your condition while you're under and your consciousness is traveling," he explained.

"But, an EEG? How expensive is that?"

I knew from my son John's medical condition that EEG studies could be costly.

"We can't risk a cerebral hemorrhage," he replied, convincingly.

I thought about a Civil War era surgeon successfully pulling bones out of Frederick Seward's brain with nothing more sophisticated than pliers. Still, Kwame was correct.

"Besides, Harris, basic EEG machines are surprisingly affordable – especially if I get one through the Armed Forces PX. We'll need to use old-fashioned, disposable electrodes and gel, I'm afraid," he continued. "Can't afford the newer models."

We agreed we'd split the cost and he placed the order. Mary would flip when she saw that bill.

The next decision was where to launch our space-time forays.

Kwame had inherited his family home on a hillside overlooking the town of Cruz Bay. He suggested we use it and invited me to take a look.

Located up a steep, unpaved road, it was an old wooden, one-story, three-room West Indian home. Bleached out yellow paint flaked from plank sides, though the tin roof was a freshly painted red. Its covered veranda was framed by delicate latticework, broken in places. The wooden shuttered windows had no glass. Screens with wooden slat frames, though, had wisely been added.

Well positioned to catch prevailing trade winds, the home had been built a hundred and fifty years earlier by one of Kwame's shamanic ancestors. Back then, Cruz Bay was a small Freedman's village.

In front of the house, an old palm grove and mahogany

tree provided shade.

"Come into my back yard," Kwame invited as he showed me the property. "My great-great grandfather was a shaman, of course. He was also clever and planted a Jumbie Tree."

"An enterprising chap," I said. "Bet the tree increased business."

Then I saw it – an immense, majestic kapok tree. Its' nearly perfect hemisphere of branches and clumps of almond-shaped, dark-green leaves reached upwards of 200 or 300 feet. Studded with five-inch-long thorns, the gray trunk must have measured nine or ten feet around and was supported by thick, tall offshoots of the trunk that resembled the buttresses of a cathedral.

No wonder in West Indian folklore it was called a Jumbie Tree and South Americans once called it the Castle of the Devil. With its thorns and buttresses, a kapok tree did seem designed to encase demons and evil spirits. What's more, odd scars and openings in its trunk resembled faces.

Kwame's spiritually rich property was the perfect launch site for my journey into the space-time ether of earlier days.

I told a dubious Mary that Kwame and I would be working at his house for several days to avoid interruptions.

Meanwhile, Kwame taught me relaxation exercises and mercilessly prodded me to do them, day after day. I'd lie down on a bed in his darkened back room, cooled by an old, iron-framed, wooden-slated, ceiling fan. Looking at the spinning fan blades was hypnotic.

Kwame made a gauze hat for me to wear to simulate an EEG electrode net. I needed to become comfortable wearing it.

"Now, we need to select mood music for your brain."

It had to be music I'd find soothing, while energetic enough to light up certain neural pathways. Kwame and I discussed a wide range of music from Celtic and medieval to classical guitar. We agreed to use one of my favorites that he'd download and edit.

To settle me down, we'd use "Orinoco Flow" by the Irish singer Enya. She'd be followed by a selection of recorded sounds of ocean waves, sea gulls and waterfalls; and, to take me over the top, Kwame would download binaural beats which are sounds in frequencies that can make the brain's left and right hemispheres work together in sync.[3]

"We need your body asleep, but mind awake," Kwame explained.

He prepared a CD with the edited soundscape.

I became accustomed to being hooked up to Kwame's instruments and the music and sounds. After days of relaxation and meditation exercise sessions, I did achieve altered states in which my mind floated freely, released from my body's weight.

In one episode, I heard donkeys braying outside the house and a steamship whistle echoing off the mountainsides of Cruz Bay. But, donkeys never come into this neighborhood – at least, not in our time.

The real breakthrough came a day later. Our target was the old Danish fortification and administrator's home on Cruz Bay. The time selected was 1900.

We began as usual. Kwame had me lie down in the now familiar room. He went about the tedious process of placing gel and electrodes in strategic spots on my head. Thin wires led from electrodes to a converter box, which, in turn, plugged into his laptop. He wrapped gauze around my head to hold it all in place. He attached the blood pressure monitor to my wrist.

I wore earphones that Kwame had spliced with a two-way microphone. We could speak with each other even as the background music played. With a thumbs up, I signaled I was ready.

I next heard Enya's "Orinoco" at low volume.

Kwame softly gave me instructions.

"Think of the sea...look down at the coral beneath the clear water...notice green fields and glistening palm fronds swaying in a light breeze above the beach...watch the sea gently breaking on white sand..."

Before I knew it, I was adrift in total exquisite, black emptiness. I rested there a few moments and then felt movement. I was confused and floating, as on water, yet physically very light as though disembodied. Then I remembered, I *was* disembodied.

I was still in darkness, but heard a sound like a zipper opening. It was a sound military remote viewers described. Then, I heard sea gulls.

Cautiously, I opened my eyes. Below me was the Danish fort. Above it flew a red flag with a white cross – the flag of Denmark. A half-dozen cannons emplaced on the wall were clean. Oil glistened off their barrels. They were ready for use. A man in a pith helmet and blue coat dozed in a chair along the palisade.

I smelled wood smoke and turned to look inland. A cloud of smoke rose from the forest canopy. There were no buildings in that direction – only forest covering the hillside. The midday sun glinted off the thin, wax-like coating of palm fronds. They glowed.

Movement caught my attention off to my right. A glorious white sand beach lined with palms ran along the entire half-moon shape of Cruz Bay. Half-way along the beach out to Gallows Point was a wooden dock. A large, wooden sailing sloop was tied up at its end.

Three women wearing turbans and house dresses caught my attention. They were wading in the water along the palm fringed beach. Nearby, four naked children were swimming and splashing. Older boys wearing very little were climbing palms to fetch coconuts.

"What do you see, Professor?"

I described the women and he chuckled. "Yes, in the days of my childhood, women would still bathe just like that. They wore clothes out of modesty."

I continued out loud, "Looking inland, where the town is now, I see a few stone and wooden houses. Donkeys with wooden saddles are tied to trees and posts. On a hill to the right is a Danish building I recognize – the Estate Enighed great house that's now our library.

"It's a beautiful, idyllic place."

"Yes, must have been blissful," Kwame replied.

"Your house must be somewhere up on a ridge above the great house," I said, feeling a twinge of panic. How could I be there and also here? "What the fuck?"

"I think it best for you to come back, now" Kwame said matter-of-factly.

"How?"

"Simply close your eyes and lay down."

In a few moments, I "awoke."

"It was glorious, Kwame," I blurted, my speech a bit slurred.

"I know. You rest now for a bit and we'll talk later. I think you're ready to go to the provisioner's shop in Charlotte Amalie tomorrow."

That night, over dinner at home with Mary and John, I had new feelings – the sure knowledge that our time together was fleeting; that after we're gone, real flesh and blood people would follow and we'd be dust in this world.

Later, we all watched a silly, old, Mel Brooks movie. After that, Mary and I went out to the deck holding hands, watching the stars.

In the morning, we had our usual hearty breakfast. I said goodbye to Mary and John routinely, as I'd done for years. I felt a little sad – and jumpy.

When I got to Kwame's house, he saw that I was tense. He gave me some lemon grass tea and sat me down.

"You know, Harris, today's trip is really not much different from yesterday's," he said soothingly. "The only difference is, if we're lucky, you will be gone a little bit longer. I'll be monitoring everything. You'll be totally safe."

"I get that," I replied. "Guess all of this is just sinking in – that it's *real.*"

"Yes, it is hard to comprehend; hard to wrap your mind around. Do you want to skip it today?"

"Not at all," I said. "This is the most important work I've ever done."

"Good," he said. "Why not go back and lie down on the bed. I'll be back in a few minutes."

I relaxed on the bed watching the ceiling fan blades spin. Kwame came in, wired me up and patted my shoulder.

"Remember, when you are out there, no one can see you. When you speak, only I can hear you. You cannot interact or interfere – even if you want to. You will have no corporeal presence there that they can see. There is no need to feel self-conscious or embarrassed by anything you see. You are totally free to simply observe. Enjoy it. Describe as much to me as you can."

"I understand," I said. "Let's go."

After a few minutes of rest and music, the sound of a zipper or Velcro straps ripping open filled my brain. Fighting down fear, I opened my eyes.

I was suspended between darkness on one side and milky red, pink, purple and gray cotton-like puffs – clouds, I realized – on the other. I thought of astronauts' photos of the Earth's horizon just before sun rise.

The blackness dissipated. More pink. More cotton puffs. Clouds in a tropic afternoon. I looked down. There were glimpses of turquoise and then deepening blue. Now, everything above and below was some shade of blue. But, was I up or down? Very disoriented and feeling a bit nauseous, I tried to focus on the place and time I was searching for.

Smells of sea salt, smoke and decaying vegetation broke into my confusion. And, I drifted.

Like an ocean sailor seeing a bird as the first sign of

land, I realized I, too, was near land. The scent of smoke awakened pleasant memories of coal burning fireplaces and steam locomotives I'd seen and smelled in Europe many years before.

Now, I could see the blue below me was the sea and I was drifting down toward it. Suddenly nearly a full circle of green mountains and islets appeared in afternoon light. The unmistakable hulls of ships of all sizes and types seemed to fill a placid basin of water surrounded by mountains and hills. A passage faced seaward between mountains.

"Jesus, all the ships have masts," I said out loud. "Even the ones with smoke stacks."

Realizing I had made it to a different era, a chill of fear gripped me. I was confused and my descent slowed to a stop. This wasn't like the pleasurable visit to St. John's charming "back-time." This was a different island; more industrial.

"Everything's okay, Professor. Tell me what you're seeing," Kwame said, as if in an echo chamber.

Somehow he knew I was unsettled. Then I remembered the EEG and blood pressure gauge back in that room.

"I …I …I'm seeing a harbor with sailing vessels of all kinds. But, some have funnels like in the mid-1800s," I said. "I must have made it. I'm here!"

Elation spread through me, driving out fear. No one alive had seen that sight.

"Yes, Professor, you made it," Kwame said calmly. "Now, relax and enjoy the view. Tell me about it."

"On the landward end of the harbor are narrow beaches on either side of a dozen or so docks. There's a town of red-roofed buildings, large and small. Many of the small structures must be homes. They are painted bright white and shades of yellow and cream. Large buildings are either red or yellow, as in Scandinavia.

"But, the town is much smaller than it should be. It

ends at the tops of three hills, towered over by surrounding mountains. Guinea grass, bushes and saplings are growing in what looks to be abandoned, terraced agricultural fields. Fingers of tree canopies flow down the mountain sides from heavily forested ridgelines.

"Ah, above town on a lower ridge is a stone windmill. It still has a wooden mast and booms on top; it appears to be in working condition. I bet if you put sails on, it would still turn the giant mill stones and squeeze syrup out of sugar cane. Nearby, a few other stone sugar factory buildings appear intact. But the forest is reclaiming them."

"Okay, Professor, move down toward the town – as though you're swimming. Think of swimming toward that town."

"All right, I'm swimming downward in a sort of slow-motion dive."

I came down to an area above the western edge of town. I stopped swimming where I had a good view.

"In town I see many people walking and riding donkeys. Donkey, mule or horse-driven carts and small wagons share the streets with people of all kinds and colors. Smoke rises from chimneys in residential courtyards – must be kitchens. This has to be Charlotte Amalie, but it's too small."

"Are you sure?"

"Of course, it's too small," I said. "But, it is Charlotte Amalie. There are the red walls of Fort Christian, the yellow barracks building with the old King's Wharf jutting out into the harbor in front of them. Row boats, and small sloops are tied up and the wharf is filled with black and white people wearing all kinds of clothing. Wooden crates, sacks of stuff, leather luggage, upholstered portmanteaus and black trunks are piled in heaps on the pier.

"Nearby, the row of long, narrow, stone warehouses perpendicular to the shoreline are just where they should be. But, I see sun glinting off what looks like narrow railroad tracks running from some warehouses out onto docks, and along some alleys between warehouses. Two black men are pushing a cart filled with sacks of something along one set of tracks. At the end of several piers are hoists – some tower over inter-island sloops tied up alongside. That's all new – er, I mean, old."

I looked out at the harbor again.

"The boats are sailing rigs or side paddle steamships, mostly. All have masts, whether steamers or not. Certainly, no diesel-propelled ships. I smell a lot of coal smoke. Black clouds are spreading upwards from several steamship funnels."

"Very good, Professor. Now slowly move yourself down into town – pretend you're swimming."

As I moved lower, I saw that just above the narrow beach on either side of town were two rows of coconut palms, providing shade for a narrow dirt road that ran between them. They were well above the water line. Those palms would provide shade and coconut milk, meat and the fruity mash called gel.

A group of West Indian children were swimming and playing on the beach. One boy used a machete to cut off the end of a coconut. He drank some and passed it to the others.

I was approaching town from the west over mostly empty fields, using the mansions ahead on Denmark Hill as my guide. Then, I saw the spires of the Catholic cathedral of St. Peter and St. Paul. But, it was only a couple of blocks from the end of town.

"Do you see anything that indicates the date?"

"Well, the Catholic church is here. It was built in 1848, I believe. Up on Denmark Hill, I see the white neoclassical Catherineberg mansion built in 1850. It's surrounded by gardens and what appear to be pastures.

"Below it, I see Villa Santa Anna as an imposing, one-story, Danish colonial-style building that was remodeled and finished in 1860. It's wooden. Too bad it burned down in the 20th century. It's high, stone embankment provides a flat terrace for the mansion and outbuildings; looks like a fortress. Why don't I just go down and look at Santa Anna's house?"

"No, Professor, you must stay on task. Do not confuse yourself. And, if this is the summer of 1867, Santa Anna's not even there. He's in New York. You can learn nothing about the gold there."

"Okay. I'm now looking over toward Government Hill. I see Government House looking brand new and bigger – freshly painted white. It was completed in early 1867. So, we're at least that close to our target time."

I went lower and entered Main Street, about 10 feet above the road. Mostly Afro-European people were going about their business. Men in simple cotton shirts and pants cut off at the knees drove donkey and oxen carts or led donkeys loaded with wooden crates, barrels and garden produce. Some were bareheaded. Others wore broad-brimmed straw hats.

Afro-European women walked gracefully erect. Some balanced baskets of goods on their heads. Many carried packages wrapped in brown burlap. Others carried fruits and vegetables in woven palm-frond baskets or cut stalks of sugar tied in bundles.

Clothed mostly in yellow cotton dresses down to just below their knees, laboring women wore madras handkerchiefs or blue or yellow turbans on their heads.

There was a Creole woman with her hair tied back by a yellow madras kerchief. On her head she balanced a large demi-john bottle covered in wicker.

I passed the Catholic cathedral, which looked normal, though newer, cleaner and with less statuary. Next came the Bank of St. Thomas on the corner of Market Square.

Its two stories with filigreed, black iron verandas and first-floor arches looked new and shiny clean.

"What are you seeing, Professor?"

"Am going by Market Square. It has no central pavilion. That was built about 1900. It's all open stone pavement now. Virgin Islanders are selling sugar apples, sea grapes, coconuts, guava berries, bananas, pomegranates, avocados, mangoes, tamarind, pineapples and sugar cane.

"Dozens of donkeys, most with wooden saddles, are tied to hitching rails. Vendors sit on wooden crates or in the beds of carts. They tip their caps to well-dressed women – white and of mixed race – in long dresses and bonnets or hats with feathers. The ladies are milling around looking over the produce, squeezing mangos, inspecting pineapples. It's all so normal, so human."

The odor of animal dung, scent of flowers and other smells I didn't recognize hit me as the breeze calmed.

Remembering Kwame, I continued speaking, "A lot of islanders are speaking a patois I can't understand, though I do hear 'Good Day,' and 'Guten Tag,' as well as 'God dag' and 'Buen Dia' spoken clearly here and there."

In this era, I reminded myself, many islanders spoke three or more European languages to do business with visiting merchants and ships' crews.

Silently I moved across the square and saw two native Virgin Island women in scarves standing under a mahogany tree. They had three wooden trays balanced on barrels. "Hot rolls, five-bit a piece," one shouted to passersby – just loud enough to be heard above the clip clop of animals and many conversations, but not too loud. That would be impolite.

"What's happening, Professor?"

"I'm still moving up Main Street, passed Market Square and now looking for our store."

Noting how tidy the streets were, I looked at the names above shop doors: Apothecary Hall must be pharmacists;

Ye Foo Chong and Company sold tea and "curios", providing evidence that China clippers stopped in St. Thomas.

On the left, I saw a two-story building with two marble columns framing its red door. High-quality, leaded glass windows were on either side; a sign of wealth on an island where most buildings had simple open air windows with wooden shutters. British West Indies Colonial Bank, a gilded sign proclaimed above the door. As with Villa Santa Anna, I wanted to go in, but knew I shouldn't.

There across the street was my objective. It was a narrow stone building: Haardemael and Andersen, Provision Dealers, with the slogan "Emporium of the Antilles" in white on a black sign above big, arched, wooden doors. They were latched open revealing a large, deep and poorly lit interior. Just inside was a front room wide open to the air. A variety of mostly white men – some in naval uniforms, others in top hats and frock coats – were entering and exiting.

"I found our target, Kwame, right where the map showed it," I said

"Good job. Go in slowly, Professor; stay focused."

I drifted in behind a naval officer. The store was lined with wooden shelves and mahogany cases with glass doors. Most of the wares were located behind a counter. There, on a stool, sat a man I took to be Mr. Haardemael – every inch a plump Dutchman. He wore a blue-striped, linen suit and, with head down and wielding a thick pencil and paper, was immersed in calculations.[4]

Immediately behind the counter were shelves with jars of chemicals and drugs. Handwritten labels identified opium, quinine, coca extract, sulfur and a myriad of other leaves and powders. A bronze mortar and pestle stood ready.

A passage between the shelves revealed a vestibule. Two clerks were busy writing on desks lit with oil lamps. Behind them, the room opened up into a long warehouse.

In the twilight were several black and white faces moving around stacks of cans, barrels and crates in that vast room. Wooden ladders were propped along walls of merchandise. Like a light at the end of a tunnel, a wide open arch at the end of the room provided a bright harbor view.

I focused again on the front room. Near where I hovered, a uniformed gentleman I took to be a naval officer stepped up to the counter.

"Good afternoon, Heer Haardemael. A fine day, is it not?" A British ship's officer, as I'd guessed.

"Ya, goede middag to you, sir," the Dutchman replied looking up. "It is a fine dag."

"I would like ten cases of vin Bordeaux and 200 pounds of Somerset Cheddar, if you please."

"To vich dock may ve deliver it, sir?"

The formality of Victorian speech was incredible. Even more incredible was hearing actual Victorians speak.

I turned from the conversation and looked more closely around the front room. Tins of several teas and coffees, jars of jams and chutneys, exotic liqueurs, bitters, gin, bottles of Madeira and Bordeaux wines and other goods were on display. Against one wall I was drawn to a tall stack of cans of Stork Brand Condensed Milk, branded with a lithograph of a stork. In fine print, I read "New York Condensed Milk Company."

A well-dressed woman with blonde hair tied back in a bun was examining a nearby shelf stacked with white crocks of Dundee Marmalade with the slogan "The British Empire Begins at Home." She moved down the aisle and picked up a crock of Fortnum & Mason's Potted Beef, "By Appointment of the Queen." That would be Queen Victoria, I realized.

Then I saw it – a row of Plantation Bitters, S. T. Drake and Co., New York, 1860. Chuckling and thinking of Confederate Captain Semmes, I carefully looked over the bottle. Brownish-amber in color, it was shaped like a log cabin with a peaked roof and had a corked spout where the chimney should be. I wished I could pick it up and take it with me.

A ship's officer lifted and sniffed one of the huge wheels of cheese stacked against a wall. One was labeled Noord-Hollandse Gouda, another West Country Farmhouse Cheddar.

"What's happening, Professor?"

"I'm in the store. Really quite remarkable. Mary would love it. Wait, I see a pile of newspapers…'The St. Thomas Tidende'," I read aloud. " '17 September, 1867' is the dateline."

For a moment, a gentleman in a gray frock coat and black stovepipe hat blocked my view. He picked up a paper and stepped out into the street.

It was then I noticed a shelf above the newspapers holding a sheaf of thick, cream-colored linen paper. Printed in black ink was "Not as Bad as We Seem, A Comedy in Five Acts by Sir Edward Bulwer-Lytton of London; Presented by The Alexandra Dramatic Association, The Apollo Theatre, 30 September."

I recalled it was a popular 19th century play. Charles Dickens had even played a character. Queen Victoria thought it "full of cleverness, though rather too long."

"This is interesting, Kwame. Here's a handbill advertising a famous London play from the 1850s. 'Not as Bad as We Seem' makes fun of aristocrats. What a great title. So, St. Thomas not only has a theater, but also a cosmopolitan audience."

"You'd better come back now, Harris. You're losing focus, delving too much in detail; drifting off target. That's enough for your first trip."

He told me to close my eyes and move upward, as though swimming from under water to the surface.

A few moments later, I heard that now familiar tearing sound like Velcro ripping open. Was it the sound of breaking through the space-time barrier?

Seconds later, I awoke in Kwame's backroom.

"A complete success!" he exclaimed. "I know you're tired...don't speak. Just relax."

And, so ended my first complete trip.

6 DINNER AT THE COMMERCIAL HOTEL

"Statistics show that of those who contract the habit of eating, very few survive."

— George Bernard Shaw, playwright, 1856-1950

It took a couple of days doing chores with Mary and John to feel normal again. We even took *Perseverance* out and spent the night moored on Salt Pond Bay in the National Park.

Then, back to my research. In 1860s Charlotte Amalie, dinners were customarily served at 6 pm – likely timed to catch the last light from the setting sun. Sunset varied little in that latitude and it was full dark by 7 pm or so year round.

I was now ready to dine with El Presidente's son, Angel Lopez de Santa Anna, and Sir Fitzroy Grannum, Managing Director of the Colonial Bank at 6 pm on October 27, 1867. The venue was the Commercial Hotel and Coffee House, located across a narrow street from the waterfront square now known as Emancipation Garden. On one side, the square was bounded by Fort Christian; the other, by warehouses and commercial buildings. King's Wharf jutted into the harbor nearby.

Kwame and I followed the now familiar preparations and procedures. I was soon on my way from his bed.

Once again, complete blackness was broken by that Velcro-like sound. Or, was it tearing paper?

Regardless, I was again floating through clouds and catching glimpses of turquoise, indigo and full blue below. This was the sea and the colors depended upon its depth, clarity and bottom. Shallow, sandy water was marked by the lightest shades of turquoise. Deeper waters were more blue. A coral bottom could show up as brownish or reddish or purple, depending upon depth and type of reef.

Suddenly, I saw the smoke from ships' funnels in the basin-like harbor nearly surrounded by bright green mountains.

"I'm over the harbor now," I said aloud. "Several steamers are here and small boats are skirting between them and town."

"Good, Professor," Kwame replied. "Keep floating downward gradually using your swimming motions."

I now saw the bright, red walls of Fort Christian with the Danish flag flying.

An old-style Baltimore clipper schooner moored not far from King's Wharf caught my eye. I couldn't see her name, but believed it to be the two-masted *Vigilant*. An American privateer during the War of 1812, she'd been built in Baltimore in the 1790s. The Danes bought her in the 1820s or 30s for use as a coast guard vessel. It also carried mail, passengers and goods between St. Thomas and St. Croix. She was in use until the 1920s.

As I closed in on the wharf, I saw that every one of the *Vigilant's* lines were hauled taut, made fast, and slack ends neatly coiled. Her sails, big lateen rigs, were neatly furled behind each mast, as were the square sails on the yard arms of the main mast. Stay sails and jibs were neatly furled between foremast and the tip of the bow sprit.

The deck below her two masts could use some varnish, but otherwise she looked great. A bareheaded, white-haired, old salt sat on the transom in the stern near the wheel, smoking a pipe.

"Make a note of this, Kwame," I said. "I'm sure I'm looking at the *Vigilant*, an old Baltimore schooner famous in the Danish West Indies."

"Move on, Professor. You are being sidetracked."

"Okay, I'm now moving to the wharf."

I slowed down and hovered ten or twelve feet above the pier. Below were crowds of people doing everyday chores. Here and there native Virgin Island men carried baskets full of fish balanced on either end of bamboo poles resting across their shoulders. Peddlers were selling sea shells and chunks of coral as souvenirs to travelers from the steamers.

Old women carried trays of cakes sprinkled with sugar on their heads. The cakes were arranged on neat linen towels and offered to newly arrived passengers.

A younger woman sat on the edge of the embankment next to the wharf selling necklaces made from brightly colored seeds and beads. Others offered slices of sugar cane and pineapples as treats for hot, weary visitors and residents.

Beyond the wharf was Emancipation Garden square, lined with large ornamental conch shells, native cabbage palms and huge ferns. Within the square were a few large mahogany trees, a grass lawn and in the center, a bandstand. Dressed in white military uniforms with peaked hats, a brass band played peppy marches to the delight of the crowd. Every wrought-iron bench was filled to capacity with older men and women.

Victorian ladies of all races were promenading and talking in small groups. Though simple by London and Parisian standards, their clothes appeared to be made of sensible linen and cotton. Whites and blues were the favored colors here in the tropics. Northern European women covered their necks and shoulders. Spanish ladies and those of mixed race were more daring, wearing more colorful sleeveless dresses and open necks, displaying a bit of skin. Long-haired children, both boys and girls, wearing little sailor outfits or school uniforms, were running around on the grass.

A young Afro-European girl was brushing a small donkey tied to a post. She softly sang:

My donkey walk.
My donkey talk.
My donkey eat
with a knife and fork.
Tinagayo,
Come little donkey come.
Tinagayo,
Come little donkey come.

My donkey laugh.
My donkey sing.
My donkey wearin'
a diamond ring.

Tinagaya,
Come little donkey come.[2]

Adult conversations in English, Spanish, German and French floated up as I moved to the center of the square. There was too much background noise to hear individual sentences. The music of trumpets, tubas and drums was too loud.

I wondered if the concert and gathering was a daily event, like the sunset celebrations in modern Key West. Above the trees I could see the red, crenellated clock tower of Fort Christian. The time was 5:30. The correct time of day, but was it the right date?

"Professor! What are you seeing?"

"I'm in Emancipation Garden at 5:30 pm," I replied aloud. "Whites and Afro-Europeans mix freely in a way that would be impossible in the American south in this era. I saw the same in Market Square on my last visit. The races interact easily and cordially."

"Following emancipation, the Danes were very tolerant of people with money, regardless of race, nationality or religion," Kwame replied. "But, do not be deceived, Professor. As you well know, labor conditions were harsh for ordinary workers. Strikes and riots did happen."

"Of course," I said. "Like everywhere else in those days."

"Get your mind back on your objective, Professor. Concentrate and do not become distracted."

Across the square was the block-long Commercial Hotel and Coffee House, made of white plaster-faced stone. On the first floor, wide arches opened onto a narrow street bordering the square. I knew the hotel lobby and dining room were located inside the arches to catch harbor breezes and shade from the square.

The second story was all open arches supported by classical style columns. Behind the columns facing the harbor was a wide veranda. People sat in comfortable bamboo and rattan chairs enjoying the concert and, perhaps, waiting for a dinner gong. A peaked wooden roof with large dormer windows made a third story. That would later be destroyed by a fire during a wild Christmas party and ball in 1873.

"Kwame, I'm the only person alive to have seen the third story of the hotel," I said. "It's an odd feeling."

"Concentrate, Professor. Focus on your target. It is 5:30. People will begin arriving for dinner."

I floated out of the square and around the corner of Tolbod Gade. There was the hotel's main entrance, flanked by columns. A narrow New Orleans-style, wrought-iron balcony ran across the second story in front of tall, rectangular windows. All were open and people were leaning against the frames or sitting in chairs to catch the breeze. White draperies were fluttering in the wind. A few men in shirtsleeves stood smoking pipes and cigars, leaning against the balcony. Several wore derby hats.

"I'm at the main entrance now" I said. "A blue-uniformed porter is carrying in trunks and suitcases from a handcart. People are hanging out on the balcony above and on either side of the entrance."

Nearest the door stood a beautiful Afro-European woman with an hourglass figure. Wearing a starched muslin dress, pink gloves and a broad brimmed hat, she held a basket of flowers. I moved closer to her and the doorway. Before long, a black enameled carriage with polished silver and brass fittings pulled up to the entrance. A driver dressed in livery jumped down to the door, which had a coat of arms featuring a British lion and crossed palm trees. Out stepped a middle-aged gentleman wearing a top hat, double-breasted, light blue, cut-away coat, white shirt, white bow tie and white pants. He had a thin, well-trimmed mustache.

The Afro-European woman stepped forward and handed him a yellow rose. "That's for love, dear," she said in perfect English.

"Yes, indeed," the gentleman replied with a slight bow and tip of his hat. "Thank you, mademoiselle." He put the rose in his lapel.

With my twentieth-century mind, I wondered, was this a Victorian proposition? But, to this day, many island women routinely call men "dear," "sweet heart" and 'love," as a matter of courtesy.

As I watched, the gentleman took a few steps forward while the porter cleared the door of people and baggage.

"Welcome, Sir Fitzroy," he said.

I had my man and followed him inside where a gentleman wearing a tuxedo-like outfit I took to be evening dress welcomed the bank manager. He led Sir Fitzroy past a front desk and into the dining room on the right. I looked back to the desk. Above it was a black chalkboard with steamship departure times and the date:

October 27, 1867. Bingo!

I turned and caught up to the manager who led Sir Fitzroy past an elaborately set table on which polished silverware was artfully arranged on a white linen tablecloth. A vase of fragile red, yellow and orange bougainvillea flowers was the center piece.

"Here you are, Sir Fitzroy; near enough to the arch to feel the breeze, but shaded from the setting sun."

"Thank you, Edward," Sir Fitzroy replied, sitting down without even glancing at a chair in the sure knowledge Edward would pull one out and place it under his rump.

"As you know, Edward, I will be dining with President Santa Anna's son this evening."

"I know, sir. We will ensure you have all you wish."

Along the dining room walls were elaborately carved mahogany sideboards with white marble tops and framed mirrors. Candles in crystal chandeliers provided soft, diffused light.

The room was beginning to fill. I looked impatiently toward the door. In the background, I heard conversations in English, French, German and Spanish. The Afro-European waiters spoke to each diner in his or her native tongue.

With a sudden break in conversation, in strode a tall, handsome, black-haired, young man wearing a blue and red uniform with gold epaulettes and braided cords. All eyes turned to him. He looked just like paintings of his father as a young officer.

Edward fawned over him and led him ceremoniously to Sir Fitzroy, who stood and bowed.

"Good evening, Colonel Santa Ana," he said. I knew Santa Anna the younger was actually a local businessman. His father must have made him a colonel in the Mexican army and, like most 19th-century men, he loved to wear a uniform on social occasions.

"Good evening, Sir Fitzroy," the young colonel said in slightly accented English. He, too, sat down without looking, certain Edward would not fail to put a chair under him.

I floated to a position above the table to ensure hearing everything.

As they gossiped about society matters and the shipping industry, waiters brought in food. Rather than serving them in proper sequential courses, however, they brought the first few rounds out all at once. Must be a local custom, I thought, though I couldn't figure what the advantage was.[3]

Plates of soup, fish and roast beef were brought out and arranged in a circle in front of each diner. Glasses of both red and white wine were presented. They could sip white with fish and red with the meat at their own initiative as they dined.

With impeccable European manners, Sir Fitzroy and the young Colonel slowly ate their food, enjoying the wines. Other diners were not so fastidious. I heard slurps, burps and the unmistakable sound of flatulence.

Finally, Colonel Santa Anna got down to business.

"This imminent takeover by the Americans is most distressful for my father. He cannot conceive of living under Yankee rule."

"I understand, Colonel, sir. It is a most distasteful prospect. More Americans seem to be arriving daily on New York packets. I suffer their twang accent in my office more often than I care to think of. But, they do have money, I must say. And, we all knew this was coming."

"Nevertheless, Sir Fitzroy, my father will not stand idle. We will be selling our properties here presently."

"I am most sorry to hear that, Colonel. Your family has been a mainstay of our society these past few years."

"Yes, I know that is so. I may stay on for a year or two. Various business affairs will need to be settled. But, my father has vowed never to return to an American St. Thomas. He finds New York odious enough."

"I am quite in sympathy with your views, Colonel," Sir Fitzroy said with a pained expression. In a more hushed, empathetic tone reminding me of an undertaker, he continued, "But, what of your gold and silver specie, Colonel? *My* vault will always be in *British* hands, sir."

"Father does not trust the Americans to rule this island and your bank sits upon it. We must move the specie to a non-American sanctuary."

"As you know, Colonel, the British West Indies Colonial Bank has offices located in the heart of the City of London – just a few steps from the Bank of England. Our vaults are the safest in the world. Our gold and silver bank notes are as solid as an anvil, sir," he exclaimed with a slap of the table. "You can reliably trade them in any nation of the world – even in America."

"I understand that, Sir Francis. That is why I asked to meet with you. Am I correct that you have priority space reserved on each Royal Mail Steamer?"

"Correct you are, sir!"

"How soon could we ship the bullion and specie to London? My father worries the Americans may try to lay claim to it with haste. You see, he has experienced some unpleasantness in New York of a legal nature."

"Sir, you are in good hands. I can secure sufficient space on the *RMS Mersey* due to depart in two days – 29th of October. She is a sound ship; a veteran of many transatlantic voyages. She has a very experienced captain, late of Her Majesty's Navy. You can depend on us, sir."

"I am certain of that, Sir Fitzroy. Let us proceed. Father will be very pleased his assets will be in safe hands before the Americans march ashore."

"Quite, so," Sir Fitzroy concurred. He then rose.

"A toast to Presidente Antonio López de Santa Anna and a free Republic of Mexico!"

The Colonel rose as well. They clinked their wine glasses and drained them. Other gentlemen had also stood and drained theirs, as a matter of courtesy.

Now it was the Colonel's turn. "To her gracious majesty, Victoria, Empress of the British Empire!"

Many more men were now standing. "Hear! Hear!" More clinking glass, more wine drained.

Now toasts at other tables were offered to a variety of monarchs and princes; more clinking glasses were drained.

So, that was that, I thought. Santa Anna's gold would be shipped to London. But, did it make it?

As I thought over the implications, waiters were bringing in the next series of courses. Salads, cheese, and custards were being arranged in front of each diner. Small bowls of what I took to be guava jelly were placed next to cheeses. John would have loved this meal, I thought.

At another table, a gentleman dipped a slice of cheese in the jelly and ate it *with his hands.* His plump wife loaded her cheese on a knife, raised it, leaned her head back and slid it all into her open mouth. I feared these might be some of the Americans worrying Sir Fitzroy with bad manners.

Then I heard the wife say, "Sehr gut." With relief, I realized they were German.

In any event, I'd seen and heard enough. No point waiting for brandy and cigars on the veranda.

"I have the information we need, Kwame."

"Good, Professor. Now let's bring you home."

I regained my body and full consciousness looking up at Kwame's wooden fan blades.

"How are you feeling, Professor?"

"Tired, Kwame."

And, very disappointed, I realized.

"I learned the gold may have been shipped to London on a Royal Mail Steam Packet. I'll need to search port records to learn more. Right now, I just need to rest."

"Take as much time as you need, Harris. Would you like some cold guava juice?"

"Yes, please."

The next morning, while John was at his guitar lesson

at St. John School of the Arts, it seemed the right time to tell Mary about my remote viewing adventures.

We were reading newspapers at the kitchen table.

"Do you recall our discussion about Kwame's ESP and his work for the Navy?"

She put the paper down, with a look of consternation.

"Yes, has something happened?"

"He taught me how to use my own powers. Turns out most everyone can find and develop them with help."

"Really," she said skeptically. "I suppose you're going to use them to talk to aliens."

"Hardly," I said, not realizing she was joking – or, maybe half-joking.

"I was joking. But, nothing would surprise me. So, what are you doing with these powers?"

"Using what some people call astral projection or out of body experience, our consciousness can travel back in time."

She looked genuinely stunned.

"I know it sounds wacky. But, it's true. I can explain the physics and scientific basis for this, if you wish. The Navy and CIA call this process remote viewing. But, they use it to spy on adversaries in our own, current time. Kwame and I have perfected remote viewing of past times."

"Was Kwame doing this in the Navy?"

"Yes. He was a top-rated remote viewer."

She still looked taken aback. So, I explained the science behind it all.

After taking it in, she regained her composure.

"Just what are you looking at back there? Where and what time period?"

"St. Thomas in 1867. We're searching for Santa Anna's gold."

"I should have known. What have you found?"

I brought her up to date. She nodded, then looked alarmed.

"Is this dangerous?"

"No, not really. Kwame is my control for lack of a better word. He monitors my heart and brain waves while I'm ...gone. He follows the same procedures and safety protocol he learned in the Navy."

"That's not all that reassuring, considering what your friends Lieutenant Taft and Admiral Turner got us into with the UFO stuff."

"All I can say is that it works and it's safe."

She thought a few moments and said something surprising.

"I almost wish you hadn't told me. Now, I'll worry. Can I be part of this?"

"The process requires Kwame and my total concentration. A third party, no matter how loving and supportive, would not help. That's why we have been working at his house. We can't have interruptions from family or pets – not even good old Molly."

As I spoke, our husky laying on the kitchen floor looked up at the mention of her name.

"I'm not sure I like this," Mary said softly. She started to cry. "Think of what happened with the UFOs. You could have died."

"But, I didn't and this is not dangerous at all. Physically, I never leave Kwame's house and he watches over me.

"Besides, this is very important breakthrough work we're doing – not just because of the gold. We're doing things no one has done before."

"I understand that."

"If it makes you feel any better, Kwame and I will include you and John in the treasure hunt as much as possible as we move forward. And, you may debrief me whenever you need to."

"Agreed," she reluctantly said. But, she was still crying.

I held her hand and said, "We have work to do."

Later that day, I went back to the library. After a few

hours I made a startling discovery. October 29, 1867, the *RMS Mersey's* departure date, was the day the islands were hit by the San Narciso Hurricane.

"San Narciso," I said to myself. "Odd name for a storm."

It turned out that the hurricane had struck the islands on the feast day of Saint Narcissus, an early bishop of Jerusalem. I wondered if he were a narcissist.

A monster later estimated as a category three or greater, the San Narcisso hurricane had grown and approached so rapidly there was little warning. Large, tell-tale barometer falls didn't occur until the storm was nearly upon the islands. No unusual cloud buildups or swells had warned seamen in time. San Narciso was fast-moving and deadly.

Even if there had been signs, who knows if people would have believed them. In the 1860s, the British and other Europeans with little Caribbean experience thought that by mid-October the hurricane season was long over. With their industrial revolution era belief in the certainties of science triumphing over nature, the British, in particular, would likely have disbelieved their own eyes – until it was too late.

When it hit, most people were unprepared. As many as five hundred lives were lost on St. Thomas. At least 60 boats sank in her harbor.

It was not surprising that I found no record of the *RMS Mersey* departing that very day. At the same time, however, she was not listed in post-storm reports as one of the lost ships.

I realized I'd need to go back and see what happened to her; I needed to go back to the day of the hurricane.

7 A BIT OF A BREEZE

"Are you a lot of women passengers to be taken care of? We are here to take care of the ship and some of you ain't up to that; Can't stand a bit of a breeze without crying over it?"

— First Mate Baker berating the panicked crew of the sailing vessel *Narcissus* as she floated helpless, blown over on her side in hurricane winds. See Joseph Conrad's 1897 classic, "The Narcissus", page 96, Internet Archive edition.

We met at Kwame's house early in the morning. We both knew this particular trip held unknown danger. I believed the scientists who said consciousness was made up of subatomic particles. Kwame agreed. Although tiny and bizarre, the particles were still solid – still vulnerable to nature, even in back time.

As he wired me up for the launch, Kwame said what we were both thinking.

"We must be very vigilant today, Harris. If you are caught in 150-mile-per-hour winds, we don't know what might happen. You must follow my instructions closely.

You must keep me informed about the weather. And, you must come back when I say so. Agreed?"

"Yes, Kwame. I agree. I'll keep close watch on the weather."

It wasn't long before I was in perfect darkness. Then, the ripping sound focused my thoughts.

I opened my eyes. Below me seabirds were circling – brown boobies, cormorants, petrels and even some frigate birds, which come to shore mostly when storms approach. I saw a couple of piping plovers – nearly extinct in our time. These and other birds were all circling in downward spirals toward cliffs and mountain peaks. They must have been going to nests – or other shelter.

As I descended through the clouds, I looked seaward. Out well beyond the harbor entrance, where water met sky, a thin line of dark clouds was slowly moving toward the island. People on the ground probably couldn't see them. And, the sun was shining. The sea was so flat, you could see the paler color of currents, like streams in a blue desert.

"I'm going down to the harbor, Kwame."

"Very good, Professor."

"Hey, there's a steamer with two masts and no paddle wheels flying the Danish flag. Looks to be about 100 feet long. Smoke rises from her funnel. She's tied along the side of a clipper ship at least twice as long. The clipper's sails are furled. The steamer must be acting as a tug boat. She's slowly pushing and pulling the clipper further into the harbor. They're in the middle of what must be a hundred boats of all types anchored or moored."

I was transfixed by the beautiful boat. "The Danish boat must be a propeller-driven steamer being used as a tug boat. But she has two raked masts and the lines of a fast schooner," I said out loud. "Must be the *Vice Gouverneur Berg* built in Copenhagen in 1863."[1]

"Good, Professor," Kwame said. "Sounds like you have reached the correct decade."

Thank goodness the *Berg* survived the coming storm, I thought. Although she did sink, she was successfully refloated; then I realized she's long gone now, anyway.

Kwame interrupted my thoughts.

"Don't get sidetracked, Professor. Keep your mind on the objective. Float down slowly to your target."

As though swimming, I descended, approaching a two-masted steamship anchored by Hassel Island. Amidships, on either side of her hull were the huge, curved wooden boxes built around paddle wheels. I slowly descended upon her.

Then, I remembered Kwame.

"I'm coming down between the mast stays of a sidewheeler steamer, aiming for an empty patch of deck just forward of the funnel. People in Victorian clothes are on deck, watching a large, black barge tied along the ship just forward of the starboard paddle wheel. A black haze makes it hard to see the barge and the Afro-European men and women working on deck near it."

I eased down, floating to about six feet above deck. No one could see me, of course.

Barefoot, white crewmen wearing short, blue jackets with brass buttons and white trousers formed a line to hold back well-dressed passengers from the barge and workers. They were trying to get close enough to look into a large open hatch. A fog of black dust floated upward.

Gentlemen had taken off their jackets. Ladies were dabbing their faces with embroidered handkerchiefs.

Observing them, I could almost feel the heat and humidity. The harbor was flat as ice. No wind – a true calm before a storm. Was it the correct storm? And, what was the date?

I "swam" back upward a few feet for a better look at the ship.

"What's happening, Professor? Remember, no one there can hear or see you."

I described the scene, "In a black dust cloud, a steady line of women with high woven baskets balanced on their heads are coming and going from a barge. Those climbing up to the steamer's deck have baskets filled with large black rocks – coal. Some are singing. Some are coughing from dust. Some are shouting at each other in a patois I don't understand.

"They wear dirty turbans or scarves and what look like thin, brown and white calico dresses that end at the knee. They are barefoot, walking with perfectly straight backs. I know the loads they carry balanced on their heads weigh 85 pounds or more. They earn a penny for each."

It's amazing, I thought. Balancing their head loads, they climbed up a ladder-like ramp from the barge. Taking a few steps on deck, they dumped their baskets into an open hatch. Must be the coal bunker. These ladies could load 300 tons of coal a day. And, a ship like this would need 1,500 tons of coal to get back to Britain. She'd burn 100 tons each day at sea.

Black men – some without shirts – stood around the hatch with rakes and shovels. Mostly naked boys jumped down into the black hole to rake out the growing pile of coal into a level mass. They were all covered in coal dust. Sweat cut streams down their bodies and splashed in black puddles on the deck.

"Once they dump their baskets," I continued out loud for Kwame, "the women climb back down another ramp into the coal barge. There, men shovel in new loads for them to take back up. It's a continuous loop.

"Passengers are watching, pointing and laughing. By Victorian standards, the coal women's sweaty, clinging, thin dresses are somewhat provocative," I explained to Kwame. "Some male passengers are grinning, drinking beer and what looks like whiskey as they watch. And, some women have glasses of wine.

"The coal women of St. Thomas were world famous."

"Yes, Professor. I read about them in history class as a

child."

I stopped talking, listening as the black workers broke into spontaneous songs. Some melodies were familiar – probably church hymns from Northern Europe. Some songs I couldn't follow.

Remembering Kwame, I started talking, again.

"A young black man is standing on a plank that seems to be part of the coal barge ramp frame. He's wearing a red, open shirt and stained, white pants, cut off just below the knee. He seems to be beating time with a small drum – like a bongo drum."

I stopped talking, listening as the time beater started a song. All the workers joined in. This time they sang in a recognizable English dialect. The first lyric had something to do with New York.

Captain he heard it, he was troubled in him mind.
Ya-he-ho-o-hu
Captain he go to him cabin, he drink him whisky and wine
Ya-he-ho-o-hu
You go to America? You as well go to heaven.
Ya-he-ho-o-hu"[2]

As they sang, rakers working the bunker swung in rhythm. Down in the barge, shovelers moved to the music, standing in a pool of thick black liquid – the bilge of the nearly empty coal barge.

Women were bringing up their last basket loads, swaying their hips to the music. As they climbed back down, they laughed, slapped each other's backs and danced to the drum beat.

Suddenly, I heard a string quartet. I looked aft where a white awning shaded the deck. It stretched from the paddle wheel casings to the stern rail. Passengers drifted sternward, now that the coal women were finished. Wooden deck chairs and a mahogany table with fruits and bottles of wine, champagne, rum and beer were laid out.

Stewards in red jackets served drinks in crystal glasses.

Off the stern flew a large flag – white with the red cross of St. Andrew and a gold crown in the center.

"Kwame, this *is* a British Royal Mail Steamer – the luxury, transatlantic cruise ship of its time. Now, I need to find its name."

"Sounds very good, Harris."

One well-dressed white woman still stood near the coal bunker ogling male workers. As they finished their work, naked boys were climbing up onto the deck carrying rakes from the bunker. Some dove off the rail into the harbor.

A steward appeared next to the woman. "Madam, if you would be so kind as to come aft, now. We 'ave refreshments for you."

A seaman walked by below me in a blue jacket with a round, rimless, black hat. "RMS Mersey" was printed in gold on a ribbon around the cap's edge.[3]

"What are you seeing?" Kwame asked loudly in a worried voice. Guess he thought he'd lost me.

"We're on target! It's the *RMS Mersey*, all right...A beautiful sidewheeler carrying rich passengers, cargo and mail – built in 1858.

"Coal workers are singing and leaving the deck with their tools. They've finished filling the bunkers. White passengers are drinking on the stern deck and a quartet is playing Strauss tunes. I'm going to explore the ship a bit more."

Sternward, I saw the companion way door leading down to officers' quarters. A bronze hook held it open. I floated down through it, descending the narrow, dark stairwell into an open mahogany- and teak-paneled area. In the center, a table was hung by brass chains so it could swing with the boat's movements. Officers' mess, I thought. Several doors with air slats lined port and starboard sides – officers' cabins. Facing aft, a single door pierced a bulkhead. That would be the captain's suite.

Facing forward, the room ended at an iron door with bank vault-like hinges and locks. The frame was sealed with glued strips of paper, bearing what I knew to be officers' signatures.

"I found the bullion room," I said out loud. "It's sealed. The ship must be preparing for its return voyage to Britain. That's why passengers are on board and the coal was topped-up."

"That must be the boat we want, Professor. But, can you see anything that indicates the date?"

The ink of the signatures was smudged. I couldn't read the date.

"Nothing down here. I'm going back up, Kwame, to try to figure what date this is."

I drifted higher, above the deck and masts, to get a better look around the harbor.

"Well, the ships are all from the mid-1800s or older, Kwame. The *Mersey* is 1858. That Danish tug is 1863. We know that much."

Not far from the steamer was the shoreline of Hassel Island, a ship service center right in Charlotte Amalie's harbor. Directly opposite the *Mersey* onshore was a long wooden and stone building – a warehouse with docks for smaller craft. White and black workmen stood around in front talking and smoking. The best-dressed man had a folded black umbrella crooked in his arm. A big puddle of water lay at their feet. Must have rained, I thought.

Above them and the building was a large, long sign – white paint on black background. I said out loud, "Kwame, the warehouse onshore about 25 yards in from my steamer has a big sign, 'Royal Mail Steam Packet Company.' These buildings date to about 1850."

I floated a bit higher and looked along the Hassel Island shoreline toward town.

There was the Danish steam-powered marine railway at the landward end. Its engine house was where it should be. It was different, however. I'd never seen it with its roof and all its walls in place.

The three-story, red building with a peaked tin roof had

a high, brick smokestack. It housed the vast beam steam engine with its cogs and large wheel that powered the marine railway.

Chains with man-sized links stretched from the building out through a one-story tall, stone-lined door. The chains led down a slightly sloped hill; they were drawn tight and affixed to a huge, green, heartwood cradle on railroad wheels at the waters' edge. In the cradle sat a big, three-masted barkenteen. It had been pulled up out of the water on iron rails. The cradle and boat now rested dry on the incline.

Workers of all races were on ladders scraping barnacles and digging out sea worms from the bark's wooden hull. One fellow in a sweat-stained brown shirt spit the cigar from his bearded mouth as he nearly fell from a wooden ladder in the struggle to pull a two-foot long, milky white worm from the tunnel it had dug into a hull plank.

It was hard, nasty work. I heard the scraping, tapping, laughing and cursing as the workmen battled the slimy creatures that looked like intestines.

Blood dripped from one man's hand as he misjudged the angle of the chisel he was using to scrape off the sharp oval shells of barnacles. Having slashed my own arm scraping these tenacious crustaceans from my sailboat's hull, I felt sorry for these men. They fought these creatures day after tedious day.

On level ground in the work yard, I saw open-sided sheds with tools, iron gears, huge nuts and bolts and other parts. There was a blacksmith's shop.

Big puddles of water filled in the low ground. Must have been raining a lot earlier in the day, I thought. Then I remembered Kwame and said out loud, "The Danish marine railway is here and operating; built in the 1840s. Incredible to see."

"Very good, Professor."

I looked out toward the harbor and continued talking.

"Offshore near the marine railway slip is a huge U-shaped structure made of big, tall iron pontoons. A narrow building is on top of one side. It has a smoke stack. The other side has a tall crane...the floating dock! One was towed to St. Thomas in the summer of 1867. We're getting closer to dating this time."[4]

"Excellent, Professor. Keep narrowing it down."

Looking further along the shoreline, seaward from the marine railway and beyond the Royal Mail Steamship building and piers, was the careening cove. Smaller sailing vessels would be emptied on a nearby dock and run aground on the shallow sand bottom. There, they'd be hauled over for hull scraping, repairs and caulking. I recognized a low stone building along one side of the cove. Today, it's a sail loft.

"The careening cove is here, Kwame ...of course, that's been used since the 1700s."

Further along the island's shoreline and still facing seaward, I saw the harbor mouth. Protecting its entrance were the stone walls and buildings of Fort Willoughby, a Danish fort strengthened by the British around 1800 when they briefly occupied St. Thomas – uninvited – to keep out Napoleon's French navy. This day, I saw cannons in the fort's gun ports, ready for use.

Above the fort on Hassel Island's peak was British-built Cowell's Battery. It was armed with two big cannons. Within the battery's stone walls was a red-roofed, white masonry building with a black-roofed porch looking seaward. Near the building, planted in the ground, was a tall, thick mast with a high cross boom. Many lines ran up to the boom and back down through ship blocks. Two huge black balls were suspended part way up the mast. Atop the mast flew the Danish flag.[5]

As I watched, the flag started flapping wildly and the lines holding the black balls bended toward town. A strong sea breeze had kicked up from a dead calm. Heavy rain now bounced off the Battery building's roof.

I explained what I was seeing to Kwame, "I'm above

the Hassel Island semaphore that signals Charlotte Amalie's harbor master about incoming ships; it's been here since 1800. The British built it with a battery when they occupied St. Thomas."

Four black men in white clothes were holding down their flapping straw hats. They stood at the battery's seaward wall looking out and pointing. A row of dark clouds was growing larger and coming closer. A large puddle of water had collected along the wall near where they stood. A white man in a blue uniform wearing a cream colored pith helmet adorned with a shined brass badge stepped off the porch and walked toward them. He carried a telescope.

A sound was growing more intense –a deep, baritone hum as though muffled in the bottom of a steel drum. With instinctive fright, I recognized the rumble of a gale, or worse. I'd heard it while sailing off the British Virgin Islands on days when small craft warnings were being issued. It's intimidating. One such stormy day, Mary became nauseous and John had a seizure onboard our *Perseverance*.

It started to rain lightly.

I looked back along Hassel Island's shoreline toward town, still trying to discover the date. Something big was missing, I realized.

"Kwame, I don't see the Hamburg-American Packet Company's coaling station and warehouse," I said out loud. "They were built in 1870."

I swam upward in the air and looked landward over the mountain ridge and beyond the marine railway building and its smokestack. A sloop-rigged sailboat was moving briskly between the railway and the edge of town. It confirmed what I suspected. Although Hassel Island and its ship repair, coaling and provisioning complexes had always been physically separate from St. Thomas in our time, it had once been attached to the main island by an isthmus. In those days, that sloop would have been aground on sand by now.

"I see the channel the Danes dug in 1860," I said out loud. "Hassel is an island this day."

The big sloop with brownish sails – and with it a scum of effluent runoff from town, including a few planks, timbers and rubbish – was moving out of the main harbor and into wider channels between Hassel and nearby Water Island. The channels and small bays would take pollution out to sea. As intended, the cut was relieving the main harbor of waste and the swamp-like miasma vapors people then thought caused yellow fever and malaria. Mosquitoes that bred in stagnant water were the real culprits, of course. Getting the harbor water flowing did help.

"Must be at least 1867," I said out loud. "But, not yet 1870."

Suddenly, it was nearly dark – like an eclipse. I looked seaward again. The sun had disappeared and from the shrinking horizon I saw four-foot swells rolling toward the harbor. A slow-moving and building cliff of high, black clouds was approaching closer and closer. The rain grew more intense.

"Shit, I'm seeing a storm – a big one," I said out loud.

"Keep calm, Professor," Kwame said evenly. "Just tell me what you see."

I asked myself and him, "Why is everyone in the harbor acting normally?"

"They don't have radar," he said, stating the obvious. "No way to predict weather."

"Not entirely true," I replied. "Captains checked their barometers regularly, and carefully observed cloud formations and sea swells. A competent seaman could forecast conditions a day or two ahead or more."

In the harbor below me, ships and boats were starting to rock as the first large swells came in. Signal flags were raised. A cannon shot echoed over the harbor, just a bit louder than the now shrieking, high treble sound of wind racing through steel cables, manila ropes, wooden blocks, lines and spars of the more than one hundred vessels below me.

Row boats, steam tenders, small inter-island sloops and smaller shallops were skirting around the larger ships, heading for shore. Lines of men pulled ashore smaller vessels that could be beached.

Big steamers began belching black smoke – stoking boilers to get up heads of steam. They must hope to leave the harbor and its dangerous lee shore for open water to better ride out a storm, I thought.

Closer to shore, I saw a warship. A royal Spanish flag flew from the two-masted steamer. She had cannons secured on the main deck. No smoke came from her funnel. But, scores of sailors scrambled up the ratlines to mast heads with axes and big hammers. They were taking down the masts and cutting away rigging.

Amazed, I said aloud, "A Spanish steam warship is cutting her rigging and dropping her masts. The Captain must expect quite a storm. An incredible thing to do. Courageous? Stupid?"

Kwame asked, "Why would they do that?"

"Hold on," I said.

When I looked seaward, the black cliff of clouds was growing higher and closer. Now, six-foot swells and bigger were approaching the harbor. Maybe the Spanish Captain was preparing to ride out a big storm at anchor. Could the masts cause a capsize? Did he know it was too late for any of them to escape the harbor?

"San Narciso," I said out loud. "Kwame, it *is* our target date – October 29, 1867."

"Keep calm, Harris."

"The killer hurricane is here," I shouted.

Then, recalling eyewitness accounts, I said numbly, "Over on St. John at the Emmaus Moravian mission in Coral Bay, the Brothers checked their barometer earlier today, saw nothing alarming and sat down to a leisurely midday supper."

I thought for a moment and said out loud, "It must now be midafternoon."

"Stay calm, Professor," Kwame urged.

Right! That was easy for him to say.

Thoughts raced through my mind. I was in an ethereal, but real state. Although invisible and silent to human eyes and ears in 1867, I was nevertheless there, composed of tangible subatomic particles. My consciousness *was* onsite. Could my particles be blasted apart by 150-mile-per-hour or greater winds?

"Professor, listen to me," Kwame said calmly. "I think you'd better come back now. We don't know what can happen."

Above Hassel Island, I could see the storm moving closer…seemingly inch by inch. Incoming swells were lifting and dropping anchored boats as the wind increased. By now, all ships had swung facing seaward and windward on their anchors and moorings.

Looking landward, I saw red tiles ripping off roofs and could feel myself being buffeted and propelled leeward toward land. Spotting the thick stone walls of the Marine Railway steam engine plant, I dove down, trying to reach it.

But, the wind was carrying me now. Concentrating hard, I swam lower, though felt out of control. A mast appeared in front of me out of nowhere. I hit it and actually felt myself bounce off. Had I lost any particles? Fortunately, I ricocheted downward to the Hassel shoreline where I landed in the lee of the British Mail Steamer building. Now I was out of the wind for the moment.

Struggling to keep low to the ground, I "swam" from the lee of the building to the shelter of a tree trunk, then, another structure and another tree. Laboriously, I finally reached the marine railway engine house and dove through the large door into a dark, machine-filled cave. The smells of grease and coal were nearly overpowering. The huge chains extending out the door were still taut, still holding the three-masted ship in the cradle at the bottom of the rail way.[6]

Workmen were running up the incline between the rails and racing in through the big door. Huge, thick shutters were manhandled into windows and bolted shut with iron rods. After the last worker entered the engine house, two vast doors closed off most of the entrance. A portion of each door was cleverly cut out to fit around the chains that would need to remain in place. Through that opening, I could still see the harbor.

But, by the time my eyes had adjusted to the dark engine house interior, it was virtually sealed shut. Now, I couldn't quite see the workmen.

"Professor, where are you!" Kwame yelled. "Answer me!"

"Kwame, I'm okay. I'm in the marine railway engine building. It's built like a fortress. That's why it still stands today. I'm going to ride out the storm here. We need to know if the RMS Mersey survives. There's no record I could find of her sinking in the storm. Remember? That's why I came."

In the dark, I could hear the men who were all around me. They were muttering and laughing nervously. The wind had the locomotive sound nearly everyone describes in a hurricane or tornado.

"Just a wee bit of wind," I heard one man say. "Not to worry."

"Aye, right you are," another said. "Remember the old ditty: 'June too soon; July stand by; August look out you must; September remember; October all over.' This can't be a hurricane."

"Give me a pull on that flask, matey," another voice said.

"Wrong you are, sirs. De 'cane is come," a West Indian voice said excitedly. "The grazing cattle come down from mountain; frogs, lizards no sing in past night. The 'cane is come!"

"See here, boy, the hurricane season ended with the September full moon. T'is just a norther blow up that'll pass," an English voice assured.

"Now you see here; the boy's correct," a Southern-accented American voice said. "I've seen a mighty hurricane come ashore in the Savannah marshes. And, it was in the last days of October or first days of November, moon or no moon. That's gospel truth. Y'all best listen."

"And, who might that be a'speakin'?" a northern American voice asked snidely. "Is that the Secesh coward who skedaddled from that lowly pirate Cap Semmes first time he called here? Er' you the traitor now livin' snug as a bug with that negress in a tatu on the beach?"

The West Indian spoke again before a fight could start, "Secesh mon, he correct. It is a 'cane. Every day bucket go a well, one day de bucket bottom mus' drop out."

"Hold your danged tongues, all of you!" an American voice of authority boomed. "And, you Mr. Billy Yank, I've told you a'fore. That dad-blamed war is long over. And, the devil to both armies."

Authority continued speaking. I wished I could see him in the gloom.

"None of you – not you Yank; not you Reb; not you Limey; I say, not one of you is fit to lead blind monkeys! Now, you all listen to me. We are all of us over a barrel in here until this blows out, see. Let us batten down all hatches, secure all shutters and doors. You, Titus, go on up the stairs and look to the windows up top."

"Yasser, Cap," the West Indian answered.

"You, Johnny Reb, go to the cupboard behind the engine room door and fetch those bottles of Santa Cruzan. I am certain we will all need a cocktail a'fore this gale blows out. Since we ain't got no bitters and gin, that rum will need to do us. And, it will do us dandy. I want the bottles right here beside me. We'll all get tots as needed."[7]

The sounds of the men talking and moving merged with the wind outside. Matches were struck. Bits of faces appeared for an instant. I smelled tobacco.

"Professor, what is happening? Please answer me," Kwame said plaintively.

"I'm safe in the engine house with workmen. I can see out a small opening where the chain comes through the door; but, the view is limited to the center of the harbor and the floating dock area. The rain's too hard to see the opposite shoreline. It's coming down as though from a high-pressure hose. At times it blows horizontally. Water is breaking over the marine railway bulkheads and the bark they were working on has lost her masts. It's leaning way over against the leeward stone wall of the work slip. But, the chain is holding her tight."

Then, something flicked by my line of vision. Then, something else.

"Wait a minute," I said to Kwame. "The wind is changing. Stuff is blowing."

A few white stones were falling – no, not stones.

"Hail," I said out loud. "Kwame, it's hail. I can't believe it."

Marble-sized frozen balls were falling everywhere, bouncing off the rails and equipment, then melting the instant they laid still on the warm stone pavement outside the engine house. A few moments after it started, it was over.

"What that hitting walls and roof?" Titus, the West Indian, asked worriedly.

Bet he never saw hail before, or snow, I thought.

"Only hail stones; ice balls, boy," the northerner yelled back. "T'aint nothing to raise your concern."

Now, I saw a whirlwind building above the water near the floating dry dock, which was still anchored about halfway between the railway slip and King's Wharf. Water was being pulled up into a wind funnel. It was turning black and twisting up into the low lying mass of clouds. Lightening sparked out of it.

"A big water spout – no, must be a tornado," I said. "Kwame, isn't a water spout really a tornado?"[8]

"Don't know, Professor. That's your department."

In a flash of lightning, I looked back inside the engine house at the men: grimy faces, moustaches, bearded mouths, drooping pipes and fearful eyes. They were all looking through the cracks and margins of the shuttered windows and doors to catch a glimpse outside. They stood among giant, greased, black iron cogs and winch wheels. Then, we were all in darkness again.

Now a strong backwind clawed and sucked at the two-inch-thick mahogany shutters and doors, bending them outward as though they were cardboard. I hid behind the immense chain and its wheel, continuing to peek through the small door opening. A clearly defined, widening funnel in the harbor was dragging everything on land and water toward it.

"To the shutters and doors, men!" Authority was shouting louder than the wind. "Hold those shutters; keep 'em shut or we're all dead meat!"

A bang like a pistol shot and a scream cut through the foreman's words. An iron bar holding one shutter closed had snapped and whipped into a man's face. Visible in the twilight of the opened shutter, he was bleeding and grabbing desperately at the window frame, fighting the suction of the vortex, as dust, papers, pieces of wood and anything else loose flew out the window around him.

"Blazes and tarnation!" Authority yelled. "Sebastian and, you, Colchester! Jump over and take hold of Crequet's arms, now! Don't let the wind haul 'im away. Gallagher and Steiner, you bring over more iron bars and wooden beams. Get them shutters closed and barricaded.

The foreman's voice betrayed no fear. Raw anger was driving him.

"Johnny Reb! Titus! Git up those stairs right now and see them windows up thar still secure! Billy, you and Nathaniel git in that engine room and have a look see. Then, climb through to the boilers. See them back windows secure! This here beam engine is more valuable than the lot of us."

"What about the residence, yonder, Cap?" I knew someone was motioning to the other side of the thick wall shared with a two-story office and director's residence.

"Do as I say, Reb. Get up those stairs! That residence is not our concern. Our lives and this engine are all we need tend to. We'll be fortunate to save both."

Then, as though musing to himself, he continued, "I know of what I speak. I seen cyclones pull men right off a ship's deck down in the roaring 40's. Those latitudes are truly frightful – none of your balmy tropics down there. No, sirs! Take heart, men. This here is nothing but a passing blow up."

Lightening continued spinning off the funnel which was now moving toward town. A large, uprooted tree slammed into one of the arched wooden doors. They held.

Suddenly, a bright, blue glow or fire, like a Roman candle, shot from the mast and yardarm tips of a four-masted, fully rigged sailing vessel anchored just outside the water spout's orbit. Had she been struck by lightning? The flare turned blue-green as I watched spellbound. The unearthly glow ended abruptly when the ship's spars and furled sails were torn off their masts.

St. Elmo's fire…it had to be that aura borealis-like light caused by electrically ionized air, I told myself.

"Did you see that, Cap? St. Elmo's fire or I'm a cherry," blurted an awestruck voice near me. "A bad sign, Cap, very bad." I could almost feel the man trembling. "We are doomed."

"Humbug! If that is St. Elmo's, t'is a glorious good

omen," an Irish voice contradicted. Must be Gallagher, I thought.

"Quiet in the ranks, men," Authority stated. "We are safe here. Safest darn place in this damn harbor."

He even made me feel better.

"Kwame; for the first time ever I'm seeing St. Elmo's Fire," I said aloud. "That water spout looks a hell of a lot like a tornado.

"Jesus, its pulling and spinning ships around like a merry-go-round. A very big steamer and at least one large sailing ship are being crushed together against the twisting floating dock. One iron dock pontoon is now sinking slowly. Men are jumping off those boats, climbing over wreckage and up onto the higher dock pontoon. Other men trying to hold on are being sucked up into blackness like pieces of paper."

As I spoke, the wind funnel moved closer to land, releasing the two ships and floating dock from its spin.

The rain let up for a moment. There sat the big, black, iron diving bell resting solidly on land by the marine railway boat slip. But, in an instant, the spout's funnel teetered back over toward us. It lifted the bell and hurled it like a baseball, landing it near the bulkhead of the new Danish channel cut – a distance of at least one-quarter mile. Yet, that diving bell weighed nine tons.

The roofs of the railway tool sheds near the harbor and everything under them followed the diving bell. The work yard was swept clean. But, the chains still held the barkenteen in place in the railway slip, though its deck planks were now ripping off and flying to the funnel.

Then, rain blotted out my view.

"Kwame, you won't believe this. That iron diving bell recently restored by the Park Service was just thrown a quarter-mile or more!"

"Professor!" Kwame nearly shouted to get my attention. "You must come back. It's been three hours. You need to come back."

As he spoke, the rain lessened to a thick, wind-blown drizzle and the white caps of the harbor waves were now visible. Out nearer the opposite shoreline, a steamer with no masts was under power, plowing back and forth amid the tops of masts and other debris from boats now settling on the harbor bottom. She was pulling her lifeboats and had thick hawser lines dangling from her sides. Men clinging to the mast tops of wrecks and floating in flotsam leaped for the steamer's lines and lifeboats and were pulled up her hull to relative safety.

"A steamer with its masts neatly cut is powering around the harbor rescuing seamen," I said out loud. "Has to be that Spanish naval vessel I saw earlier. That Captain knew exactly what a hurricane can do and was prepared. Now, I see a launch being lowered from her with a dozen or so men on board. She's maneuvering over the swells and toward a large, sinking merchantman."

The brave men in the launch pointed their boat into the wind and waves. A large swell lifted it up, up. It climbed up some more on that wave. The launch's bow and then the whole boat was briefly suspended in air as the wave crested and broke out from under it. The wind caught and twisted the launch as she fell into the trough, men holding on. Another wave took them under. It was as though they had never existed.

The Spanish steamer, though, continued her work. I looked seaward along Hassel Island's shoreline. There, bobbing in the waves, facing windward and secured by three anchors was the *RMS Mersey*. She'd lost her top-gallant masts and all her yardarms and booms, but her funnel was in place and she was afloat – alive.

The tornado now moved onshore, just outside the town's limits. The rain slackened, though it was still blowing a gale. I was certain, though, that the worst of the storm had passed.

"Okay, Kwame, I'm ready. But, I'll get blown away if I go out there."

"Everything is all right, Harris. Relax all your muscles right where you are; calm down, breathe deeply, close your eyes. Think of a clam sea. Think of your wife. Just rest. I know you're tired."

The voices of the engine room men dissipated. I was again traveling through inky blackness...the sound of Velcro ripping open...

"Now, Professor, slowly open your eyes."

Wooden ceiling fan blades rotated above me.

"You're back! And, no worse for your journey. Professor, just lie still while I check your vital signs."

He noted the blood pressure gauge and listened to my heart with a stethoscope.

"You're fine – blood pressure a little high, but rest will cure that."

Too tired to speak, I fell asleep.

Later, sitting on his porch with beers, I explained what we now faced.

"The good news is the *RMS Mersey* survived. That's also the bad news. Now, we have to find what happened to her and the gold."

"But, didn't you discover there's no record of her leaving port?"

"Precisely. That's why I have to go back the day after the storm."

"It will not be pretty, Professor, as you know," Kwame said gently.

"I know that," I replied. "Now I understand what you were saying about the remote viewers being sent to places like that Civil War hospital to harden them."

"This could be upsetting and pose a psychological danger, Harris. Can't you continue searching the records for new clues?"

"Wish I could," I replied sincerely. "But, it's now clear to me that the records for at least 24 hours are likely in disarray or completely lost in that storm. I've read blood curdling, eyewitness accounts of that catastrophe.

"And, I've seen dead bodies – once a bloated one caught in bushes along the Anacostia River in Washington, DC; another was a drowning victim on a Greek island."

"That's not the same and you know it," Kwame said sternly. "Maybe we've reached the end of this treasure hunt. It may be madness to continue."

"No, it isn't. And, I'm going back."

8 A POOP PORT IN A STORM

"The town was in a fearful state; so many dead lay under the ruins of fallen homes that the stench was abominable and the same state of affairs existed in the harbor, where every vessel suffered more or less from the hurricane."

— C. J. Fennell, Assistant Surgeon of *HMS Doris,* the first naval vessel to arrive in St. Thomas following the San Narciso hurricane.[1]

First, I noticed the odor. Sea water, wood, coal smoke and decaying animals – or were they human cadavers? Probably both. I had just broken free from the blackness of the void and was becoming aware of the smooth sea below and bright sun above. Ahead was the harbor entrance. Directly below was a small island I recognized – Buck Island.

"Where are you, Professor?" From his monitoring, Kwame knew I was now on site.

"Am above Buck Island. I see what's left of the *RMS Wye* …broken masts, torn rigging, a section of her stern, her funnel – all strewn across the rocks. The swells move wreckage and bodies up and down as though a carpet. Many white carcasses are collecting in the little harbor where we go snorkeling with sea turtles…hard to imagine."

I knew the *Wye,* sister ship to the more famous *RMS Rhone,* which also sank that day off Salt Island in the BVI, had tried to escape the harbor. Sadly, it was driven onto little Buck. Fifty-three sailors lost their lives there.

"Look away toward the harbor, Harris. No need to dwell on that."

"Okay, I'm moving toward the harbor. The lighthouse the Danes built on the point where Frenchman's Reef hotel now stands is gone. All that remain are some stone foundation parts that must have been cemented to cliff rocks."

I looked across to the other side of the harbor entrance up to Cowbell's Battery and its semaphore mast. The mast was gone as was the roof and porch of the building. I wondered about the officer with the pith helmet and his four West Indian subordinates. Were they blown off the hill top?

"Harris, what are you seeing?"

"Am entering the harbor now. Masts are poking above the water all over the place. Guess the smaller vessels sank and righted themselves on the bottom. Spars, trunks, casks, planks, cordage, sails and bodies are floating everywhere in a very still sea.

"Small sailboats and row boats manned by dazed white men in ragged clothes are moving everywhere pulling the dead out of floating rubbish. I see a couple of live seamen clinging to mast tops. Good for them!"

Moving closer to the Hassel Island shoreline, I approached the Royal Mail Steam Packet complex. All the docks and building roofs were gone. Pilings remained. Several small sailing vessels had washed among them, up onto shore. Men in pith helmets and slouch hats were scurrying over and through the wreckage looking for survivors and bodies.

"Kwame, I see the *RMS Mersey*. She's lost a lot of rigging. Fortunately, her main and mizzen masts appear whole, though stripped clean. Her funnel is intact. She's just where I left her, anchored close to Hassel's shore. A schooner is sinking near her. The *Mersey* won't depart today. That's for sure."

Farther along the Hassel waterfront, the roof of the massive Marine Railway engine house had withstood the cyclone. The men who rode out the storm there had been lucky to work for that company and to have had a good, strong leader.

Moving closer to Charlotte Amalie, I passed the floating dock still afloat amid a jumble of ships and debris that had crashed into and collected around it. The huge merchant ship *British Empire* was barely recognizable. There was no mistaking her, though. She was the second largest ship afloat – though barely – after the iron-hulled, sidewheeler *S. S. Great Western*, the British behemoth designed by Isambard Kingdom Brunel that laid the first successful transatlantic telegraph cable in 1865.

Another large steamer, *RMS Columbian*, also lay shattered. She was bobbing along with the remains of the *British Empire* amid all kinds of flotsam and jetsam. Seamen crawled over both shipwrecks and the floating dock looking for survivors and bodies.

Ironically, the *Columbian* had just arrived in harbor yesterday, just in time for the hurricane. I thought about the specie still aboard her. It was worth $2 million that day and probably 100 times that now.

Looking toward town, on the empty beach, where French Town is now located, were the hulls of four or five steamers smashed together. Their funnels and masts were intertwined and lay over each other's decks. There, too, men were crawling over hulls and searching through rigging.

"Kwame, I'm going to King's Wharf to try to learn what's happening with the *Mersey*."

Approaching town was heartbreaking. The docks in front of the warehouses were mostly gone, some as cleanly sheared off as though done with a chainsaw. Others, collapsed and twisted, floated in shallow water with other wreckage and bodies.

In town, at least half the roofs were gone, palms stripped bare, streets filled with bricks, roof tiles, tree leaves, branches and palm fronds. Goods spilled out of stores onto the pavement and white men in shirt sleeves moved like zombies through the rubble. The Danish army barracks across a lane from Fort Christian had lost its roof and parts of every visible wall. Fort Christian itself looked untouched, although a lot of debris had washed up around its harbor facing ramparts.

Across Emancipation Garden, the Commercial Hotel had lost part of its third story and its harbor- facing wall was plastered with bits of green fronds and ground-up leaves stripped from trees. It was as though a wood chipper had chopped the roughage into mulch and plastered it on the hotel. Though still flying, its flag was in tatters.

Above town, the mountains looked like a winter forest on the mainland after an ice storm. Trees were bare, broken or uprooted. The stone windmill I'd admired during my first trip had lost its wooden mast and superstructure. Other sugar mill outbuildings were missing roofs and parts of walls.

The scene on King's Wharf was surreal. A crowd of Afro-Europeans in fancy dress were dancing to drums, singing in patois, laughing, telling stories and slapping backs. I recognized the distinctive amber color of rum in cheap clear bottles being passed around. A few men were stretched out on the wharf sleeping in the sun.[2]

As I got closer, I saw a British ship officer, in a disheveled uniform, standing in a rowboat yelling up to the crowd on the wharf, "Ten dollars for any and every man who will follow me out there!" He pointed to the harbor. "That is where the duty of every decent man is to be found today."

Other ships' officers must have been saying much the same thing in Spanish, French and German. All were ignored.

"Kwame," I said out loud. "Is there an island tradition of partying the day after a hurricane?"

"Is that what's going on, Professor?"

"Yes. A celebration of deliverance is my guess."

"That's exactly right, Harris; I heard of those from elders," Kwame explained.

"So, I'm seeing a 19th-century hurricane party, Kwame. But, the venue is grotesque."

Even as Virgin Islanders partied on, sailors in various states of undress were rowing and paddling to the end of the pier in ramshackle, small boats and rafts stacked with bodies. A couple of Danish soldiers helped lift up the cadavers and toss them into what looked like a hastily built shanty at the end of the dock. The dead included women and children – passengers who, like most, had chosen to stay aboard their steamers rather than seek hotels onshore.

I moved to an officer in Danish uniform who seemed to be supervising activity on the pier. A British maritime officer, with deep circles under his eyes and an arm in a sling, stood next to him speaking in a loud, nervous voice, "I do hope your negroes will assist in this vital task, Major. We must get those bodies underground quickly or we will all die of disease."

In frustration, the Danish Major pushed back his white pith helmet, wiped his forehead with a handkerchief, and replied in excellent English, "I am very well aware of our circumstances, sir. And, they are not my negroes, Commodore. As you well know, they are free and happy to have survived these past 24 hours. Many of these men worked hard yesterday to save lives and boats. Soon, though, they will suffer the most from deprivation of safe food and water that will come in the wake of this storm. They know that, sir, and I know it."

That ended that conversation. Looking toward shore, I saw none other than Sir Fitzroy Grannum, silver-headed cane in hand, looking every inch a proper, starched English gentleman as he pushed celebrating Afro-Europeans aside, striding out onto King's Wharf toward the Danish Major and British Commodore.

"Good morning, gentlemen," Sir Fitzroy said. "How did you fare last night?"

Sir Fitzroy, of course, had fared quite well up on Government Hill in his stone mansion, secure behind high, thick walls.

"As well as can be expected, sir," the Commodore replied. "We've lost two Royal Mail Packets and another, the *Mersey*, is damaged. Sixty men are missing in the harbor and an unknown number on the *Wye*, which tried to escape to open sea. She went aground out on Buck Island. As to passengers, we don't know yet how many were lost. That is all I know at present."[3]

"You would have lost more souls, if not for the gallantry of Commander Don Garcia Tudela of the *Vasco Nunez de Balboa*," the Danish Major interrupted. "He was lost yesterday when his long boat capsized while attempting to rescue stranded seamen and passengers from sinking vessels."

So, that heroic Spanish warship I'd seen was named after the explorer Balboa who discovered the Pacific Ocean. Interesting.

"Correct, Major," the Commodore replied. "I personally saw the *Balboa* saving souls during the worst of it. I was on Hassel Island in our building trying to bring order to chaos."

The Commodore's eyes went misty as he recalled yesterday and the horrors of the night. Then, he remembered something, "Speaking of courage, Major, may

I offer you the deepest condolences of our Royal Mail service for your loss of gallant young Captain of the Port Sternberg; so tragic to have drowned after saving the lives of more than thirty seamen."[4]

I hadn't seen Captain Sternberg's heroics, but had read about them in a newspaper dispatch.

"I thank you, sir," the Danish Major bowed his head. "We laid Captain Sternberg to rest this morning. I must tell you, sir, that a crew of negroes died with him. They all manned his long boat, making repeated forays into that churning, hellish harbor."

Looking out over the water, the Major continued. "We've buried 100 people this morning, thus far."

Sir Fitzroy wasn't impressed by the maudlin conversation.

"Commodore, when will the *Mersey* be fit to depart for home?"

In addition to managing the Colonial Bank branch, Sir Fitzroy was a director of the Royal Mail Steamship Packet Company.

"Well, sir, let me think a moment," the Commodore instinctively looked out to the ship as he calculated. "I made a preliminary survey of the *Mersey* this morning. Her hull is sound, engine and side wheels are in good order, funnel secure. We can repair her running rigging, spars and such within 24 hours, I should think."

"And, her cargo, Commodore?" Sir Fitzroy was no doubt worried about Santa Anna's treasure.

"The valuable items and dry goods cargo are dry and secure, Sir Fitzroy. They are locked and guarded by the *Mersey's* officers and available crew. As for perishable goods, sir, I believe Captain Barnstable will be able to make good speed at sea and make up for time lost to this storm. Spoilage will be minimal."

Sir Fitzroy grunted, "When will she depart?"

"By the morning of the second of November, sir, *RMS Mersey* should be ready to depart."

"Very well, Commodore. Make every effort to see that happens. That is the Company's top priority at this time."

"Yes, sir. We will make it so."

The Commodore, however, winced and motioned Sir Fitzroy to step aside away from the Major, for more privacy.

"Sir, a Tortola sloop arrived an hour ago with the most dreadful news, if true. Half the buildings in Road Town are destroyed. And..."

"Spit it out, man! What else?"

"Captain Woolley and the *RMS Rhone* are lost, sir."

"Impossible," Sir Fitzroy blurted impatiently. "She was safely anchored in Great Bay of Peter Island. Furthermore, the *Rhone* is known to be unsinkable."

"No, sir. Any boat can sink, I assure you. Sadly, the report is that Captain Woolley took her out for the open sea and ended on the rocks off Salt Island. Only 25 men of nearly 300 passengers and crew have been found alive, thus far."

Sir Fitzroy went white in the face.

"Good lord, there was 60,000 pounds sterling in specie and bullion on board."

Sir Fitzroy needn't have worried about the gold, however. The *Rhone* sank in shallow water just off Salt Island. All her treasure and most cargo of value were recovered by divers using the latest apparatus. Many of the bodies, too, were brought up and are buried in a desolate part of Salt Island. Afro-British fishermen and salt miners risked their lives to help rescue survivors and recover the dead. They were honored by Queen Victoria, who gave them annual pensions.

Despite heroics, the fact remained that in just a few hours a horrific total of three Royal Mail Steamers were lost. These included the *Rhone* that many believed unsinkable because of her innovative, water-tight compartments and modern, bronze-propeller-drive system. Indeed, upon being told by a crewman that the *Rhone* had run up on some rocks and was doomed, Captain Woolley replied, "Good Lord, is it even possible?"[5]

Hundreds of passengers and crew went down with the lost mail steamers and other British vessels. San Narciso's toll, though, was far worse. American, Danish, French, German, and Spanish ships, passengers, crew, cargoes and hundreds of Virgin Islanders were also lost.

I'd seen, smelled and heard enough of the San Narciso hurricane. Today's back-time visit had become upsetting, to say the least.

"Kwame, we've gotten what we need. Time to come back. I have homework to do."

It took a couple of days on St. John to recover from that unnerving journey to October 29, 1867. Then, I needed to get back to work. On a sunny day, Mary, John and I took the car ferry over to St. Thomas. They dropped me off at the library and then went shopping. From the third floor of the antiquities section, I looked out the window at the harbor, just visible over the roofs of stone warehouses.

"So many lives lost," I said to myself. "Why did I survive?"

I left the library for a break, walking down to the waterfront where construction of Veterans Drive in the 1960s had filled in and paved over the old beach and the remnants of warehouse wharves and shanties. King's Wharf, too, is gone. But, looking across the harbor to Hassel Island, the Marine Railway engine house was still standing, without a roof. The residence and office wing had also collapsed; hard to believe all those men I'd spent those dreadful hours with just a few days before had now been dead for a hundred and fifty years.

There, in the harbor, I could see the approximate position of the old floating dry dock where so many died. Now, commuter seaplanes carrying passengers to and from St. Croix take off and land there on several runs each day.

All those colorful and courageous people who had survived the hurricane had, of course, died in the end.

Then I caught hold of myself. I couldn't have survivor's guilt. An observer, a witness, was all I was.

Nevertheless, I was fighting some very strange emotions as I walked back to the library.

Still in some confusion, I sat at the microfiche table, going through West Indian English language newspapers for November, 1867. I needed news of the *RMS Mersey*.

After a few tedious hours, I found her. An Antigua newspaper had published a letter from a *Mersey* passenger dated November 3, 1867. It reported a disaster. She had sunk off Sombrero Island, following some serious starboard paddle wheel trouble. Fortunately, all 225 passengers and crew were saved.

Thank goodness she sank, I thought. No one had died and the treasure might still be within reach.

I needed more details. An online search uncovered a January 10, 1868 Parliamentary Inquiry into the loss of *RMS Mersey*. Because the Royal Mail Steam Packet Company was technically in partnership with the Royal Navy, each ship built received a subsidy. In return, each was constructed so that it could easily be converted into a warship, if needed.

So, the British government had a stake in the Mail Packet fleet. And, they took the loss of each ship very seriously.

The Parliamentary report told a fascinating tale. Under the command of Captain Edward Barnstable the *Mersey* did depart St. Thomas on November 2, 1867, as the Commodore had promised Sir Fitzroy. No doubt, passengers were relieved to leave the disaster of St. Thomas behind.

By early evening, she was steaming in a quiet sea beyond Virgin Gorda, entering Sombrero passage, the wide body of water between the outlying British islands of Anegada and Sombrero, the most easterly isles of the

Caribbean. The passage was really part of the open Atlantic and the islands marked the last land before Africa.

Only a few miles from the wide-open Atlantic, the *Mersey's* lookouts missed a mostly submerged wooden wreck off the starboard bow. When they did sing out, Captain Barnstable managed to turn the ship to port, but the starboard paddle wheel struck the wreck, damaging its axle. The captain hove to in calm seas and, using chains and tools, a repair was finished after seven hours work. Or so he thought.

The *Mersey* was back underway in the dark. By the Captain's reckoning, he should have seen the light atop Sombrero Island by 12 midnight. He hadn't. Royal Mail Steam Packet regulations called for a ship's master to hove to and wait for daylight when he suspects a navigation error at night. But, Captain Barnstable felt under pressure to make up the time lost to the paddle repair and the storm at St. Thomas. He kept steaming.

Suddenly, the *Mersey* scraped a coral head at the southeastern extent of the long, treacherous Horseshoe Reef. The fourth largest reef in the world, Horseshoe extends down westward from Anegada, edging Sombrero Passage and almost reaching Virgin Gorda.

Upon striking the coral, Barnstable stopped the engine and sent men below with bullseye lanterns to inspect the hull and bilge. Everything was fine, they reported. But not really. They'd missed an unusually large drip from the stuffing box where the starboard paddle wheel shaft went through the hull.

"Shit," I thought to myself, thinking of our own *Perseverance*. "Another damn stuffing box problem."

It seemed the shaft was slightly bent from the earlier accident. With every revolution of the paddle wheel, the box was opening and the leak was growing worse.

Meanwhile, the Captain backed off the reef and steered southeast to avoid the rest of Horseshoe Reef and

Anegada Island. It wasn't long before he spotted the light atop Sombrero.

Satisfied he had cleared Anegada and Horseshoe, Barnstable was about to order a new dead east heading to take them across the Atlantic to the Canary Islands off Africa. But, the ship felt sluggish. He checked the inclinometer with his bullseye and saw a starboard list that was barely noticeable standing on the quarterdeck.

He and crewmen went below and eventually discovered the iron casing of the starboard stuffing box had cracked open. Water was spraying in. Worse, part of the adjacent iron hull had cracked from the asymmetric pressure.

Captain Barnstable immediately shut down the starboard paddlewheel and ordered the shaft hole and hull crack stuffed with oakum and blankets. He ordered the steam-powered bilge pumps set at maximum.

The leak persisted. The starboard list grew more pronounced.

Studying his Admiralty charts, he saw a slight harbor and sand beach on the leeward, Caribbean side of Sombrero Island. Under sail and assisted by the port paddle wheel, Barnstable headed for it.

Realizing his ship would sink, Captain Barnstable hove to about two miles off Sombrero harbor, lowered the boats and started transferring passengers and nonessential crew to shore. Three hours later, with a skeleton crew, Barnstable reset the sails, engaged the port paddle and attempted to reach the harbor where he hoped to beach the ship or, at least, sink her in shallow water. He almost made it.

The *Mersey* did sink in relatively shallow water. Barnstable and his remaining crew abandoned ship and made it to the beach. Later, back home, the Captain was reprimanded and ended up skippering a desk in London.

That was as far as I could go with the Parliamentary Inquiry report. The ship had sunk in shallow waters, making recovery of cargo relatively easy – even in the 1860s.

But, unlike, the *Rhone*, which sank in indisputably British waters, the *Mersey* rested off an island claimed and occupied by Americans – a claim and occupation disputed by the British.

Under an obscure American law – the Guano Islands Act of 1856 – U.S. citizens could then seize any unclaimed or unoccupied island rich in guano – bird and bat feces. A source of phosphates, guano was golden as fertilizer for the American South. Its soil was depleted from decades of plantation cultivation of just a few crops – mainly, cotton and tobacco.[6]

Sombrero Island, about one mile long and a quarter mile wide, had as much as 200 feet of solidified guano droppings covering its rocky surface.

"Quite a pile of shit," I said to myself, while conducting research online. A valuable pile, as well.

Nevertheless, although Sombrero was a British possession, it was an isolated speck in their vast empire. With neither fresh water nor a good harbor, the desert island was uninhabited and ignored.

Two American businessmen claimed it in 1858 and started guano mining. The Brits can be excused for not noticing this territorial invasion. In the decade or so from 1850 and into the 60s, they were otherwise engaged in exiting the exhausting Crimean War, fighting several conflicts against Maori aborigines in New Zealand and invading Abyssinia, among other imperial ventures.

By 1860, the Americans on Sombrero had built a spacious manager's house with wide verandas, barracks housing 200 British and Danish West Indian workers and huts for 12 white supervisors. A small railway was constructed to carry wagon loads of mined guano down from the island center and out onto a long wooden dock. There, the ore was loaded onto ships bound for southern ports.

The free West Indian workers, though, weren't accustomed to the tyrannical discipline of southern overseers experienced in supervising Afro-American slaves. One foreman named Snow was particularly hated. The New York Times describes what happened in an insurrection that began August 13, 1860:

> "[The men] were engaged in loading a car and the chosen murderer being on the top of it, took advantage of the foreman as he was stooping on the ground below, and hurled a tremendous lump of guano at his head, crushed his skull with the blow, and left him for dead on the ground. Considerable commotion followed among the whites upon discovery of the attempted murder, and the negro who committed the deed was immediately arrested by Captain Burnell of the Emma Tuttle, and Captain Benthall of the bark Warren of Baltimore, placed in irons and conveyed on board the latter vessel." [7]

The West Indians protested and broke into food and liquor stores. They partied, frightening the white supervisors who then closed themselves up in the manager's house. Eventually, the supervisors made peace with the workers and all enjoyed an unexpected vacation, lasting several days. Order was finally restored upon the arrival of two additional U.S. vessels.

Working conditions must have improved. The Sombrero Guano Company increased production with sales driven by advertising. The October, 1860 American Farmer Advertiser ran this ad explaining the futility of choosing any other type of guano:

> SOMBRERO GUANO - The data are incontrovertible on the superiority of Sombrero Guano as the richest and most efficient manure, and are suggestive of the futility of any attempt to bring other similar guano into competition with it. Precedence belongs to Sombrero Guano only because of its much greater richness in phosphoric acid, but also for the reason that nearly the whole of that constituent occurs in the guano as actual Bone Phosphate of Lime.

By the beginning of the Civil War, about 80,000 tons of guano were being imported annually into the U.S. Sombrero Island was among the closest sources of high-quality guano.

The worker insurrection and commercial success of Sombrero mining, however, did attract British attention. Union ships bound to and from Sombrero Island also caught the attention of Confederate raiders. Among the *C.S.S. Alabama* claims for damages on Secretary of State Seward's desk was $35,000 for a small, New York ship destroyed near that guano island.

By the time of the *Mersey* wreck in 1867, American guano mining was being done under a lease granted by Her Majesty's government, which later took direct control of the island in 1870.

On November 16, 1867, a Royal Naval vessel, the *HMS Vindictive*, arrived at Sombrero to salvage the *Mersey*. It brought divers equipped with the latest Siebe suits. These were large, gray, one-piece garments made of India rubber designed to be fitted into lead shoes, each weighing ten pounds. The suits had a heavy, leather collar ringed with heavy screws. A brass helmet with a glass eye (protected by copper wire work) was bolted on, sealing the suit. An air hose passing through the helmet was connected to a hand-cranked air pump on the deck of a raft. One hundred pounds of weights were added to the suit, which in total weighed more than 180 pounds. Divers were given a crow bar and ax before descending down a ladder to the wreck.

An 1859 diver described what it felt like:

"I had to be assisted by two attendants to the ladder. When I was submerged and could see the water outside the helmet, I felt suffocated and my temples felt as though they were being pressed in by a vise – like a tempest. But, when I was half-way down, the pain disappeared."[8]

Salvage was slow and dangerous. By end of day, November 17th, 12 bales of cotton, several cases of champagne, beer, soda water and other cargo had been brought up from the *Mersey*. The reinforced, zinc-lined treasure room, however, remained locked tight. The divers decided to continue removing all cargo and valuables from the surrounding compartments before using axes and chains running from winches on the surface raft to break into the treasure storeroom.

Like a received hail Mary pass at the end of the fourth quarter, however, the game suddenly changed in favor of us modern treasure hunters.

9 "VILLAINOUS RASCALS"

"When they got within hail, they fired a musket at us, cheered and came on board. They were the most villainous-looking rascals that anyone had probably ever beheld."

— Captain Sabins out of Charleston, describing his merchant brig being boarded by Caribbean pirates in 1822.[1]

It was about 4 pm, November 18, 1867. One of the divers was in the midst of his final descent to the *Mersey* for the day. Suddenly, those standing on shore were knocked down by the wobbling beach. The diver below had just reached and was standing on the *Mersey's* upright deck. He was knocked over as the ship lurched. Sand and sentiment clouded his view. Using his lifeline he signaled he was coming up.

By the time he was out of his suit on the raft, the sea was receding away from the island, uncovering most of the still attached masts and paddle wheels of the *Mersey*, leaving boats tied up to the island pier sitting on a sandy bottom. Old-timers knew what would happen next. The diver, a veteran of many years West Indian service, ordered his assistants quickly off the raft into their boat. They rowed for their lives to the *HMS Vindictive* anchored nearby. By now, most of the *Mersey* hull was exposed.

With little warning, a twelve-foot cresting wall of water washed in over the ships, flooding the narrow beach. Although the *Vindictive* was unharmed, the next morning the divers discovered the *Mersey* had been flipped entirely over, masts snapped, paddle wheels splayed outward, and iron hull bottom up.

The *Vindictive's* captain, charged with the *Mersey* salvage, calculated that the earthquake had been centered in the middle of the Virgin Islands. The magnitude and direction of the tsunami wave pointed to an origin somewhere between Tortola and St. Croix. He decided his resources would be needed immediately in Road Town and St. Thomas.

He was correct. The quake, estimated at 7.5 on the Richter scale, was caused by tectonic plates moving in the Anegada Trough, a deep underwater trench along the edge of the Virgins. St. Thomas, still recovering from the devastating hurricane, was hit hard, as was St. Croix.[2]

Abandoning the *Mersey* salvage, the *HMS Vindictive* steamed through the Virgins, finding new devastation. Among the lost and damaged vessels was the *RMS La Plata* that had been anchored near Hassel Island.

St. Croix, which had escaped the worst of the October 29 hurricane, was hit hardest by the quake. Louis van Housel, an officer on board the American naval frigate *U.S.S. Monongahela* anchored off Frederiksted, St. Croix, described what happened November 18 , 1867:

> *"Our vessel began to quiver and rock as if a mighty giant had laid hold of her and was trying to loosen every timber in her frame. Officers and men ran pell-mell on deck...The vibrations continued the space of perhaps a minute, accompanied by a buzzing noise somewhat like ...the hum of innumerable swarms of bees...Various suggestions were made by old and young [as to*

what was happening]. 'It's an earthquake, sir!' shouted an old blue jacket from the bow."

Following the quake, when the water started receding under them, the *Monongahela's* captain ordered the anchor chain cut so it did not pull the ship's bow off as the tide sucked all outward. A few minutes later, when a 20-plus-foot tsunami came in, the surf carried the 227 foot ship over the first row of warehouses and coastal road, then yanked it back, depositing it upright on the beach.[3]

While disaster history is always entertaining, I needed to find out what happened to the *Mersey*.

A search of all applicable databases provided no record of any further salvage attempt. The iron hulled *Mersey* had turned over, apparently locking in all remaining valuables – including Santa Anna's gold.

I'd reached another roadblock. It was time to bring Mary up to date and talk it through.

"And, the *Mersey* must still be resting off Sombrero," I explained. As we discussed it all, Mary was varnishing the teak kitchen cabinets.

"I've never even heard of Sombrero Island," Mary said. "Is that one of the British Virgins?"

"I'd never heard much about Sombrero, either, until I researched sailing trade routes. Aside from guano miners, the most important thing about the island to sailors has been to avoid hitting it. There is absolutely nothing there."

"You mean there are no moorings like in the BVI?"

"That's right. It's empty except for an automated lighthouse. By 1900, the guano deposits were played out and everybody went home. There is no fresh water, little vegetation and only a narrow beach."

"Hard to believe the wreck hasn't been explored. I don't care how barren the place is," Mary said skeptically. "Aren't all wrecks around here tourist attractions for divers?"

"Good point. The famous ones in the Virgin Islands

certainly are," I admitted. "But, *Mersey* lies off desolate Sombrero. It's a dependency of Anguilla, but 40 miles away. And, it's 60 miles from Anegada. That's way too far for Virgin Island dive boats to easily reach. And, Anguilla itself is struggling to attract tourists to its home island. Sombrero seems to be ignored."

Mary shot me a critical look, but did nod her head in a positive way.

"I get that. Why doesn't anyone else know about the *Mersey*?"

"I don't know if anybody else knows. But, I've got to tell you, she was very difficult for me, a naval historian, to discover. Remember, between the hurricane and tsunami of 1867, hundreds of boats of all sizes and types sank in these islands within just one month. Many of the others and their cargoes were within easy reach."

Mary nodded and continued, "You think *Mersey* was lost in the shuffle."

"Something like that," I agreed. "Plus, if she had been further salvaged, there would be a record and I can't find any."

She had the kitchen teak looking a lot better.

"Here's more important information," I said, picking up the conversation a couple of hours later. I had thought of something else.

By then, it was near sundown. Mary put her work aside. John was watching yet another splendid sunset, punctuated by evening bats taking flight from hidden nests in our high palms and roof eaves. He loved nature. Every animal was a friend.

"Santa Anna's son put all El Presidente's property – even clothes and furnishings – up for sale in early 1868. Had a Royal Navy or Royal Mail Service salvaging operation taken place, they would have returned identifiable assets to owners. And, at that isolated, exposed location in the 19th century, no one else could have mounted a recovery operation."

"You're saying that if the gold was recovered, the son might not have put all the family property up for sale," she said. "If I were having a yard sale, I sure wouldn't do it so soon after two of the worst natural disasters that ever hit St. Thomas. The value of everything must have been close to zero; a real hardship sale."

"Exactly. That's how I see it. We know Santa Anna wanted to leave St. Thomas. But, his son was a business man. They wouldn't have held a fire sale, unless they were desperate for cash."

Mary stretched her legs and curled up on the couch motioning for a drink – Jim Beam on the rocks.

When I returned, she had another good question.

"Your conclusions all sound logical. But, how do we get out there? I'm not sailing 60 miles southeast in our *Perseverance* and neither are you – not after your adventure last year sailing to the Anegada Trough."

I had to agree. Sailing into the unknown chasing a UFO in a thirty-year-old, 32-foot sailboat had, in retrospect, not been the best idea.

"I bet Harry Elliott and his *Black Knight* would sail there, if I pitched in for the diesel fuel and gave him a share of any recoveries," I said hopefully. "Then there's Lord Claymore's *Bonne Chance*. She'd make it and he's already said he's interested in a treasure hunt. Plus, both Harry and his Lordship are experienced divers."

"Let's think about this," she interjected. "Neither boat is in the best of shape, but I'd vote for *Black Knight*. That 110-foot, steel schooner can handle a lot."

"All we need to do is get there, anchor, and dive," I explained. "It will be obvious if the *Mersey*'s been tampered with. There'd be a big hole in her iron hull."

"Let's think about this some more," she said, ending the conversation.

Maybe we didn't need to go there physically to check out the wreck. Why not remote view it?

The next day, I phoned Kwame. After pleasantries, I

got to the point.

"Have you ever remote viewed a target underwater?"

"I once located a Russian submarine several hundred feet below the north Atlantic," Kwame answered matter-of-factly. Then he perked up. "Are you thinking of the *Mersey*?

"Yes, and I don't feel comfortable going underwater to check her out. I'd like you to take this trip – if you're okay with me as your monitor."

"Certainly, Professor," he replied. "I understand entirely. Viewing underwater takes getting accustomed to. Your natural reaction is to panic and get to the surface – or hold your breath."

"Thanks, Kwame, we don't have time for me to experiment. We need to get this one right."

Before hanging up I wanted to clear the air on something else.

"Kwame, we've been through a lot. Why don't you drop the Professor bit and just call me Harris?"

"You must understand. During my years in the service, I learned the value of chains of command and use of titles. It is good for all. You are in charge – the Captain; as was decided that day when we talked over Morgan's buccaneer code for dividing up recoveries."

"I remember that," I admitted.

"I have also found that in a crisis or when planning a course of action, it is helpful to the one in authority to use a title such as Captain or Professor. It strengthens the self-esteem of a commander and strengthens him in making decisions. This is important."

I couldn't argue with that. We rang off and I moved to the next task.

After consulting nautical charts of Sombrero and its leeward beach, I narrowed the location of the wreck to one-half square mile. Since the target was 330-feet long and 44-feet wide, it should be relatively easy to spot.

It was. Kwame found it within a few moments into his

"trip" and gave me the coordinates.

"I'm seeing a long, boat-shaped mound surrounded by elk horn coral and covered with algae, soft coral and sponges," he said, his voice coming from his otherwise seemingly unconscious body.

"There are two circular reefs on either side of the main mound and plenty of reef fish," he added.

"Good, Kwame, the circles must be from the iron frames of the paddle wheels. Are there any holes or deep depressions in the hull mound?"

"No, looks solid."

"Excellent, can you view inside?"

After a few moments of silence, I saw his corporeal body's breathing rate accelerate and EEG lines peaking. So, this is what it's like to sit helpless as a friend goes off into the ether, I thought. He must be struggling to get through the hull.

"Kwame, where are you now?"

"This is definitely a hull and I'm inside in the dark. I sense and feel a lot of decayed wooden decks and bulkheads; pipes, iron beams. There is at least one, big, square structure intact. It's hollow inside."

"That could be the zinc-lined treasure room, still sealed by the iron door," I explained. "They used galvanized zinc on the walls to protect stock certificates and paper currencies from moisture. That must be what you're sensing."

"Yes, that could explain it," Kwame said.

"You've done very well, Kwame. Time to come back."

My elation at finding the *Mersey* intact lasted only about 24 hours. The spell was broken by an unexpected, serious threat.

The next day began innocently enough. It was Saturday. After kayaking the mangroves that line the coves of Coral Bay's pristine Hurricane Hole, we were back home relaxing. Mary was reading the papers online, while John played his guitar. I was searching regulations governing salvage of wrecks in UK territorial waters. Anguilla and Sombrero are British "overseas territories."

"Did you see this, honey?" Mary interrupted my research. "This story in the New York Times about Seahawk Enterprises, Inc.? It seems to be a treasure hunting company that's searching the records of Lloyds of London Marine Insurers and the Insurance Company of North America. They're looking at insured ships lost between 1850 and 1870; they want ships carrying gold back from California and South American gold mines."

Looking up from my laptop, it took me a moment to comprehend what she said.

"Let me see that." A chill went up my back.

Seahawk Enterprises was a corporation publicly traded on NASDAQ with about $25 million in annual revenues. Headquartered in Jacksonville, Florida, it had a 250-foot exploration vessel, submersible robots and every other high-tech sea gadget one could imagine, and more.

"Jesus," I said. "We can't compete with them."

"No," Mary said. "They must have deep pockets."

"Well, Seahawk won't find it looking through insurance records. The *RMS Mersey* was not insured. Because of the peculiar link to the British government, Royal Mail steamers were self-insured to avoid any interference by private companies or their investors. In the event the Royal Navy needed those boats, they wanted a free hand."

But, gold from the mines was shipped to London on RMS steamers. It was hardly a secret that St. Thomas was their headquarters in those years.

It couldn't hurt to check. I quickly learned that a Tad Sprinter of Seahawk, Inc. had visited the Charlotte Amalie library's antiquities section just a few days earlier. Like it or not, we had a race on our hands.

"You'd better make a move now or give it up," Mary advised.

"You're right."

So, the next evening a selected group of professionals

met at Skinny Legs bar: Kwame, Sir Keithley (aka, Lord Claymore), Harry Elliott, Richie (the best industrial diver in Coral Bay), and me. We were all of that certain age when opportunity rarely knocked at our doors. An offer of free drinks was more than enough to get this crew assembled.

We took a table along the rail overlooking the sand horseshoe pits and makeshift bandstand. Donkeys brayed nearby in the mangroves.

"Gentlemen, I've asked you all to come this evening to discuss a rare opportunity; the chance to recover a treasure in gold and silver likely worth tens of millions of dollars. And, it's in relatively shallow water – less than 100 feet – in the lee of an uninhabited island 40 miles away from any authorities. The only thing separating us from the treasure is a 150-year-old iron hull."

Lord Claymore responded first, "What's that ye say, matey? Easy pickins? But 'ow far from 'ere? And, under what flag?"

"Good questions and there are many more," Harry Elliot said, pushing up his red Mount Gay Rum cap and squinting, thinking it all through.

"The treasure is off Sombrero Island about 70 miles east/southeast from where we're now sitting. Sombrero is uninhabited, has little vegetation. There's a short, narrow beach, a few 19th-century shacks plus the automated lighthouse, as most of you know. It's a dependency of Anguilla, an overseas territory of the UK. Anguilla itself is 40 miles southeast of Sombrero."

"What boat are we going to use?" Richie asked, stroking his long, red beard thoughtfully.

"Afore ye answer, we've an immediate need," his Lordship broke in. He ordered another round, pointing at me. "Put it on 'is tab, lass."

An hour later, Kwame and I'd answered all their questions, leaving out the remote viewing part. It was our scholarship that had gotten us this far. And, everyone agreed it was worth mounting an expedition. We'd also voted to follow the tried and true Captain Sir Henry Morgan formula for divvying up spoils. None could argue with that.

"Now," Harry asked, as we got down to planning. "Let's say we're anchored at Sombrero and the Anguilla's 48-foot, fast patrol boat comes by? What then?"

"I gather you've worked those waters before," I replied to chuckles from the others.

"The best thing to do is sail to Anguilla first, check in legally with customs and then proceed to Sombrero," I continued. "The only boat we take is the *Black Knight* and her launch. We say we're bird watchers interested in Prickley Pear Cays and Sombrero, which are bird sanctuaries."

"What's that ye say, lad? Birdwatchers are we? And us comin' in the *Black Knight*, a 'undred and ten-foot black schooner built in 1899? Do we look like fuckin' bird watchers?"

I glanced at Richie, overweight, with his salt-stiffened beard rising horizontal as he leaned back to chug a Heineken. There sat Keithley with Pusser's stains on his chin and clothed in khaki tatters, fingering his graying pony tail. Harry, standing and listening, wore one of his best selling Coral Bay T-shirts with 'Age and Treachery will Triumph Over Youth and Skill' printed above a skull and crossbones.

"No, Sir Keithley, we don't," I admitted. "But, we'd look more like middle-aged bird watchers if we brought along wives and girlfriends. And, if we spent some dollars on tourist stuff in Anguilla's port, it would help. They'd appreciate any tourists this time of year – even us."

"That might work," Harry said. "As *Black Knight's* captain, I'd be checking everyone in at their customs house. If we cleanup and have women with us, it will look okay."

Sir Keithley grunted, "Women on board are bad luck."

"Don't be silly, Keith," I said gently. "That's just an old wives' tale."

The others chuckled. His lordship looked perplexed.

"Ol' wives' tale is it?" Keithley spit the words, getting peeved as he drained his glass. "Why t'is common knowledge a bare, big-breasted beauty is best suited for a figurehead beneath a bowsprit, don't you know. But, up on deck out a sea, a live one distracts the lads, tempting ol' Neptune to raise cane."

"Now Keithley," I said, "Right here in Coral Bay we all know that some of the best crews on charter boats are women. Why, look at Corsair Cathy, she's a captain."

"We mightn' make an exception for comely Cathy," he allowed with a leer.

"There you are, my lord. We're hoping Cathy will crew for us on this trip," I explained. "Speaking of crew, Harry, can we assume Bronco will come? We need more strong arms."

Bronco was a tough mariner in his late 30s or early 40s. Short of temper, no one messed with him. He was loyal to Harry, though.

"He wouldn't miss this one. But, remember I'm Coast Guard licensed for only 12 people and some will have to sleep on deck."

"Great," I said, relieved. "Let's toast our new Coral Bay Bird Watcher's Society!"

We all raised glasses and beer bottles. Lord Claymore, now in his cups, shouted, "Hoorah!"

Later that night, I shared with Mary the plan for what we'd do when we reached the *Mersey*.

We'd raise the treasure and take it back to St. John. We'd then appear to follow British law by declaring it to the United Kingdom's "Receiver of Wrecks," as required by the Brits' Merchant Shipping Act. We had 28 days in which to do so.[4]

Once declared and after a waiting period, Her Majesty's Government would likely decide who owned it (probably "the Crown") and award the "salvors" (us) a significant percentage.

But, before reporting it, we'd divide amongst ourselves enough to cover our expenses, time and a good profit. After that, we'd report the remainder and follow the British government's instructions on how to proceed.

Eventually, based on past practices, I was sure we'd be awarded a healthy dose of more treasure. It would be a win-win in the grand tradition of Sir Francis Drake and Sir Henry Morgan. Maybe I'd be knighted.

First, we had to put together our expedition and get to Sombrero before Seahawk, Inc.

In addition to divers, we needed an air compressor, underwater lights and cutting torch, heavy lines, a strong, steel-mesh basket and suitable containers to put the treasure in. What equipment Harry Elliott didn't have, we could borrow or rent from other islanders. Some items, we'd make ourselves.

We already had four experienced divers. Harry Elliott and his tall, muscular and sometimes acerbic crewman Bronco (his real name unknown, like so many St. Johnians). Then there was Richie, the congenial king of Coral Bay mooring maintenance, and, of course, the cantankerous Sir Keithley. They all had salvage experience.

Corsair Cathy was also a diver and we were sure she'd join our merry crew. Getting her onboard was Mary's task. She was in charge of provisioning, recruiting Cathy and two other able-bodied women to pose as wives or girlfriends of Richie, Kwame and Keithley. John would also come and assist us where needed. He actually loved bird watching and could make us look legit.

As to time needed, we would allow a maximum of ten hours to get to Road Bay, Anguilla's port of entry. We'd plan to arrive in the afternoon, clear customs and explore the port village of Sandy Ground. We'd spend some money on souvenirs to look like tourists. Next morning we'd depart Road Bay and motor sail to Sombrero. It was about 4 hours away.

The first morning at Sombrero, we'd locate the wreck, anchor as close as possible and get to work. To cut through the rusted iron hull and flimsy decayed wooden bulkheads to the treasure room should be relatively easy. Finding and raising the gold and silver should also be straightforward. I'd found the *Mersey*'s blueprints at the Royal Mail Steamship Packet archival website. And, of course, I'd also seen the ship and its treasure room with my own eyes (so to speak) off Hassel Island.

We'd allow three days at Sombrero, working around the clock on diving and retrieval.

Then, a return trip to St. John of 10 hours at most. It would be a fast downwind sail home.

We planned for a maximum trip of 120 hours or five days. We needed five days of food, water and beverages plus emergency medical supplies for ten people.

It was late in June, the end of the season, and everybody could clear their schedules. We would leave the Thursday of the long, July-4th weekend.

That Monday, however, a strange boat was sighted coming into Coral Bay between Le Duc Island and Ram Head point. Richie spotted her first, while working on a mooring at the entrance of Coral Harbor. He phoned Harry on his cell.

It was a trawler-rigged motor boat. By the time it dropped anchor in the middle of the harbor, a half-dozen or more people were watching her from land and their own boats. Mary, John and I were on *Perseverance*, cleaning her up and checking the auto bilge pump and electrical system since we'd be leaving her untended on the mooring during our trip to Sombrero.

I grabbed the binoculars and looked over the stranger. It was a 35- to 40-foot trawler type craft adapted for diving and other work – like a small tug boat. A wind shift swung her around on her anchor. I could now read her stern:

Seahawk 2, Jacksonville, FL.

Above her wheelhouse, the boat's communications mast boasted all the antennae and bulbous radar and satellite stuff money could buy. I also bet she had sonar and bottom scanning equipment.

"Shit," I yelled out loud. Seahawk Enterprises, Inc. had arrived.

I phoned Harry. He asked Richie and Bronco to hang around the dock and boat yard. We knew *Seahawk 2*'s crew would be coming ashore and that was the only sensible place to do so.

It wasn't long until an inflatable tender left *Seahawk 2* filled with five men. It came to the end of the dock. Richie and Bronco were fiddling with some fitting on the pier, looking busy.

I later learned that as the Seahawk men approached, Richie looked up and in his finest, good-natured, mid-western manner broke the ice.

"Good day, boys. Beautiful boat. Where do ya hail from?"

The five men were dressed in light-weight, blue uniforms with "Seahawk" and a swooping, menacing osprey embroidered above their breast pockets. A well-groomed, gray-haired guy stepped forward offering his hand.

"I'm Skip Perch, captain of *Seahawk 2*. Pleased to meet you."

"I'm Richie, and this here's Bronco."

Bronco stood up from where he'd been squatting on the dock. Flexing his six-foot, muscular body, he shook longish black hair from his face and squinted at the visitors.

"Welcome to Coral Bay," he managed.

Richie continued with the pleasantries, "We've got a small boat yard, chandlery and a great bar right along the path through these mangroves and sea grapes."

"So I've heard," Skip said. "We're down from Florida,

came in by Virgin Gorda. Any problem if we spend the night at our anchorage?"

"None at all. You'll want to hit Skinny Legs for refreshments and music."

"That's the plan," Cap Skip said. "Do you have fuel here?"

Richie acted disappointed, but helpfully asked, "How much do you need?"

"Well, our tank's 200 gallons and we're probably down about 50 or so."

"You'll have to go to Cruz Bay, then," Richie replied. "Hey, it's Carnival time on St. John. You could have some fun over there."

"Afraid we're on a business trip," Skip said. "We're a research vessel scanning the bottom offshore for phosphorites and seafloor massive sulphides."

"Huh? What's that in English?"

"Phosphorus and potentially valuable metals found near undersea tectonic plates," he replied patiently. He motioned his men to go ahead to Skinny Legs as he continued talking, possibly trying to pick Richie's brain.

"Well, we sure have tectonic plates out in the Puerto Rico Trench and Anegada Trough," Richie replied. "That's a pretty small boat, though, for working those seas."

"We're simply a scout, you might say," Skip replied. "We scan a designated region and, if we see something promising, we call in our 250-foot research vessel to take a closer look."

"Ain't that something," Ritchie said, folksy-like. "How does your crew do all that? You ever employ local divers?"

"We can handle our own mission just fine. It's all done with scanning technology. Hell, aside from one able-bodied seaman, my three other crew are all tech geeks. Our mother ship has remote underwater robot vehicles and highly-trained deep sea divers who'll take over, if we find something."

"That's too damn bad," Richie replied. "We've got a few good divers right here who'd welcome a gig."

"Then, I now know where to come. Good meeting you."

"And you, Skip. Likely be seeing you guys in Skinny's in a bit."

As soon as Skip disappeared up the path, Richie made a phone call.

Mary, John and I had finally rowed to the dock as Richie was speaking on his cell. I overheard part of his conversation, "Phosphorites and sulfides, my ass! –Ya, the whole crew's at Skinny's now."

Bronco stood by flexing muscles and cracking knuckles.

When Richie got off the call, he told us about the *Seahawk 2* crew. I was disheartened and we proceeded directly to the car and went home.

Later, Harry phoned to give me an update.

"The *Seahawk 2* crew are drinking heavily at Skinny's and will spend the night at their anchorage. Then, tomorrow they go to Cruz Bay to get fuel and, hopefully, spend some time at carnival."

"Sounds like we better get moving ASAP," I said. "Mary says she's got the food and other supplies."

"And, I topped up the fuel yesterday in Cruz Bay," Harry said. "Guess we could leave Wednesday morning, if everybody else can get away a day early."

"Let's shoot for that. We'll fill the pick-up with provisions and bring it all to the dinghy dock tomorrow morning first thing. It may take two trips."

"We'll have boats waiting to take it all to *Black Knight*."

Meanwhile, Mary had successfully enlisted Corsair Cathy. As expected, she was an energetic, perky and expert helper. With blondish, curly hair and a trim figure, no one was surprised to learn she hailed from southern California.

A relatively new arrival in Coral Bay, Cathy had gained her captain's license and established a healthy charter business – both sail and motor boats – within three years. She was always ready for any boating or partying challenge. Even Coral Bay's most grizzled old salts like Keithley were charmed by her good looks and competed to help her with advice.

Tuesday, as we loaded supplies and equipment on the *Black Night*, Sir Keithley spent the day in Cruz Bay, watching the Seahawk men. He started at the carnival village set up by the customs house. Leaning on the rail of a strategically located bar stall, Keith watched the *Seahawk 2* as she pulled up to the customs dock and then crossed the lagoon to the fueling pier owned by Caneel Bay resort.

Those chores done, the boat motored around the Danish battery and Government House peninsula and beyond the ferry dock to anchor in Cruz Bay. Keithley left the bar stall and walked along the waterfront to his next observation post: the simply and accurately named Beach Bar, located right on the water with a good harbor view.

The *Seahawk* crew did come ashore. They mingled with colorful carnival partiers, visiting food and beverage stalls like everyone else. By the time Keithley hitchhiked back to Coral Bay in late afternoon, he reported the *Seahawk* crew were "snookered."

"Even ol' Cap Skip was wobbly – too many smooth, refreshing rum punches in the sun, I'd say. And, they was still at it when I left."

The consensus was that *Seahawk 2* would not be departing at dawn the next morning. But, we would.

10 CORAL BAY BIRDWATCHING SOCIETY'S FIELD TRIP

"Most serious birders compile a Life List. It's a list of all the bird species they've identified with absolute certainty...Life Lists are extremely important to many birders. Wherever particularly interesting birds congregate, you can bet that birders will be there searching for the rare ones."

— Jim Conrad, "The Life List," blogged October 12, 2001.[1]

Mary, John and I slept on *Perseverance* at her mooring that Tuesday night. Just before dawn, Harry picked us up in his launch as he drove around the bay collecting compatriots from boats and the dinghy dock.

It must have been nearly 6 am by the time we were all assembled on *Black Knight's* planked-over steel deck. Harry, Kwame, Bronco and I were clear-eyed and ready. Keithley and Richie, not so much. Corsair Cathy and Mary were as ready as they'd ever be. Two other middle-aged

Coral Bay women — Marla and Sissy — and John were resting on the deck half-asleep.

A whiff of diesel fume and moderate vibration announced Harry was firing up the *Black Knight's* 200-horse-power, six-cylinder Detroit Diesel engine. He'd salvaged it from an old Greyhound bus in Florida many years earlier.

When he appeared on deck, he motioned to Keithley who looked startled.

"Lord Claymore, would you say a few words as we start our voyage."

As the sun inched above the water on the pink horizon, we gathered in a circle. Sir Keithley stood straight, removed his hat, rubbed his bloodshot eyes and took a deep breath.

"Lord, may I drink a bowl of brimstone with the devil 'imself if we don't beat them fancy Sea'awk bastards to the prize. By all that's holy and unholy, I bloody well know we will, by Jezuz."

"Amen," Mary said and we all mumbled the same.

"Raise sails, weigh anchor!" Harry yelled. Bronco and I were winching up the great lateen sails aft of the masts, as Corsair Cathy hit the deck switch on the electric anchor winch. Then she and Mary raised the jib and head sails. John went up to the bow sprit and rested in the safety netting, his binoculars in hand, believing we really were birdwatchers.

A ten-knot, easterly wind flapped the sails in a clear sky as we motored out of Coral Harbor. Once out in the bay, we easily fell off onto a tight port tack. We'd be beating upwind the whole distance to Anguilla.

To make time and reduce the number of tacks, the engine would be used. At our reasonably anticipated speed of eight to twelve miles per hour, we'd be in Anguilla in 10 hours, as planned — maybe sooner, depending on the wind.

An hour and a half later we passed the BVI's Ginger

Island to starboard and the line formed by
Round Rock and Fallen Jerusalem islets and Virgin Gorda
to port. We were exiting Sir Francis Drake Channel that
had led us from St. John through the British Virgin
Islands. The wind stiffened as we entered Sombrero
Passage, wide open to the Atlantic on our port side and
the Caribbean to starboard.

We fell off onto a close reach and picked up speed
from a freshening wind as we sailed southeast, a course
that would take us a little below Anguilla. The added
speed was worth a slight diversion. We could get back on
a true course later.

The boat healed to starboard about 25 degrees and
easily shipped the 4- to 6-foot waves crossing her port
bow.

"I'd be scared to death out here, if we were on
Perseverance," Mary observed as we leaned on the port rail
enjoying the swells. "We'd be healed way over, getting wet
with spray."

She still remembered getting sick as we rounded Ram
Head one Easter Morning in a gale with cresting waves
nearly knocking us on our beam.

"Yes," I agreed. "The *Black Knight* is a more stable,
comfortable ride."

By late morning, we were a little more than halfway
there in open sea. In the stern wheel house, a radar blip
attracted Harry's interest. He sent Bronco to fetch me.

"You see this, Harris. This boat's been following us on
nearly the same course for the past hour or so. Looks to
have emerged from Drake's channel like us."

"*Seahawk 2*, no doubt. Is she gaining on us?"

"Well, we're probably making about ten knots, maybe
better. A reasonable cruising speed for a trawler that size
is 10 to 12. But, we've altered course by falling off to pick
up wind speed. They don't need to. So, they're slowly
pulling closer than us to Anguilla because they're on a true
course. In a couple of hours they'll likely pass us to

windward. And, I can't push this 25-year old engine much further."

"Guess there's nothing to be done but watch and expect the best," I told Harry.

"That's a funny way of putting it – 'expect the best'," he replied

"Well, even if they beat us to Sombrero, they don't know precisely where *Mersey* lies. We do."

Even as I said it, I knew with their bottom scanning gear, it would only take them a couple of hours to locate the wreck.

Sir Keithley stood at the stern rail shouting curses at the trawler, though she was not yet visible to the naked eye.

At noon, Mary and Cathy passed around homemade chicken salad sandwiches. They offered iced tea and water to drink. That didn't sit well with some.

"Where's the beer, Harry?" Bronco asked.

"If we're going to make it through five full days, we need to learn to conserve resources," Harry replied. Then, he thought about it. "Guess we can have one each. Here, Keithley, take the wheel and stay on course."

"Aye, Cap," Keithley replied, looking fairly shipshape in a new khaki shirt bought just for this trip. A binocular case hung from his neck. He'd even cleaned and stitched up his Royal Navy hat and trimmed his beard.

Harry and I went below to the ice chest and grabbed beers for those who wanted them. Bronco, Richie and Harry were game. Surprisingly, Keithley declined; a good sign, I thought.

"I'm stayin' this 'ere course," he muttered.

Everyone else was up eating lunch amidships where a brown canvas awning offered shade.

After a bit, I walked back to the wheel house to check on his lordship and the radar. Damned if I didn't smell rum, but could see no bottle. Keithley was concentrating on the wheel and carefully watching waves and sails through the open glass windows.

The blip on the screen was bigger and running to the windward of us, as Harry had predicted.

"Shit," I said.

"Don't you be worryin' yourself, lad," Keithley said, with a sparkle in his eye. "The Lord will provide."

"You're awfully biblical today," I commented.

" 'Trust in God and Dreadnought,' as old Lord Admiral Jacky Fisher said," Keithley replied with a wink.

I went forward and gave Harry the update on *Seahawk 2*. I said to myself, "After all we've been through, we're going to lose at the eleventh hour to pin-striped, Wall Street-listed assholes."

As though he guessed what I was thinking, Richie came over and sat next to me.

"Are those shysters catchin' up?"

"Looks like it."

"We're doing our best, Harris. That's all we can do. Put all else out of mind. That's all a sailor can ever do."

He patted me on the shoulder and winked.

"Good thoughts," I replied sincerely. Richie had a good heart.

An hour or so later, Harry and Richie were dozing in the shade. Bronco was half way up the mainmast rigging keeping watch for first sighting of Sombrero and Anguilla on the eastern horizon. The ladies were sunning. John was asleep under a beach towel.

I looked back to the wheel house and could swear I heard singing. Moving back quietly on the starboard side I approached the house.

"...you got me on my knees,
I'm beggin' darlin' please.
...won't you ..."

Sir Keithley seemed to be singing Eric Clapton's classic "Layla." As I rounded the starboard side of the house, he raised his open binocular case to his lips and sipped.

"So, Keithley, now you're singing hymns and taking

communion. Quite a conversion."

"Yes sir, Harris, me' boy. Hell, I can navigate and sail better drunk than sober. Think of ol' Sir Francis Chichester. A 'ero, 'e was. Sailed clear 'round the globe fueled by nothin' but gin and wind."[2]

"I read his book, but don't remember that part."

"Where are those pricks now, Professor?" Keithley asked, nodding at the radar.

"Looks like they're about even with us to windward. Still can't see them visually."

Mary walked back to see what was happening. Keithley immediately stood straighter, closing his binocular case.

"Good day, Mary."

"Hello again, Keith. I enjoyed your words this morning."

"My pleasure, madam," he replied gallantly.

She moved over next to me.

"Where's *Seahawk 2*, honey?"

"About even with us off to windward. I'm afraid they'll beat us into Anguilla and probably to Sombrero."

"Fuck," she said. "How can we compete with that group? All that technology?"

"They don't know precisely where *Mersey* is," I said hopefully. "We do."

"That's something, anyway," she replied. "You know, watching the screen won't change things."

She headed back up forward with the others.

But, I kept watching the screen, imagining the blip was moving faster than it was.

"Care for a snort, Professor?"

"Why not?"

I took his binocular case flask and took a sip. And, then another.

"Thanks, Lord Claymore. I needed that."

"Course you did. Every birdwatcher needs 'is binoculars."

I went back to staring at the radar. Not even remote

viewing could help us now. It was a race we would lose.

Kwame came back.

"How's it look, Professor?"

"Not good. They'll get onsite first and with their equipment, they'll quickly find *Mersey*."

"Just remember, you knew 'dis road was fulla bumps an hole' as my auntie says. It's a miracle we've gotten this far."

"True enough, Kwame. All we can do is keep moving and go around 'dem hole.'"

I glanced at the radar. The blip pulled ahead of us.

Since Sir Keithley was still awake, reasonably alert and on course, I went back up amidships under the awning.

"Harry, they just moved ahead of us to windward."

"Nothing for it, Harris, but keep going or give up."

Bronco, who was resting in the rigging with a binocular and another beer, sang out, "Sombrero off port bow on the seaward horizon. You should just be able to just see it on deck."

With binoculars, I saw a shape on the horizon that looked more like a top hat than a slouch sombrero. Guano mining had turned gentle hillsides into nearly vertical bluffs. A lighthouse stood on the top of lower land – not far from where I knew was a ruined 19th-century chimney and a few collapsing buildings.

Everyone grabbed binoculars.

"It's all brown and white," Corsair Cathy said. "Where are the trees?"

"It's mostly rock and guano," I explained. "Miners long ago stripped off most of the soil and vegetation."

"We can't see the beach," Harry said. "Probably some bush and trees along it."

"Doesn't look like a place to party," Cathy said.

"No bar or liquor store – or even water on that rock," Richie observed.

"Anguilla just visible off port bow," Bronco shouted.

We all looked. Our first destination was just visible; a

short, inviting line of green.

"What are all those mountains in the far distance?" Cathy asked.

"St. Martin," Harry replied. "Half French, half Dutch."

"Anguilla only has a few hills and physically it's only about half the size of Washington, DC," I added. "St. Martin is east and south of Anguilla and has those mountains you're seeing."

I went aft to the wheel house. Mary followed.

The blip was moving further ahead of us. They'd clearly beat us to Anguilla by a couple of hours.

Worse, it was midafternoon and, as often happens here, the wind died down. We were slowing. Seahawk, Inc. was winning a race they didn't even know they were in.

"Shit."

"You know, honey, Sombrero's right over there," Mary said pointing. "What if we simply go there now?"

"Too risky. If we don't check in at Anguilla customs first and then get caught at Sombrero, they could seize the *Black Knight* and maybe arrest us. You know how the BVI can be about foreign charter boats. Anguilla's probably the same."

"We keep going, then," she said. She kissed my cheek and went back amidships.

Harry ordered a course change. We tightened up the sails, heading closer to the wind. Now we were moving directly toward Anguilla, but had lost some wind speed.

I went back to watching the blip. The *Seahawk 2* was already nearing the channel separating Prickley Pear Cays from the main island of Anguilla.

"What's she doing now, Professor?" Sir Keithley asked, taking another slug from his case.

"Beating us into Anguilla. She's picked up speed; we're slowing."

"The day's na' over yet, mate," he replied, grinning.

Was he drunk? "Whatever," I thought. He still had us on course. And, Harry would soon want to come back and take over the wheel as we neared Anguilla.

I walked back up amidships.

"A trawler visible off the bow," Bronco yelled.

"Fuck," Harry said. "We can't get much more speed from our engine and it wouldn't matter anyway."

"What's the problem?" Corsair Cathy asked. She, Marla and Sissy weren't aware of the whole story. Fortunately, Cathy had had a few drinks and her question was mostly rhetorical.

Richie was watching the trawler with binoculars.

"Hold on," he said excitedly. "Some gray-black smoke's coming off her stern!"

"What?" I exclaimed. "That boat must be the best maintained in the Caribbean. What could go wrong?"

"Well, it's *still* a boat," Richie replied.

Now we were all watching. *Seahawk 2* slowed as more smoke billowed out of her stern.

"Is it a fire?" I asked.

"Don't look like one," Richie replied.

"We're gaining on her!" Harry yelled excitedly. "I'll get back to the wheel house in case they call for help on the radio."

Soon after he left, the smoke from *Seahawk* petered out. She slowed to a crawl. Then, she turned into the wind and oncoming swells and stopped. Prevailing wind and current had her sliding backward.

"If they're smart," Richie explained, "they'll lower their oversized dinghy with the big outboard on it, start her up, and throw a line from it to the *Seahawk 2's* bow. The dinghy can hold *Seahawk* into the wind and waves while they work on the engine. They don't want to be adrift taking waves and wind on the beam."

A few minutes later, that's just what they did.

As we drew closer, we could just make out two men sitting in chairs on her stern. With one in the dinghy, that left two – the captain and mate, probably – working in the engine room.

I walked back to the wheel house.

"Any signals from our friends?"

"Nothing, yet," Harry replied. "If they call for help, we're obliged to come to their aid."

"Boy, would they be surprised to see us," I remarked. "Their new Coral Bay friends just happen to be passing by."

"I'm sure they've already recognized us," Harry said. "*Black Knight* is fairly obvious. They couldn't have missed her the other day."

"If they don't call for help, we're not obligated to radio them, are we?"

"No," Harry said. "We can and will just sail on by."

Sir Keithley was listening as we talked.

"They ain't goin' nowhere soon; I guarantee it."

"What's that, Keithley?"

He chuckled.

"Divine intervention, lads, with a little 'elp from me and my old shipmate, Nigel."

"What do you mean?" I asked.

"You remember Nigel – from Isla Margarita? He sailed in a few days ago."

I remembered him; Keithley's old Royal Marine friend from Grenada days who came to Coral Bay a couple of times a year. Last year, he'd told quite a tale about Grenada's first Prime Minister, Sir Eric Gairy, during my UFO investigation. He'd been proven correct.

"Nigel's hard to forget," I replied.

"That 'e is, mate, that 'e is," Keithley agreed. "So, Monday night, when I 'eard from Richie that them wankers over there were all at Skinny's, I got to thinkin'."

He had our full attention.

"There's an old formula Her Majesty's Marines are taught. One pint a saltwater for every 20 gallons of diesel fuel; t'is all it takes to stop and kill a diesel engine. Just a matter of time."[3]

"What do you mean?" I asked, flabbergasted.

"I mean when I 'eard from Ritchie they was nearly 50 gallons short of fuel and were 'eading over to Cruz Bay the next day to top 'er off, why Nigel and I collected some five-gallon Jerry cans, don't you know. Five of 'em!

"Then, we rowed over to that fancy stink pot of theirs, picked the lock on their fuel intake and siphoned out twenty gallons of *their* diesel into four cans. Then, we filled the fifth can four times with seawater and poured it in their tank to replace the 20 gallons we'd taken. Are ye follow'n?"

Harry scratched his head, as I did the math.

"Continue, Keith," I urged.

"T'is simple enough. They 'ave a 200 gallon fuel tank, see. One pint for each 20 gallons comes to 20 gallons saltwater for the full two 'undred. But, we 'ad to take 20 out, so the fuel gauge 'ed show no difference, don' you see?"

"Great job, Lord Claymore," Harry said, slapping him on the back.

"Yes, t'was. And, ol' Nigel got 20 gallons of good diesel for 'is boat for 'is trouble."

I was speechless for a moment, as Keithley laughed.

"You saved our expedition, my Lord," I said. "But, how long will they be stuck?"

"That engine's finished," Keithley said proudly. "Nothin' for it but to get another."

"Amazing," I said. Then I came to my senses.

"Let's keep this among ourselves, Keith," I said. "Just us three and Nigel."

"Me lips 're sealed, Professor. And, don't you worry, now. By the time them plonkers discover it was bad fuel, they'll have no idea where they got it. Might blame Caneel Bay's pump; or mightn't they 'ave got it in San Juan or Santo Domingo? Or any place else they may 'ave stopped on their way down from Florida?"

"Well, they sure didn't fuel up in Coral Bay," I said, feeling more relaxed about it.

Sir Keithley took a pull from his binocular case, but came up dry.

"Now, Professor, when your missus was provisionin', 'ow much Pusser's did she lay in?"

"A couple bottles, I think. I'll go down and get you one."

Before going below, I stopped. "You know, it might be advisable to buy a couple more on Anguilla."

"That it might, Professor," Sir Keithley replied. "That it might."

We soon passed by the disabled *Seahawk 2*, now a couple miles off to our port and drifting back toward the Virgin Islands. She never did issue a "Mayday" that we heard.

By 4 pm, Harry had brought us to an anchorage in Anguilla's Road Bay. He and Bronco immediately collected everyone's passports and took the launch into the customs dock. We needed to check in before 5 pm.

Since we appeared to be a respectable American family (certainly not treasure hunters), Mary, John and I went along with them to scout out the village of Sandy Ground. Everyone else stayed aboard until Harry successfully checked us through customs.

It didn't take long to walk through the whole town. There were a couple of typical West Indian beach bar eateries, a green grocer, spirits shop and marine chandlery, among other attractions.

Our first stop was to buy a couple of bottles for Sir Keithley. Then, we hit a tourist shack. We each bought T-shirts with Anguilla's coat of arms: a centered shield with three dolphins swimming in a circle. Underneath was the government motto, "Strength and Endurance."

Although their currency was the old British Eastern Caribbean Dollar, they happily accepted U.S. dollars. Two of theirs equaled one of ours. So, everything seemed like a bargain.

After Harry and Bronco checked everybody in, the

entire Coral Bay Bird Watchers Society trooped over to the Reggae Reef beachside grill to celebrate its first field trip.

"Here's to the birds!" I exclaimed as the first toast.

"I've always liked chippies," Sir Keithley blurted.

"Not that kind of bird, my Lord," I said. "*Real* birds, not British 'dolly birds'."

"I daresay some real dolly birds are on this 'ere beach in season."

As for food, John and I had curried goat with mashed breadfruit. Everyone else had fresh seafood. Beer was consumed in great quantities. John stuck with lemongrass tea.

We broke up the party early – about 9 pm. We'd depart at sunrise for Sombrero. It would be a long, hard day.

Under purple, pink skies we raised anchor and motored out with the beautiful palms and white sands of the two Prickley Pear Cays to starboard and the curved 15 miles or so of the northern half of Anguilla to our port. Soon, it was light enough to see Sombrero looking ominous off our starboard bow. It looked like a maritime version of the Devils Tower National Monument in Wyoming.

In the distance, a marine tug could just be seen towing what looked like a trawler.

"The *Seahawk 2* is finally arriving in Anguilla," Harry said chuckling and nudging me. "They'll need to tow her to Phillipsburg on Dutch St. Martin to get any real help with that engine – if it can even be repaired."

Since we were heading west-northwest and they southeast, we never got close enough to see much of them.

"Good riddance to 'em," Sir Keithley muttered.

We were approaching Sombrero now, getting a good view. We heard and saw a variety of sea birds circling the island and diving into the water to get breakfast.

We could see a few bushes and trees – even a couple of palms – on the leeward side along the beach. Bushes ran part way up the "hat," which looked to be an islet connected only by a sandy beach to the rest of the island –

a citadel-like flat surface up on rocks thirty yards or more above sea level. That's where the lighthouse and 19th century mining ruins sat. They looked like the remains of a World War 1 battle – crumbling concrete, brick and rusting, erector-set-like iron structures.

Old maps showed the island had a true sombrero-like silhouette. The peak of the hat was in the middle with slopes forming the rest of the island. It was all in one complete piece. Guano mining had seriously carved up the landscape. Had they cut and carried away all 200 feet of the stuff?

The historian in me was fascinated, but we had a different job to do. Using his GPS, Harry found the *Mersey's* coordinates we'd given him. The target was about a mile and a quarter off the beach. We all lined the rail peering down through crystal-clear water to a bottom of sand, coral and sea grass. A large oval sandy spot surrounded by elkhorn coral seemed relatively empty.

I noticed some odd, circular reef on either side of the long mound – the splayed paddle wheels.

"That's got to be it," I said to Harry, Kwame and Bronco, who were standing next to me amidships.

"I'm sure it is," Kwame said. I remembered he was the only one who had actually seen the site.

"One way to find out," said Bronco. Within minutes Harry had lowered the chain and wood ladder and Bronco descended in his scuba gear carrying a garden trowel in one hand.

Mary, John, Kwame and I got on our snorkel gear and went down to observe from the surface. Everyone else watched from the railing.

Bronco was in the center of the oval, digging with his trowel. Plumes of sand blurred our view. Suddenly, he raised his hand and made a "V" for victory sign. He'd struck iron. Flakes of rust floated up.

"It's only about 50-feet deep," he said when he surfaced. "If I banged hard enough, I bet I could beat a hole in that hull – it's pretty brittle."

"Excellent," I said, as we treaded water. "All we need to do is figure out which end is the bow and which is the stern. After we measure approximately back to where the compartment should be, we can make the hole."

We all returned to the *Black Knight* deck and held a counsel of war. First, Harry checked the radar – not another vessel anywhere between us and Anguilla and us and Anegada, lying invisible over the northwest horizon.

"Pays to travel off-season," Harry said.

Then, we got down to business.

Kwame, who was our expedition's medical officer, explained to us neophytes, "It's great news that *Mersey* lays in only 50 feet of water. That means our divers can spend much of our three days here working below. But, they can each spend only a maximum of 100 minutes down there at a time. And, only three dives a day each. We don't want decompression sickness or other problems."

Kwame continued, facing Harry and Bronco directly, "We must be strict about the time each diver stays below, gentlemen. We do not want to call Anguilla emergency services for help."

"We get it, Kwame," Harry said sincerely. "We'll be careful."

Then, we got down to hard work. We moved the *Black Knight* as close to the wreck as possible with bow and stern anchors put out to hold here there. Eventually, we'd be using her winches and hoses and needed to be nearly over the *Mersey*.

Next, Bronco and Richie suited up, went down the ladder and jumped in, pulling a hose Mary and Cathy fed them. It was bigger than a garden variety, but smaller than a fire hose. It was attached to an air compressor on deck manned by Harry.

Kwame and I were in the water with snorkels watching our divers. They'd give us hand signals that we'd relay to deck.

When the divers reached one end of the oval area, Richie raised two hands.

I yelled up to Harry, "Turn on the air!"

In a burst of bubbles and sand clouds, Bronco and Richie were manning the hose, blowing sand and debris off the hull. Clouds of sand and bits of sea vegetation drifted upward with thousands of air bubbles.

A half hour later, I could just make out one of Richie's hands appear above the clouds, which now included rust flakes.

"Turn off the air," I yelled. When the divers surfaced, we learned they had cleared and found the keel of the hull and contours of the bow.

We all went back on deck and I got out the *Mersey's* blueprints. At the keel, the hull was 250 feet long. The captain's cabin and officers' quarters were in the far stern and took up about 40 feet. The treasure room was located just forward of their quarters. If we entered the hull 45 feet from the stern, we should hit the treasure room.

"OK, guys," I said to Harry, Sir Keithley, Ritchie, Bronco and Kwame, who were all gathered around the chart table where I was working. "If we measure 205 feet from the bow stem you uncovered and follow the keel aft, we should find our spot."

They cheered.

"We have a 30-foot measuring stick that can be read under water," Harry explained. "We can use that and stakes to measure it off."

"Do we need to clear off the whole hull?" Richie asked.

"No. We don't want to destroy any more coral or risk damaging more of the hull than necessary," I said. "What do you think, Bronco?"

He smiled and said, "We've enough hull uncovered to measure from stem to stern. We'll get close enough to our spot and then clear a few feet of hull back there."

"Sounds like a plan," Harry said.

By then it was midday. We all ate lunch. Harry

checked the radar.

"Shit, a boat's coming from Anguilla. What the fuck will we do?"

"Not to worry," I said. "I have a plan. Now, Mary, John, Marla, Sissy, Kwame and Keithley take the launch to shore with binoculars and start birdwatching. If you get too hot on that rock, go ahead and take a swim off the beach. Cathy, you get into your bikini and lay on the fore deck in the sun on that lawn chair we brought."

Harry and I went back to the wheel house and watched the radar. Richie and Bronco tied a tarp over the compressor and all the hose. Then they stowed the diving gear below.

Everyone else was approaching their assigned positions.

The blip soon became visible as a communications mast on the horizon.

"Can't tell if it's the police or not," Harry said.

We were all sweating and breathless.

Slowly, a deck house appeared.

"Could be anything," Richie said tensely.

Finally, it appeared.

It looked to be about a 35-foot motor catamaran – the kind used for snorkeling charters. We saw a gaggle of tourists in the stern under a canopy. A few were suntanning on the deck.

As the cat approached, Cathy stood up climbed out the bowsprit, waved and pantomimed a dance and drinking a bottle. They all waved back and, fortunately, moved off away from us, closer to the rock "hat" part of the island and the beach connecting it to the "citadel" portion. There they anchored.

Black Knight was off the other end of the citadel and its beach – too far for the tourists or their crew to see clearly what we were doing. Soon, tourists were in the water, snorkeling and swimming.

We decided to wait an hour or so, before resuming work. Everyone could use the rest, anyway. Meanwhile, we kept our binoculars on the party boat.

It wasn't long before some of the older snorkelers returned and climbed back aboard her.

"I can taste the cold rum punches," Richie said, as he watched. And, they were all given glasses as they stowed their snorkeling gear.

Meanwhile, our birdwatchers could be seen on our end of the island moving through the bush and up over the rocks to the top of the citadel. Mary and John went back down and got in the water to cool off. Keithley was moving toward the old buildings, looking for plunder, no doubt.

Soon, all the tourist snorkelers were back on their boat with drinks in hand. Most of them were laying around deck sunning by the time they raised anchor and went back toward Anguilla.

"Bet they stop at the beach bars on Prickley Pear Cays before returning to Road Bay," Harry said.

"That's just what they'll do," Richie agreed. "A nice day charter."

We were all soon back to work. Richie and Bronco were underwater measuring off and staking the *Mersey's* hull. Then Harry and I handed down the air hose and I jumped back in with my snorkel to act as communicator.

They had found and cleared the aft section of the hull we were looking for. Their staked target position proved to be only four feet off the real spot – a great job of virtual dead reckoning on the sea bottom.

After coming back up, they returned to deck. Richie refilled air tanks. Since the *Mersey's* keel was the strongest and thickest part of the iron hull, we'd need to make a hole on one or the other side of it. Rather than punching through with brute strength, we agreed to use the cutting torch to make a cleaner and safer entryway into the ship. The hole would be made on the section of bottom hull closest to the *Black Knight*.

Underwater cutting was Harry's specialty. He and

Bronco descended carrying a bronze wand with a narrow hose connected to a propane tank on deck manned by Richie. I snorkeled on the surface nearby as communicator. When they were ready, I gave Richie the signal.

This time, an eerie, greenish-orange and white ball of light was at the center of bubbles and flakes of rust rising to the surface. In about an hour they'd cut a four- by-four-foot square in the iron hull. The two of them used crowbars to pry it up and open so it wouldn't fall inside. They pushed it aside and shined a light in the hole.

Bronco started going inside. But, Harry grabbed his leg and pointed to the watch on his wrist. It was time to go up. They'd had their 100 minutes below.

"We could see what must be the bottom of the wooden floor of a compartment a couple feet above the bilge," Harry explained when they surfaced.

"That sounds right," I said, but thought it could describe the bottom of any compartment.

It was now about 3 pm. Bronco and Richie had as much diving time as they should for one day. But, Corsair Cathy and Sir Keithley were still fresh. Harry was game for more, after a rest. Meanwhile, he monitored the radar. We didn't need any surprises. All was clear.

Sir Keithley and Cathy suited up. They'd have the honor of breaking through into what we hoped was the treasure room.

"Lord Claymore, please be gentle getting through the wood floor," I cautioned. "We want as little destruction to the site as possible. We also don't want a lot of debris falling on the gold."

"I hears ya," he said, as he descended the ladder. "I'll be as delicate as a sheep among wolves. No worries, lad."

Cathy followed him down the ladder. She carried a steel mesh basket connected by a thick line running up to the deck and through a series of blocks forward to the anchor winch. Richie was going back and forth over the line and winch, checking and double checking everything.

I was back in the water as communicator. Kwame was beside me.

In a cloud of brownish water and chips and slivers of rotten, mushy wood, the divers easily poked through the floor. Flakes of silver floated up. Must be the zinc lining, I thought. Without special handling, anything wooden brought to the surface would simply disintegrate. But, we were after metal.

Cathy and Keithley disappeared through the hole into the inner hull. They wore underwater headlamps. Bubbles and debris clouds drifted up from their position.

Kwame and I watched and waited, breathless with anticipation. After about five minutes Cathy appeared, grabbed the steel mesh basket and brought it into the hull.

But, she hadn't signaled a thing to us. We waited in suspense for another 15 minutes.

Cathy then appeared, gave us a "V" and motioned for the basked to be raised.

"Raise the basket, Richie," I yelled. "We hit the 'mother lode'!"

I heard wild cheering up on the boat. Under water, I could see Cathy standing on the *Mersey's* hull to guide the line pulling up the basket as Ritchie slowly raised it with the winch. When the basket emerged from the hull, I could see metal shapes – even imagined gold and silver colors. I swam over to the line to guide it safely up.

Between the line and *Black Knight's* hull, Harry had positioned the launch. Bronco and Harry were there carefully guiding the line up so it didn't swing into the ship's hull and break loose. When the basket finally reached the surface, Kwame and I were in the launch, too.

In the basket were bars and coins of a dull brass color and what I recognized as tarnished silver. Harry took his pen knife and scrapped a brassy bar – shiny gold.

After back slaps and high fives, I suggested we get that basket up as fast as we could so we could lower it again to bring up more. We were in a race against time. Although we'd done extraordinarily well the first day on site, we only had supplies for three days there. And, we could be interrupted at anytime by unwelcome visitors or weather changes.

We needed to recover as much as possible, as soon as possible. And, we did.

Working two-person shifts, our diver teams managed four dives each our first 24 hours on site. We'd raised what I estimated to be one quarter of the treasure.

On deck, we'd preassembled boxes made of treated wood to hold the loot as it came up. We didn't see the point of going to the trouble and effort of lowering it all into the hold, only to have to raise it up again back home. We didn't have the time or manpower for that.

Harry had arranged eight four-by-three-foot boxes for gold bars. He'd carefully placed them around the deck to maintain stability.

For the coins, we'd brought along two dozen double-stitched bags made of old sail cloth. John was kept occupied by organizing and putting away all the coins. Those bags we put below deck.

The second day, we again made great progress. But, the same charter boat had come back at noon. This time, we all pretended to be partying on deck – waving and making provocative gestures to the tourists. Harry even had rock music from his CD collection blaring out deck speakers so they could hear it over the water.

By the end of the second day on site, all receptacles for bars and specie were full. But, there was still more, much more to bring up. We found ship's buckets, pillow cases, cans and other containers and filled them up with loot. Sir Keithley found a glass cutter in one of the tool boxes and cut the necks off empty beer bottles. These, we also filled with coins.

11 ADDITIONS TO OUR LIFE LISTS

"February 24, 1671, Captain Morgan departed from Panama, or rather from the place where the city of Panama [previously] stood; of the spoils whereof he carried with him one hundred and seventy-five beasts of carriage, laden with silver, gold, and other precious things."

— "The Buccaneers of America," by John Esquemeling, "one of the buccaneers who was present at those tragedies," Project Gutenberg edition of this book first published in 1684. Morgan had sacked and then burned the Spanish city of Panama.

By sunrise of our third morning off Sombrero, we needed to make a tough decision. Over coffee and breakfast, we talked. If we were still there when the tour boat came back a third time, they'd get suspicious and Anguilla is a very small place. It was certain that the tour boat crew knew the police. No innocent tourists (like us) would spend three days at barren Sombrero.

Also, we now had every conceivable container filled with loot.

"We should stop while we're ahead," I cautioned everyone. "The Anguillan patrol boat could come at anytime and we still have to get back to Coral Bay without being boarded by our Coast Guard. We'll be a lot less suspicious sailing back in day light."

"Just two more dives," Harry said. "We could do it and still be out of here by 11 am before the tourists arrive."

"Okay, but the second diving team has to allow time to figure out a way to put that cut-out hull section back in place and cover over our work. We want to disguise the entrance and leave everything as clean as possible."

Our last two dive teams brought up gold bars only. We tied these together in squares and secured them on deck around the masts. Harry and Bronco were the second team down that morning.

They'd taken down a thick, gray, waterproof tarp they'd found in *Black Knight's* hold. After an hour of work, we raised the last basket of gold and they spread the tarp over the hole with a few extra feet on each side. Then, they used stakes to secure it in the sand.

Gently, they placed the square of iron, which only weighed half as much underwater, over the tarp. It held. Then, they pushed sand over it all, and went forward and spread sand over the other section of hull we'd exposed.

We were all back on deck and ready to depart by 11 am. With some reluctance, we raised the anchors and began our sail home – hours earlier that we had originally planned. Nevertheless, I was certain we'd recovered tens of millions of dollars in treasure. There was much more still down there and we could always come back.

We'd been very lucky. Mary was right when she said, "the harder we work, the luckier we get."

Although it was an easy, comfortable downwind sail back to the Virgins, Harry and I were tense and hung out in the wheel house worrying. For starters, the boat was top heavy. We also could be stopped and searched at any time. As Sir Keithley happily steered us home, Harry and I took turns watching the radar until we grew bleary eyed.

After three hours or so, the mountain on Virgin Gorda was in sight off the starboard bow. It was then that a big blip appeared. It was moving quickly out of Sir Francis Drake channel on a converging course with us.

"Fuck, now what?" I shouted.

"Keep yer cool, Professor," Keithley advised. "Take it as it comes, lad. Nothin' else for it. Likely, nothin' to do with us, anyway."

"By its signature, it must be close to three hundred feet long," Harry observed.

"Hand me that binocular case, my lord."

"Gladly."

Harry and I both took swigs.

"I don't believe this shit," Harry said. "Look, here's another sizeable blip coming in fast out of the northeast from the Atlantic. It's also on a convergent course."

"Jesus," I said. "Our deck is literally awash in treasure."

"Nothing coming in over the radio," Harry said nervously, pushing his cap up and wiping the sweat from his forehead.

Everybody else was amidships under the sunshade. We still had plenty of beer and other essential provisions. Sensibly, most crew members were lounging under the sunshade hoisting quite a few bottles so we wouldn't be burdened with unloading them full when we reached port.

We didn't bother alerting them. There was no point. There was nothing anyone could do.

"If we're to be seized and arrested, t'is best to be lit up," Keithley observed.

"Hey, Bronco," Harry yelled. He came back to the wheel house.

"Take a look at these blips."

"I see them, but don't believe what I'm seeing."

"Neither do we. Go up the mast with binoculars and see what we're looking at. But, don't tell the others."

In a few minutes, he was back.

"Looks like some kind of research ship coming out of Drake Channel. Her hull appears to be yellow."

"Great news," I said, relieved. "Not Coast Guard white."

"Yup, but the one coming in from the Atlantic looks like some kind of Navy spook ship – battleship gray, antennas, satellite dishes coming out everywhere and a helipad on her stern."

It was only a matter of minutes before the yellow research ship was visible from deck. She kept coming toward us from the BVI. Off her communications mast she flew a private flag – a gold eagle or something on a blue field.

"Shit," I said. "Is that an eagle or a fuckin' osprey on that flag?" I asked no one in particular.

"It looks to me like that symbol Cap Skip and the boys wore on their Seahawk uniforms," said Richie, who'd come aft when he saw the first vessel.

"Must be the Seahawk mother ship," Harry said. "Think they put 'two-and-two' together and came up with us?"

"Wish we 'ad a rifled cannon," Sir Keithley said quizzically.

"Wish I had my forty-five pistol," Bronco said.

Now the superstructure of the naval vessel was just visible from deck on the horizon.

"She's got a U.S. flag," I said, feeling better because we were not in American waters. "Not a fuckin' Union Jack; no offense, Keith."

"None taken, lad."

"We're technically in British waters, I guess," Harry observed. "Either still in Anguilla or now in the BVI."

The yellow research vessel was closing on us.

"Let's jibe and head west," Harry said. "We can then bypass the BVI on our starboard and avoid *Seahawk* and Sir Francis Drake channel altogether. Then, we can come up on Coral Bay from behind Norman Island."

"You want to jibe this ol' girl, 'arry? With 'er decks

weighted with 'eavy metal and 'er layin' as low in the water as I've ever seen? Cap, think it over."

Keithley was right to caution Harry. We had a nice stiff breeze behind us. Jibes can be dodgy.

"Wait," Richie yelled with excitement, pointing to the Naval vessel whose hull was now visible.

"She's launched a helicopter!"

"Now, we're truly fucked no matter what course we take," Harry said despondently.

"Let's watch the copter and listen to the radio," I advised. "No sense doing anything else."

With amazement, we saw the helicopter take a course toward the research vessel. Then, it circled above it. The Naval ship changed her course toward the research ship. We listened tautly to the radio.

"Attention *R/V Seahawk*. This is *USS Jeannette*, please stop and prepare to be boarded."

"Now, me ol' eyes 'as seen everything!" Sir Keithley shouted.

"*USS Jeanette*, we are a private research vessel sailing in British territorial waters. By what right do you impede our voyage?"

"*R/V Seahawk*, we are authorized by Her Majesty's Government to patrol these waters in the absence of the Royal Navy."

"Rule Britannia!" Lord Claymore shouted. "Fuckin' A!"

"*USS Jeanette*, we have not violated any British or U.S. laws or customs procedures."

"*R/V Seahawk*, the United States Naval History and Heritage Command asserts that you conducted underwater archeological work on a sunken U.S. Naval vessel while in U.S. territorial waters without permission as required by law. Please hove-to and stand-by to be boarded."[1]

The *Seahawk* changed course into the wind, slowed to a crawl and waited as ordered.

"God bless America's Naval historians!" Richie yelled, punching the air with his fist.

We all cheered. Sir Keithley patted me on the back.

Within moments, our whole crew was up in *Black Knight's* bow, watching the drama. A U.S. Navy launch had been lowered and was approaching *Seahawk*. It had a manned, 50-caliber machine gun mounted on its foredeck.

"Wish we 'ad one of those," Kiethley said wistfully, pointing to the gun.

"Unfuckin' believable," I said. "We've spent nearly three days illegally plundering a 150-year-old British wreck and *they* get pulled over."

"The Navy works in mysterious ways," Kwame said. I hadn't noticed he'd come up next to me.

"It sure does," I replied and then thought out loud. "You know, it seems a funny coincidence that a Naval spy ship comes in from the Atlantic at the same time a Navy-backed expedition is exploring the Puerto Rico Trench for unidentified submersible objects or alien artifacts right out there," I pointed.

"You and I both know the commander," I added, thinking about how I met Kwame. There were a lot of coincidences – too many, maybe. Still, we did have the treasure and the Navy was leaving us alone.

"Apparently, the *R/V Seahawk* was illegally diving on a wrecked Naval vessel in the Virgin Islands," Kwame said.

"How could they know Seahawk, Inc. was doing anything in these waters?"

"Don't be naive, Professor. With satellite surveillance on drug interdiction missions in this region, they know what's going on. It *is* Naval Intelligence."

I was stunned into silence. It could be coincidental, I thought. They could also know about us from satellite passes – but, they're not stopping us. It was all confusing.

Completely unmolested, though, we passed by the *Seahawk/Jeanette* incident and were soon comfortably in Sir Francis Drake channel, watching our glorious islands pass by.

It was sunset when we made fast to the *Black Knight's*

Coral Bay mooring. But, our work was just beginning. Now we had to discretely off load all the treasure, divide it up and find safe places for each of us to hide our shares.

We really needed a warehouse or empty hall.

We were all sprawled out over *Black Knight's* deck tiredly brainstorming.

Mary came up with a suggestion.

"The Coral Bay Blues Bar is closed and empty. As you know, it's right on the water next to the mangroves. Boats could unload there pretty much out of sight from land. We could tell Jenny we want to rent it for a private party."

"Good idea," Harry said. "But, what do we pay her with? 1850 gold dollars? Silver pesos? Gold bullion?"

Harry made a good point.

"Let's think this through," I interjected. "First, if we agree the Blues Bar is a good idea, I think Mary and I have some money saved that could pay for it – maybe even rent it for a week."

"No good," said Harry. "Too many people would see us moving stuff between the boat and the bar."

"What about the car barge dock over at Enighed Pond?" I suggested. "In theory, anyone can rent a spot short-term to work on a boat or something."

"Good idea," Bronco said. "Then we could drive trucks and cars right up to the boat and unload comfortably."

"Sounds okay," Mary said. "But, what about U.S. Customs? To use that dock, would we need to check in?"

"Fuck that," Richie said. "In 25 years, I've gone all over the place out of Coral Bay and never once checked back in."

"Good point, Richie," I said. "Most people don't bother to check in when they return to Coral Bay."

"Hell," Harry said. "If I checked back in here, they'd think it was unusual – maybe even suspicious."

Several grunts of agreement came from our group.

"Harry is captain of *Black Knight*," I said. "It's his decision and sounds like he's made it. Next question?"

"Nevertheless, do we need to worry about U.S. Customs, if we use the car barge dock?" Mary restated her inconvenient question. I think we were all prepared to simply ignore customs, regardless.

"I can answer that," Kwame said. "It's a USVI Port Authority facility, not a federal point of entry. As long as you pay, any VI vessel that needs it can use the dock — assuming there's space."

"Thanks, Kwame. Do you know whom we should call for permission to use it?"

"Yes, I went to elementary school with the harbor master."

"Hell, I didn't even know they 'ad a 'arbor master," Sir Keithley observed.

"Okay, Kwame would you check on availability? We can split the cost. Is that all right, Harry?"

"Sure, sounds good. Better than trying to unload her at her mooring."

Kwame looked at his watch.

"Seems like midnight, but, it's only 8 pm. I can call him now."

"Wait," I said. "Don't we need a cover story? Harry, didn't you used to go to Trinidad regularly for loads of lumber and other stuff?"

"Yep. I brought back mahogany and teak, plumbing fittings, some cistern tanks and other odds and ends I could sell here."

"Good. That's our cover for the harbor master. Harry just got back from Trinidad and needs to unload. Any objections anybody?"

It was agreed and Kwame made the call. It being off season, there was space on the dock. We could move *Black Knight* there the next morning, providing we gave a third party a 'good will' payment. No customs needed. No questions asked.

"Ok," I said. "Harry, can we move her over first thing in the morning?"

"Sure."

"Mary, we're going to need a bunch of tarps to cover up everything we're unloading. Can you go over to St. John Hardware first thing and pick up a bunch?"

"No problem. Do we need anything else?"

"Some extra line would help," Harry replied.

"A couple cases of 'eineken would do well," Sir Keithley threw in. "Nigel will 'elp us unload for a case, I'd wager."

"Sounds good," I said. "Now, what about security for the boat tonight?"

"Why don't you and me sleep on her?" Harry suggested. "Anyone want to join us?"

"I bloody well will," Sir Keithley said. "I'll just pop over to *Bonne Chance* and get me Royal Navy Browning 9 mm."

"Hell," Bronco said. "I'll get my Colt 45."

"If Bronco's getting his, I'm sure as hell getting mine!" Richie said.

"You mean that 12- gauge, pump-action shot gun of yours?" Bronco asked.

"Yep. That baby is a Mossberg 500 seven-shot edition; same as used by the military in Bermuda. I wouldn't sail south of Antigua without it."

"Don't blame you," Bronco replied. "If it's good enough for Bermuda's forces, it's good enough for us."

"Just the thing for an active birdwatcher," Sir Keithley added.

"That may be overkill, gents," I said. "But, if they're legal and make you feel better, why not?"

"My thinking exactly," Harry said. "You can't be too safe. And, I'm sure that Seahawk bunch knows what we've been up to. They're not stupid."

"We'd best be prepared to repel boarders, Cap," Sir Keithley said. "Nigel will 'elp us, sure as this night will be a long one. He's got an old Armalite assault rifle on 'is boat from service days. Wouldn't it be grand, lads, if we 'ad us a little fight?"

I, for one, didn't think so and hoped to God we had a quiet night.

Everyone got in the launch and Harry took them to their boats so they could get their weapons. I could hear Sir Keithley merrily singing an old Irish rebel song in the distance over the harbor.

"And it's down Along the bog road, that's where I long to be.
Lying in the dark with a Provo company,
A comrade on me left and another on me right
And a clip of ammunition for my little Armalite."[2]

I insisted that Mary, the other ladies and John go back to the dock. They would need to collect and bring as many of our trucks and cars as possible to the car barge dock the next morning.

Kwame and I waited on deck. I broke the ice, which was getting thick.

"I hate to say it, but Harry's right, Kwame. The Seahawk people must know what we did and that we recovered something from the *Mersey*. The question is what will they do?"

"It does stand to reason that they know, Professor," Kwame replied. "For all our sakes, I'm glad I'm a good Navy Corpsman."

"Exactly," I replied. "I hope we don't get into a fight, but if we do you must stay under cover. We might really need a medic."

By the time everyone got back onboard, it was about 10 pm. Keithley had brought Nigel with him.

"Cap Harry and the rest of you lot," Sir Keithley said loudly. "As a retired Royal Marine Sergeant Major, Nigel 'ere would like to 'ave a few words. We'd best listen very carefully."

Nigel, like Keithley, was dressed in well-worn khaki. This evening, though, he wore a faded green beret with a tarnished brass badge: a crown astride a globe with "Africa, Europe and Asia" inscribed over it. He had shaved his red, wrinkled face and cut off his gray pony tail since I'd last seen him.

Nigel came forward, standing erect as though on a parade ground. He was every inch a Sergeant Major this evening.

"You see, gents, it's like this. If an enemy wants to take this 'ere treasure while it's still in one place, they must attack tonight. Am I right?"

Everyone murmured affirmatively.

"Right," Nigel continued. "They know that. We're sitting ducks 'ere at this mooring. T'is right where anyone can and *will* find us."

Harry pushed his cap back and scratched his head.

"What should we do?"

Nigel smiled and continued. "We'd be a might harder to find and attack in the open sea. If you've 'nough fuel, we should go out."

"I have the fuel," Harry admitted. "You're right. At sea, we'd be harder to find and we can maneuver."

"Quite right," Nigel agreed.

I was thinking about how someone might attack us and made a comment.

"It stands to reason that if someone knows we have a treasure onboard, they wouldn't use rocket propelled grenades or cannons on us."

"Very true, Professor," Nigel responded with a slap to my back. "They'd only use small arms. That gives us much better odds."

"Well, Nigel, very glad you joined us and brought along that Armalite!" Harry exclaimed.

"Wouldn't miss it for the world."

Keithley stepped closer.

"Nigel, me mate. We may finally get a sea battle." He chuckled and continued. "Glorious, simply glorious," he said, rubbing his hands in anticipation.

"That it will be," Nigel agreed.

So, we weighed anchor and set the jib and head sails for

maneuverability and speed assist. But, we'd rely on the engine so the main deck, masts and booms would be clear of running lines and sails. At about 11 pm, we rounded Ram Head, leaving Coral Bay behind and steered west southwest for Frenchman's Cap, a rocky uninhabited bird sanctuary on the way to St. Croix.

The plan was to round the Cap and head back to St. John on the western Cruz Bay end of the island. On that route, we'd be out of easy sight of authorities on St. Thomas and St. John. Ironically, though, any bad guys in a boat looking for us could still spot us on radar.

We assigned two, three-man watches to be changed at 3 am. One man would be at the wheel, one in the wheel house scanning radar and watching astern, the other on the foredeck watching the sea ahead of us. At the sign of any trouble, the foredeck man would wake the rest of us.

Bronco led the first watch with Keithley at the helm and Richie up forward. Everyone else slept on deck with any weapons they had.

It was a cloudy night with no moon, good for sneaking up on someone, but, also helpful for those of us trying to sleep. Exhausted from the Sombrero adventure, I fell into a deep sleep almost immediately.

Sometime later, my arm was being shaken. Was it a dream?

"Wake up, Harris," Richie said, releasing my arm. "There's a suspicious boat."

Harry was already awake, telling everyone to keep very low on deck. Anyone watching with night vision binoculars would try to count our number.

I followed Harry and Nigel back to the wheel house. Harry relieved Bronco, who went forward to rest. I relieved Keithley at the wheel. Kwame was on foredeck watch. The time was 1:45 am.

"We're nearing Frenchman's Cap," Harry explained. "The blip on my screen is coming from Charlotte Amalie.

It just cleared Buck Island. It should be visible, but I see no running lights."

The last time I'd seen Buck Island, the wreck of the *RMS Wye* and bodies of her crew carpeted that islet's little bay and beach. I put that out of mind, concentrating on the here and now.

"No running lights," I said. "That can't be good. How big do you think she is, Harry?"

"Somewhere between 40 and 50 feet. Sure wish we could see it."

"Without running lights, she's up to no good, gents," Nigel said. " 'ow soon before we converge?"

"Hold on, look there's Frenchman's Cap," Harry interrupted. We could now see the crests of white swells breaking on her rocks off the starboard bow. The noise of water smashing into granite was becoming overwhelming – an ominous reminder of how insignificant we really were.

Harry took the wheel and we rounded the Cap. I watched the punch and fall of crushed waves breaking on its towering, nearly shear, rock walls. A sense of foreboding gripped me.

Harry was concentrating on the *Black Knight*. Once we rounded the Cap, we were on our course back toward the distant shimmering lights of St. John.

"Now then, Nigel," Harry said, giving me the wheel. "I think that boat will overtake us in a half hour or less. They're moving a lot faster."

"May I suggest, Cap, that you command from the wheel house with the Professor 'ere on the wheel?" Nigel said. "That would put all our armed men plus Kwame on deck."

Harry nodded and Nigel asked an interesting question.

"What do you think that boat's made of?"

"Could be steel or aluminum, but I'd bet fiberglass. It's cheaper, lighter for speed and easier to maintain."

Nigel nodded.

"How thick is your steel hull?"

"Why, the old *Knight* here has a good half-inch of steel,"

Harry proudly answered. "They don't make them like this anymore."

I handed the wheel to Nigel as he and Harry worked out a plan. I went forward to look for coffee. First, I spotted Richie.

"Ever shot anything with that rifle?"

"It's a shotgun; I used to go huntin' in Indiana as a kid and was a pretty good shot. But, I never shot a person, only deer."

"Could you?"

"If they're shooting at us, I'll shoot back – guarantee it." He said it firmly and I believed him.

I looked over to Keithley. He was practically shaking with excitement and anticipation, fondling his Navy pistol. All his pirate dreams were coming true: Christmas and Guy Fawkes Day wrapped into one fun-filled week.

And, there sat Bronco on a secured stack of gold bullion, back resting on the main mast, his 45 in his lap. I needn't ask that dude if he'd use his weapon.

Harry quietly called me back to take the wheel. Nigel crouched astern of the wheel house. He was virtually sprawled on the deck, Armalite ready for use, as he stared astern watching and waiting for our visitors.

"There," he shouted. "Look at the lights on St. Thomas off astern of us on port side. You see how they flicker off and on briefly in a line – that's their boat passing between us and them."

"I have them on radar; can't be but two miles or so away."

"Funny thing about this situation," I said. "Neither them, nor us can call for help; not with all our contraband on board and not with whatever weapons they must have."

"Quite right, Professor. We're all alone this night." Nigel said, as the black shape trailing us started taking form.

"Shit," he yelled. "Get down." As he spoke wooden chips and splinters from our wheel house exploded into the air in a clean line port to starboard.

I was already kneeling on deck, but still had the wheel. We were on course. Harry had fallen to the deck in the wheel house. Nigel was crouching as though taking aim with his rifle.

"What happened?" Harry asked, now kneeling in the house.

"Automatic rifle fire," Nigel said. "By the time I saw the flashes, the bullets were already hitting us. The bloody bastards."

"Are you okay, Harry?" I asked. I saw sweat on his forehead, despite the cool night breeze. My heart was beating faster and suddenly my palms felt sweaty. The biochemistry of fear, I realized, wishing I had a weapon.

"I'm fine," Harry replied shakily. "Just scared shitless."

"That was a warning," Nigel continued, cool as the proverbial cucumber. "Their fire crossed our stern, right above our 'eads. They must have night vision."

"What are we supposed to do?" I asked.

" 'old steady, lads. They're gainin' on us. But, may not know we 'ave weapons. Let's keep 'em guessing till they get closer."

Time seemed to slow down as we watched the now more defined black shape approaching our stern off to port.

"Cap," Nigel said to Harry calmly. "Crouch down and go forward. Tell Richie, Bronco and Keithley we've been fired upon in case they didn't see or hear it. Tell 'em to remain below the top of your steel bulwarks and any other cover they can find. They should be ready to fire off our port side behind cover."

Harry nervously bent over, readying himself to move forward.

"Harry," I said, "ask Kwame to get behind cover with his medical kit and stay put."

"Good thinking, Professor," Nigel said. "Now, keep calm, Cap, and remember our plan."

"What do we do?" I asked Nigel.

"I'm watching 'em. If I sees a muzzle flash, I'm firing right back at it. Meanwhile, we just watch and let 'em close in some more. You crouch as low as you can and still handle the wheel."

Harry was back, sitting on the deck, using binoculars to try to see more of their boat.

"Their silhouette looks to be a motor boat with a wheel house and small cabin amidships. The rest appears to be open deck – can't see any people."

"They're likely wearing black and blackened their faces. Just keep calm, watch 'nd wait," Nigel said, still crouched, still aiming his rifle at their boat.

He suddenly fired several rounds in ear busting explosions, just as another line of wood chips burst from one side of the wheel house to the other – this time the strafing was a few feet lower.

Everyone was all right. Nigel continued aiming, waiting for another target.

"They now knows we're armed," he chuckled. The black boat silhouette seemed to slow a bit.

"Think you hit any of them?"

"Most likely, mate," Nigel replied matter-of-factly. "My guess is a bloke with a night scope on 'is assault rifle was in the bow, maybe even standin' up. 'e didn't expect disciplined return fire aimed right at 'is barrel flash; no sir, 'e didn't."

Everything went silent. It was timeless for what seemed like several minutes. We all watched the black shape coming closer, but at a slower speed.

"Now what?" Harry asked, crouched on the deck of the wheel house.

The black boat, now a bit more defined, sped up, moving forward, but at an angle away from us. We could just see the white wake from her stern.

Nigel was still aiming, following them with his rifle.

"This doesn't change our plan, Cap," Nigel said calmly.

We lost sight of them and Harry felt comfortable enough to stand and look at the radar on his control panel.

"She's going closer in shore nearing Great St. James Island; now she's turning to her starboard a couple miles off our bow."

Great and Little St. James were two small, thinly-inhabited islands in between St. John and St. Thomas. We wanted to pass both of them to our port, motoring through the widest body of water between the St. James islands and St. John.

"She's turning now, speedin' up a bit; coming straight at us off our bow."

"Time for me to move forward, Cap," Nigel said, putting a big silver whistle and lanyard around his neck. "Keep calm and alert. Just wait for my signal."

Harry was glued to the radar.

"They must be a mile or less ahead of us, now," Harry said as he slowed our engine.

"Still movin' closer, Harris, where's Nigel?"

Then, we both heard a whistle.

"Harris, slowly turn us to starboard until I say 'stop.'"

As we turned, Harry further reduced our speed to all that was necessary for headway and to complete the turn. He told me to stop and crouched down.

Now our whole port side was facing the St. James islands and the enemy boat. Too bad we didn't have cannons to give them a broadside, I thought.

Harry was back at the radar.

"Damn, they haven't slowed much, headin' right for us; maybe only a couple hundred yards away; now 200 yards; now 100; 75; 50 yards coming right at us."

"Get down, Harry."

We heard a rapid series of high-pitched explosions, as Nigel reopened fire.

Then we heard boom, boom, boom, boom from Richie's shot gun and more of Nigel's automatic fire.

Suddenly, wood chips, splinters and sparks were flying

amidships from railings and steel bulwarks. More chips exploded from our wheel house. Faint light shone through fresh holes where Harry's head would have been, if he'd been standing. The wheel house windows were shattered. But, he and I had remained crouched low.

Nigel was still firing back at their flashes. Everyone else was flat on deck, below the steel bulwarks.

They must have strafed us with at least two automatic rifles that time, I thought.

Then, their boat veered off back toward St. Thomas.

Harry was now standing, bent over the radar. The enemy was moving toward St. Thomas.

"She's nearly ashore on St. Thomas off the Ritz Carlton's beach. Now she's quickly changin' course back toward us." Harry was yelling loud enough for everyone on deck to hear.

Shit, I thought, the Ritz Carlton. What would the rich people make of this? Maybe they'd think it was fireworks or some pirate pageant. Drunks at the beach bar would be delighted. Guests from New York would be unfazed.

"Nigel," Harry shouted, interrupting my thoughts. "Looks like she's coming back for a run across our stern!"

They likely want to take out the wheel house and wheel, I thought. Suddenly, we seemed very exposed.

Nigel was shouting back to us.

"Cap, keep calm. Wait one minute. Then, very slowly, move us back to port, parallel to 'er course."

Harry understood. He waited, telling me, "She's comin' at our stern; now 150 yards out! Harris, slowly turn us to port until I say 'stop.'"

I did just that, once again bringing our port "broadside" to bear on the enemy.

"She's still comin' at us — maybe, 75 or 50 yards out; now, she's veering away to her starboard," Harry shouted so Nigel could hear.

Wood chips and sparks flew around us, again.

At the same instant, Nigel's rifle responded and we

heard four booms from Richie's shot gun.

We were now heading slowly toward St. Thomas and the last position of the enemy. Harry got up and crouched over the radar.

"He's still turning to his starboard, stern toward us," he shouted. "He's headin' back toward shore; now turning to his port, coming back – looks like he wants to run across our bow. He's speeding up."

"Cap," Nigel yelled back to us. "Wait two minutes. Then, slowly turn to our starboard."

I could see Nigel's strategy now. Whenever the enemy was speeding up and committed to a course trying to cross our bow or stern, we'd slowly turn at the last minute so our port side firearms could open up.

Harry was kneeling over the radar, as I turned us to starboard.

"They're comin' at our port side now – 50 yards out," Harry yelled.

One, two, three, four booms from Richie and another burst from Nigel met them. Richie and Nigel were aiming at their wheel house, which they could now clearly see.

More sparks and chips flew in the air across our deck. Laying down and firing over the bulwark, Richie and Nigel poured more fire into their fiberglass wheel house; must look like Swiss cheese by now, I thought.

"Still comin'," Harry yelled. "Twenty-five fuckin' yards. I don't believe it. She's slowed and veer'in a bit to her starboard, now wobbling back to port; comin' toward us again."

The spitting of Bronco and Keithley's pistols had joined Richie's booms and Nigel's bursts, as the *Black Knight* fired her full broadside. Despite the gentle breeze, which had kept us all cool, I now smelled something like the odor of fireworks.

By now, our target was actually below *Black Knight's* much higher side. Our guys could fire down into her.

A few wood chips and sparks flew off our masts and

booms as those on the motor boat fired upward. But, they couldn't hit anything on our deck firing up at that angle. Our guys were returning fire, reloading, and firing more.

"She's slowed considerably, but still comin'," Harry yelled. "God, she's going to hit..."

An ear splitting, grating concussion knocked Harry and I flat to deck. Fortunately, our shooters had already been flat. I crawled around the deck house and looked forward. Some smoke was coming up from below our port side. Nigel, Bronco and Keithley were picking themselves up and staggering bent over with firearms ready as they cautiously looked over the bulwark at the enemy boat. Richie and Kwame were out of sight.

Nigel fired a burst of what must have been 50 bullets downward. Keithley opened fire with his pistol. Bronco looked down very carefully, took aim and fired five shots. We could hear some screams, but couldn't tell where they were coming from.

The booms from Richie's shotgun were noticeably absent. I worried about what was happening up there. I crawled on the deck to look past the wheel house. Smoke billowed up from the enemy below us. Neither Richie nor Kwame were visible. Oh shit, I thought.

No time to think, though. Now I was hearing a sickening, scraping, rumbling sound moving slowly from amidships toward our stern.

Nigel ran back to us, yelling to Harry to make speed.

"Get back on the wheel, Professor!"

The scraping sound was the metal equivalent of fingernails on a blackboard – piercing. In this case, it was their fiberglass hull on our steel side.

Nigel pointed his rifle downward and opened fire again. Bronco came back to join Nigel in shooting downward. Keithley came back, as well, and reopened fire. The scraping sound neared our stern.

"Get down, Cap and you too, Professor," Nigel shouted.

Harry and I dropped to the deck. We could just see a splintered, crushed fiberglass bow section drifting by. What was left was folded back like an accordion. Their boat was listing hard to stern; wheel house nearly cut in half; cabin afire. In the darkness and with all the smoke we could see no men on board her. I did see some fluorescent orange forms floating around the wreck; probably men in life jackets. Bronco aimed and squeezed off another couple shots.

"Cease fire," Nigel said.

Black Knight quickly left the wreck astern. Nigel was now crouching on the transom, rifle still aimed at them in case another burst hit us. Clearly, though, they were finished.

Harry and Bronco went below with flashlights. *Black Knight's* hull was sound, though dented inward about an inch around sea level amidships on the port side.

When they appeared, Harry was visibly relieved.

"No problems. We can simply bang it back out; sure as hell pays to have steel."

Harry laughed and said, "One time a drunk kid in a fiberglass speedboat hit us off the Soggy Dollar bar on Jost Van Dyke. He sank, but we didn't have hardly a scratch. I fished him out and took him to the beach."

Then, Harry called everyone aft. Aside from Richie, who'd gotten a teak splinter in his upper arm from a blown-off piece of railing, no one was hurt. It was a miracle.

Kwame had been tending to Richie under cover before the enemy made its final assault.

"I'm okay, no big deal," Richie said, smiling. "We sure showed them they can't fuck with Coral Bay!"

"Take it easy; darn lucky it didn't pierce the axillary artery," Kwame said. "It's going to hurt. Keith, give him that Pusser's bottle."

"Aye, 'e needs it."

By now, we were all standing around the wheel house, relieved, laughing – filled with the curious mirth of survivors – and suddenly very tired.

"T'is a miracle, it is," Sir Keithley said. "They never 'ad a chance, really."

"Right you are Keith," Nigel replied, slapping him on the back. "Your first sea battle, my Lord. Congratulations."

"Thank ye; thank, ye. T'was bloody grand!"

I looked at my watch. It was only 3 am. Amazing. The fight had seemed like hours and hours.

"A little too much like shooting fish in the barrel there at the end," I said, thinking of Bronco carefully taking aim and firing downward until there were no more targets.

"Professor," Nigel said, turning so he could address everyone. "These people are professionals – for-hire mercenaries, probably with African and Middle East combat experience; working for whoever the 'ell pays 'em most – oil companies, African dictators, drug cartels and sod knows who else. What would 'ave 'appened to us if they'd taken this ship?"

No one answered.

"I'll tell you, they would 'ave 'erded us down below under guard, taken this boat out to sea, met up with a larger ship, unloaded all the treasure, then scuttled *Black Knight* in deep water with all of us locked below. Lost without a trace, we'd be."

"Who were they?" Kwame asked.

"Bet they were hired by Seahawk, Inc. to get the treasure and pay us back for their trawler," Harry said.

I thought about my run-in last year with mercenaries – they were killers rented out for a fee by the Houston-based oil and military services conglomerate, Harlingen Corp. They made billions in the Iraq and Afghan wars with their thugs earning a reputation for ferocity bordering on sadism. Could it have been them?

My musings had been correct. Seahawk Enterprises,

Inc. had hired Harlingen to acquire the treasure from us. The *Harly 5*, a 44-foot, fast-response boat designed for military and law enforcement, had come to get it from Puerto Rico where Harlingen protected a pharmaceutical factory. Special mercenaries with Middle East experience had been flown in to board us, take the loot and dispose of us.

The night of our sea battle, though, we could only guess who are protagonists had been.

"I agree with Harry," I said. "They must work for Seahawk. They're the only ones who know about the *Mersey* and our trip to Sombrero."

Nigel cleared his throat loudly to get our attention.

"Now then, gents, we must get our stories straight."

We all stood still, listening. It sure paid to have a Royal Marine Sergeant Major on board.

"As far as the women know, we spent an uneventful night in Coral Bay. We'll simply arrive at the car ferry dock this morning as planned."

"Richie, here, hurt 'is arm working moving treasure," Sir Keithley suggested. "Am I right, lads?"

"Yes," we all yelled in chorus.

"We banged the side of *Black Knight* when we hit that new, metal channel buoy off Chocolate Hole," Harry offered.

"That's right, boyos. Quite right," Nigel agreed. "That's the Gospel for this 'ere night. Now, let's clean up all these bullet shells and toss 'em over the side; same with the wood chips, glass and other useless stuff."

Cleaning up settled us down. As we passed Little James island to port, Harry slowed the boat to a crawl and suggested we all take a rest. The current was gently taking us toward the St. John car ferry port. We had plenty of time to get there.

By daylight, we were entering the large lagoon that is called Enighed Pond – really a somewhat narrow, deep bay used as our car ferry and "industrial" port. We brought *Black Knight* to the cement deep water embankment, parking her next to the old island car ferry *Roanoke*.

A relic that would be welcome in any maritime museum collection, the *Roanoke* was having some serious engine trouble and other chronic problems. Mechanics worked on her mighty, 50- year-old diesel while welders and riggers worked to repair her car ramp.

Waiting for us on the embankment were a variety of birdwatchers' pick-up trucks and aging Suzuki Samurai cars. All were suitably dented and rusted. As Mary says, "You can't have nice things on this island."

We had already figured out an equitable distribution of the loot. As president of the Society, I'd get the biggest share. As co-equal, senior vice-presidents, Harry and Kwame would get the next biggest shares. And, following traditional buccaneer articles of service, the other crew would divide up the remainder of the loot evenly. Everyone had earned their shares. All were happy.

Dripping with sweat and exhausted by the past 24 hours of exhilaration, fear, hell and hard labor, I briefly recalled my plan to contact Her Majesty's Receiver of Wrecks to declare our find and set aside a portion for them. "Fuck that!" I shouted out loud.

Working under cover of tarps, the cargo was off loaded onto pick-ups and SUVs, which made round-trip runs to various residences and hiding places. Mary reminded me we had an unused cement cistern from a previous structure on our property. We'd always meant to hook it up to our working cistern to double our water supply. Now we had a better use for it – a secure vault for our portion of the booty.

Everyone was exhausted by 10 pm that evening. But, we'd successfully emptied the *Black Knight* of its cargo. It had been a most remarkable night.

No one needed to tell members of our Society the importance of "omerta." The Coral Bay boating community lived and thrived under a code of silence.

The next challenge was how to turn this historic treasure into usable money.

12 DOING THE LAUNDRY

"Why bother with investment theory? Theory. We hated
it in college. What practical use would the Pythagorean
Theorem or Deconstructionism have in our daily lives?"

— question posed by Morningstar's online "Portfolio 500
Investment Classroom."[1]

Gold was $1,200 per ounce. Silver sold for about
$20 an ounce. We had hundreds of pounds of
both, including rare Double Eagle $20 gold coins
minted during the California Gold Rush. We also had
vintage Mexican Republican silver pesos from the mid-
19th century. Hell, we even had a couple of buckets of
silver Danish West Indian rigsdaler and daler coins. And,
then there were the gold bars.

But, we couldn't buy anything with any of it. How
could we sell the loot without raising suspicion? We
needed a way to launder it all. Unlike South American
drug lords, however, we lacked obliging international
bankers.

Every member of our Bird Watchers' Society had the
same problem. Before doing anything, we agreed to meet

after all had rested up. Then, we'd meet to discuss it all.

The next evening, a party was held on the *Black Knight*, safely back on her mooring.

"We can't simply start selling it *en masse*," I explained . "That would be too suspicious. We need to find several numismatic dealers and traders in gold and silver; then feed them items slowly in small quantities over time."

"Numis what?" Sir Keithley asked.

"Coin collectors and dealers. We can't give them the true source of our booty. We need to seek out small dealers who won't ask too many questions about the provenance."

"You mean fences ?" Bronco asked, confirming my impression of his background. But, he'd risked life and liberty for Harry and the rest of us. That was good enough for me.

"For lack of a better term, yes, Bronco. But these are people who specialize in rare coins, gold and silver."

"Ought to be businesses like that in San Juan, Miami and New York," Harry said.

" 'ow about right 'ere in Tortola?" Sir Keithley asked. "The BVI is quite a tax 'aven, now. Even bloody Russians park money there."

"True enough, Keithley," I said. "You're still a British citizen, right? And, you Nigel?"

"Quite, right, sir."

"Good, that may come in handy. I guess we need to *carefully* ask certain people we might know how to manage our investments. Also, we can do discrete online searches."

"We must find several buyers to avoid overloading one," Harry pointed out.

We agreed to start looking and meet again in a week. Needless to say, we were all very frustrated, though amazed at what we'd accomplished.

John, of course, was well aware that we'd come home with a pirate treasure. It was hard to explain why it was all hidden.

"It's like the Native American or Danish artifacts dug up on the Virgin Islands, John," I explained over dinner. "It takes a while to find out who legally owns them. Then, we decide what we're supposed to do with them."

"Who did the stuff we found at Sombrero belong to?"

"Good question. Back in 1866, I believe most of the stuff we found belonged to Mexican president Santa Anna."

"But, he was a murderer and bad guy," John responded.

"Yes, he was and he's long dead. And all the money he had was stolen from other people. Most of the American gold coins we found came from the U.S. Government to pay for the Gadsden Purchase."

"Then who owns it now?"

"Another good question. We may own it, but we have to figure out some legal things. Meanwhile, don't say a word to anyone about our Sombrero adventure or the historical artifacts we found."

"What's the Gadsden Purchase?" he asked next.

"Go Google it on your lap top," Mary told him. "That was something you were supposed to learn in American History."

While he was working on that, Mary and I went to the porch to admire the evening birds and bats. Bats can eat as many as 1,000 mosquitoes an hour, so we'd all learned to love them.

"You know, Harris, weren't you intending to report the treasure recoveries to the Queen's Receiver of Wrecks and then see what happens? This treasure is becoming a burden. It's scary. We don't want to deal with fences or crooked coin dealers."

She didn't have a clue just how scary it was.

"Yes, declaring it to Her Majesty's Receiver of Wrecks was my plan. But, I had no idea then how much we'd find and how many people we'd need to get involved. You know, the Royal family has a half billion dollars in assets and makes millions more from rents and the British Government. They don't need Santa Anna's blood money."

"Still," Mary insisted, "we could legally report it and then receive a good portion back after they decide ownership. That's how you explained it before."

"Yes, but, they would hold it for a year to see if any other claims turned up. If somebody does claim it, we don't have the money to hire British lawyers to fight for it."

Mary thought a moment. "Couldn't Sam help us?"

Quite frankly, I'd forgotten about Samuel, our older son. A lot had happened since I last spoke with him about the Chiclet factory in Queens. Mary was correct to think of him. He was an attorney working as a trial lawyer for a New York plaintiffs firm. He'd gone to New York Law School and was moving ahead nicely in a tough career.

"Jeez, he just made junior partner," I replied. "You really think this is the kind of case his senior partners would approve of?"

"There's money involved," Mary said, laughing.

"Yes, that's another thing," I replied. "His firm would take a healthy percentage.

"Beyond possible legal problems, we need to think about the other birdwatchers who helped us," I continued. "They deserve to be paid.

"Plus, reporting it to the UK could open up a whole new set of problems here. There could be taxes, customs duty and who knows what else."

"Who knew this could be so worrisome?" Mary asked.

"Too bad we can't just sail to Port Royal, Jamaica and buy up land with the loot like Sir Henry Morgan did."

"Things were simpler back in buccaneer days," Mary agreed. "Well, we don't have to decide all this right now; let's catch up on the news."

We were now on the couch. Mary was reading newspapers as I searched online for rare coin and antiquities dealers on my lap top.

"Harris," she interrupted. "Listen to this item from St. Thomas Source:

> *The US Coast Guard reports that wreckage of a 44-foot power boat class frequently used by military and law enforcement agencies was found washed up in Christmas Cove on Great St. James island. Four men appearing to be in their 30s were found dead nearby. Two other men were alive, but seriously injured. They were taken to Schneider Hospital in St. Thomas in critical condition, then airlifted to Puerto Rico. The boat, Harly 5, was registered in P.R. to Harlingen Corp. Authorities refused to answer further questions."*

So, it was those bastards after all.

"Boy," I said. "Sounds like a drug deal or something gone bad. We know Harlingen works with anyone who'll pay their price. Maybe those mercenaries were helping one of the drug cartels with security; could have been a falling out among thieves and Harlingen's boys lost."

"Yes, despite it being paradise, this can be a very rough part of the world."

To my relief, Mary let the subject drop.

It was now late July. I needed to go back to my College office on St. Thomas to get ready for the fall term. It would take my mind off our more pressing problems.

Back at the office, though, I was still struggling with the treasure dilemma. There remained time to report it to the Brits. Would the other Society members go for it? What if we went back to the *Mersey* for more? We could then report that find as though it was our first.

It was all getting complicated and troubling.

The phone rang.

"Dr. Harris speaking," I answered, my mind adrift elsewhere.

"Ah, my good doctor. How are you today?"

"Very well, Commander Taft," I was actually happy to hear his voice. He sounded jovial. "To what do I owe the honor of your call?"

"I thought you'd like to learn that while in USVI waters the *R/V Seahawk* illegally dived on a U.S. Naval vessel of Civil War vintage. It was a supply ship, the *Susquehanna* captured by Confederate Captain Rafael Semmes off St. Croix. She was carrying copper from an Argentine mine bound for Connecticut munitions factories.

"Semmes took her without a fight and put on board a prize crew to sail her and her captured men to St. Thomas. He'd planned to set the Union crew free and sell the boat and cargo. But, the *Susquehanna* sank in a storm."

I cringed at his mention of the *Seahawk*. I thought back to Kwame discussing satellite surveillance on our way back from Sombrero. Did they know? If so, what would they do to us?

"Very interesting, Commander," I replied, keeping calm. "I know a bit about Semmes' adventures, but hadn't heard about that."

"He left *Susquehanna* out of his memoirs and scratched it from the log. It was too embarrassing. Fortunately, the crew did make it to St. Thomas in open boats and the Danes turned them all over to the U.S. Counsel in Charlotte Amalie. He reported everything to Secretary Seward, who noted it for the record."

I was asking myself when Taft would bring up Sombrero.

"Fascinating," I said. "But, how did *Seahawk* learn about the boat?"

"Probably studied the Alabama Claims submitted by Seward to the British. The *Susquehanna* and her copper cargo were listed, I believe."

"Copper prices are high right now, Commander."

"Indeed, Professor. And, being greedy, that young hedge fund billionaire who owns most of Seahawk Enterprises decided to locate and drop by the *Susquehanna* while en route to Anguilla for another big prize. He was preceded by a Seahawk scout boat that somehow became disabled at sea. It was towed to St. Martin. Now, it's awaiting delivery of a new engine."

"Serves 'em right. I don't much like corporate treasure hunters. They destroy historically significant wrecks. All they care about is loot."

"We agree. That's why we recently tightened the rules governing salvage of U.S. Naval vessels and even foreign military ships wrecked in U.S. waters."

"I've read about it. It's all good. So what will happen to Seahawk?"

"We discovered artifacts from the *Susquehanna* on board *R/V Seahawk*. They will pay a hefty fine and, more importantly, be barred for two years from any salvage of U.S. or foreign naval vessels in U.S. waters.

"But, there's more. When we told our British cousins about it, they barred Seahawk from their territorial waters for two years."

"What a shame. But, I guess the hedge fund kid has plenty of money to tide him over."

"Not as much as he had. When news of the actions against Seahawk became public, its stock price plummeted. Think about it. They're now banned from seeking any war vessels including sunken Spanish galleons in Florida waters and much of the Caribbean. Two years is a long time for Wall Street analysts to watch a company sit still."

"Well, that is good news. Glad to see the Feds won a fight against corporate greed."

"I thought you'd appreciate that. Speaking of unsavory businessmen, that was fascinating news about those Harlingen mercenaries. They could have been old 'friends' of yours," Taft said with a touch of wry humor.

Shit, I thought. Does he know the whole story of *RMS Mersey*?

"Here's the real reason I called. I understand you may need a discrete commodities broker. I have contacts at a company that knows how to handle delicate assets. For a percentage, they can take care of everything – paperwork, tax issues, legal matters, everything."

Huh? Were they going to bail us out?

"Could that 'company' be based in Langley?"

"You know, I am in intelligence and know good people in several agencies."

"That's very, very interesting. Why would they want to help with my investment portfolio?"

"First, the Navy takes care of its friends – even you, Professor. There are people in that company who owe me a favor; plus they can make a few bucks off this under the table, off the books."

"Fascinating. That could be a big help. And, you'd be doing this out of friendship?"

"It's also come to my attention that in recent months, you've learned a very valuable historical research skill that helps you view the past; learned it so well that you may be the best in this highly specialized field."

"That's flattering, but I'm not sure where you're going."

"I'd like you and, if you wish, your new friend Kwame, to become independent consultants to us. The Navy has a long list of historic mysteries that could affect national security and it's time to clear them up. The Caribbean and South America would be wide open territory for your consulting firm."

Should I ask Taft about Kwame being a spy for him? Thinking quickly, I decided against it. That would be a question for Kwame himself. Meanwhile, I wasn't going to look a gift horse in the mouth.

"Well, I'll have to ask Mary about this," I replied. "I do still have a job at the College, you know."

"Harris, with the help of the investment advisor I have in mind, you and your family will be more than financially secure for the rest of your lives. I know you love the research side more than academic bureaucracy and teaching. Didn't they have the nerve to cut your pay?"

"Correct as usual, Taft."

"I thought so. Why don't I have Mr. Smith give you a

call about those commodities?"

"Can he also help my friends with their portfolios?"

"I'm sure he can."

"Well, first, I must talk this all over with Mary."

"Understood," he said.

Then, as an afterthought, he added, "Don't forget to wear that lucky Sombrero on your way home."

"Thanks, I will."

Clearly, he knew the whole story. It had to be Kwame.

That night, watching yet another gorgeous sunset on our porch, I briefed Mary on Taft's phone call.

"If you want to start a consulting firm, I think it's a good idea," she said. "And, I won't object to working with that company on our investments."

I was relieved.

"I have one condition," she warned. "We must sell *Perseverance*. After what we went through on the Sombrero trip, I don't want to go out on any more sailboats under 100 feet."

"Agreed."

From home I phoned Taft on his secure line.

"Mary agreed. Harris and Associates is at your service."

"Splendid, Professor. Mr. Smith will be in touch directly. I'll phone at some point soon to go over possible consulting assignments."

Next, I called Kwame and arranged a meeting next morning on the benches overlooking the National Park Service dock. It was the spot we had agreed so long ago to work together under Captain Morgan's rules.

With the sun just appearing over the mountains behind Cruz Bay, I walked along the harbor and saw Kwame sitting on the bench. I didn't know whether to be angry or relieved that he had proven to be a sort of guardian angel.

We each nursed a cup of coffee as we exchanged pleasantries. I got down to business.

"I spoke with Commander Taft yesterday," I said, looking him in the eye. "He knew everything about our research, the treasure hunt and our naval battle."

To his credit, Kwame nodded and smiled.

"How did he know all that?" I asked.

"My auntie says, 'alligator lay egg, but him no fowl.' What she means is that things are not always as they seem." As he spoke, he leaned back on the bench and stretched his legs, sipping coffee.

"What's that supposed to mean?" I asked, growing agitated.

"It means that Commander Taft had a hunch that you would be interested in remote viewing and would want to try it. If you did, he wanted me to train you, if I thought it wise."

"Just as I thought. You tricked me!"

"No Professor. No. *You* came to me and asked for remote viewing help. I was content to have a comfortable retirement and try to forget it all."

I couldn't argue. I had pursued him.

"That's true. But, then you obviously kept Commander Taft informed."

"I did. It was out of loyalty to him and concern for you. I'd never done remote viewing work outside the safety of the Defense resource center and labs. The Commander reassured me that we could proceed so long as I kept a close watch on your vitals during your journeys. He also said you could be a very, very valuable asset should you prove skilled at remote viewing. The commander wanted to be kept informed. I saw no problem with that."

Everything he said did make sense.

"What if Taft had interfered with our treasure hunt and recovery?"

"He did not," Kwame said quietly.

It was true. No harm and a lot of good had come from his keeping Taft informed.

"We will soon be a hell of a lot wealthier," I said, pointing out the obvious. "I'm not ready to retire, though."

"I'm not either," he mused. "It would be too boring."

"Well," I replied, "we have an opportunity to do regular and, I'm sure, fascinating consulting work for the Navy. Are you interested in continuing our collaboration?"

Kwame thought for a few moments.

"It has been much more exciting than fishing and working on charters. Yes, I would like to continue working with you."

Sternly, I said, "I must remain in command and be the main point of contact with Taft, though. Please don't contact him without my knowledge. Okay?"

Kwame abruptly stood and saluted.

"Yes, sir, Captain."

I laughed.

"We don't need military discipline around here."

I did like the title, though. Years ago, "ship's captain" had popped out of a computer as one occupation suggestion following an employment aptitude test.

THE END

****

IF YOU'RE A FAN OF THE EXPLOITS OF PROF. HARRIS...

Don't miss Professor Harris' first adventure, **Undocumented Visitors in a Pirate Sea**, available on Amazon.com as paperback and Kindle.

Working for U.S. Naval Intelligence, intrepid maritime historian Thayer Harris, PhD, investigates the mysterious body of a Marine washed ashore on the Caribbean island of St. John. In the process, Professor Harris discovers a

60-year record of UFO activity in the Caribbean basin and high level abuses in Washington.

History and national security politics meet science fiction in this mystery grounded in exhaustive factual research and informed conjecture. Read Chapter One below.

Undocumented Visitors in a Pirate Sea
An Investigation of Certain Caribbean Phenomena by Dr. Thayer Harris

— Excerpt —

1 THE DEAD MAN'S CHEST

"The New Frontier is here, whether we seek it or not. Beyond that frontier are the uncharted areas of science and space, unsolved problems of peace and war, unconquered pockets of ignorance and prejudice."

— Senator John F. Kennedy, Democratic Party Presidential Nomination Acceptance Speech, July 15, 1960

Feet propped up on the gray, steel government-issue desk, sweat dripped from hands as I tapped on the keyboard. A whirling, humming ceiling fan did little to cool the room. Lethargically, I was fine-tuning lecture notes for the next term. But the view of the palm-fringed beach down the hill from my office was more enticing than struggling for new anecdotes and humor to engage students in Caribbean Maritime History 101. Sailboats swinging in unison to their moorings, as a breeze propelled white clouds across an azure sky and turquoise bay, were hypnotic.

Finally, drowsiness and a sinus headache caused, no

doubt, by various molds growing in the former Navy barracks housing faculty offices drove me outside. There a fresh wind and strong midday sun startled the neurons and synaptic clickings in the old memory banks and I was fully awake again – despite the heat and humidity.

Suddenly, remembering the day of the week and items on my calendar – a challenge at times in these slow, warm latitudes – I looked down the brick paths for my scheduled noon day visitor. It isn't every day the maritime history professor of the Territorial College of the Virgin Islands gets a visit from a U.S. Naval Intelligence officer. A glance at my watch revealed he was late and that was a good thing.

I had no idea why he was coming to visit me – Thayer Harris, a historian whose last significant research had been completed years earlier. That work, done back in Washington, D.C. when I was an American University post-doc adjunct professor, had concerned Cold War naval activity in the Caribbean. It had also covered the phenomena of unidentified submersible objects – still unexplained, still unidentified.

Now securely tenured, I was more interested in family, sailing and exploring sugar plantation ruins in Virgin Islands National Park than career development. My six foot, lanky (albeit, filling-out) frame and salt and pepper hair were easily recognizable to Park rangers.

While waiting, I surveyed the college grounds. Above the campus the mostly green mountain sides were speckled with brown and yellowing trees and bushes. With April already upon us, leaves were dying and dropping. Funny how "Fall" occurs in the Spring down here. Spent Bougainvillea flowers were falling, floating around lawns like crinkled pink, yellow, red and orange tissue paper. And, the first of the "mists" formed by Saharan dust carried across the Atlantic on the Trades had appeared just a week earlier. Today, though, was clear.

No question. Summer was approaching. Tourists and

snow birds were
flamboyant trees
The loud, cackling
with longer tail fe
gulls and terns w
north from where
of here.

As I watched
Ford SUV (the g
islands) drove thro
hill leading to the
Above these forme
officers' row of two

green plywood office and
"Are those from Ir
"Both, actually,
intelligence anal
and other mi
work at th
D.C."

the rest of our campus. The structures, built before World
War II, and the land under them were a post-Cold War gift
to the United States Virgin Islands from the United States
Navy.

On a hill overlooking the grounds, an old stone wind
mill testified to the 18th and 19th century years when the
principal islands of St Thomas, St John and St. Croix had
been colonized by Danish sugar planters, merchants and
traders (mostly Danish, Dutch and English) and
administered as the "Danish West Indies." In 1917, the
United States bought the islands for $25 million because of
their strategic location vis' a vis' the newly built Panama
Canal and north to south shipping lanes. St Thomas'
outstanding deep water harbor was a big plus and the
Navy built a formidable base and airport there.

The SUV arrived, parked in an oval of shade, and a
suitably clean-cut, 30-something man emerged. He quickly
climbed the steps to the History Department's lofty offices
where I awaited him on the stoop. A gold-plated belt
buckle and various badges glistened on his summer white,
short-sleeved uniform. He stopped and saluted.

"Dr. Harris, Sir?"

"Lieutenant Taft, I presume?"

With introductions over, I invited him into my pale

looked over his ribbons.

q or Afghanistan, Lieutenant?"

I did two tours based in Bahrain as an

st and managed a couple of fact-finding

sions in both Iraq and Afghanistan. Now I

e Office of Naval Intelligence in Washington,

had read about the rigors and perquisites of adquarters life in Bahrain – the Fifth Fleet's base and one of the wealthiest and most luxurious principalities in the world.

"Well Lt. Taft, what brings you from Washington to our humble tropical outpost? Not too many Pashtuns or muhjardins here. And, no sightings of Taliban naval craft that I know of. Still, plenty of sand."

He wasn't amused and we hadn't yet established eye contact. Without responding, he abruptly pulled a typed manuscript out of his brief case and plopped it on my desk.

Bloody hell! It was my paper on Unidentified Submersible Objects – USOs. No good would come from it, my wife Mary had warned years ago. Was she to be proven correct?

"Your former History Department chairman at American University had the sense to pass this on to the Office of Naval Intelligence. Thirty years ago, it was considered one of the more credible, objective analyses of these mysterious objects or craft. You mostly relied upon mainstream media reports and the few military officers and defense contractors who spoke about them. And, of course, the UFO buffs were sources. I gather that people spoke more openly about such things in those days."

Yes, I recalled vividly. People were more forthcoming back then, less worried about non-disclosure pacts and secrecy laws; and, of course, the abuse and ridicule associated with open discussions of USOs or UFOs had not yet been institutionalized in the media.

An image of Dr. Mecklenburg, American University's history department chairman, mailing my paper to Naval Intelligence came to mind. Or, perhaps, the wizened old academic merely ambled with his cane across campus on a nice day, traversing Ward Circle and Nebraska and Massachusetts Avenues to personally drop it off at Naval Intelligence offices. They were only a block from our campus, after all. Now the property has been subsumed by the Department of Homeland Security and the old Naval Observatory, a few blocks away, is the official home of U.S. vice presidents.

Like so many well educated white men of military age, good breeding, and above average intelligence in his era, Dr. Mecklenburg served as a naval officer during World War II – probably in intelligence, given his academic achievements. No doubt he kept-up his contacts in the "club" after the war.

But, Dr. Mecklenburg – God rest his soul – couldn't be faulted. And, Lieutenant Taft sitting here before me was both insightful and disarmingly forthright – a young innocent, perhaps. I thought of something to say about Dr. Mecklenburg's generation.

"People were more open and honest in the post-World War II years. Today, do we have anyone like Admiral Roscoe Hillenkoetter – an early CIA chief, for goodness sake – who publicly said UFOs are real and called for Congressional hearings? Or, would a British Admiral of the Fleet such as Lord Hill-Norton, the former head of the Ministry of Defence, today publicly say as he did that UFOs are real and then badger the House of Lords into holding a hearing on them, as they did? But, Admirals Hillenkoetter and Lord Hill-Norton were World War II vets and heroes. Not ones to be intimidated by bureaucratic functionaries or secret operatives."

"I agree, Professor. And, I learned about them in your paper."

"You're probably too young to have heard about the

UFO sightings by Presidents Jimmy Carter and Ronald Reagan. I bet those incidents never made it into your history books at Annapolis."

Having noticed his Naval Academy ring, I felt free to opine self-righteously.

"On the other hand, I'm sure you were taught that Jimmy Carter served in Admiral Rickover's nascent nuclear submarine service. The President was very proud of being a submariner."

"I knew President Carter was an Annapolis man and submariner, but must admit I had no idea he and President Reagan had witnessed UFOs," he said a little skeptically. "But, we did learn the protocols on how to deal with reports of unidentified flying or submersible objects, as I believe you know."

I did know the military once had instructions on how to handle sightings and reports, but was out-of-date on the details.

"I knew the Air Force and Navy had protocols, but heard they had been rescinded when researchers made them public. Are they, or revised versions, still 'operative', as you people say?"

"That's a question I am not at liberty to answer," he said off-handedly. "How did you learn of the Carter and Reagan sightings?"

"Well, Jimmy Carter told his story to several newsmen, freely admitting he had no idea what it was that he saw; but said he did see a maneuvering object in the sky. And, Ronald Reagan described his tale to no higher authority than the Washington bureau chief of The Wall Street Journal. Carter and Reagan were both governors when the incidents occurred, and, of course, they, too, were of a generation of leaders who spoke their minds. Right or wrong, you knew where they stood."

I made a note to myself to check on the details of the Carter and Reagan sightings. More information might now be available.

As I thought about the Presidents, I realized I had been rambling on, but still didn't know why the Lieutenant was sitting in my office.

"So, I assume you're here because of my paper."

"Yes, sir, I am. It's complicated. I'm investigating the death of a retired Marine Corps gunnery sergeant. His name is Roger Baskins, age 65, place of birth: Gulfport, Mississippi. His last base was Pensacola. His body washed up on St. John's East End on April 5th."

Since my family and I live on St. John, we knew about the body. In fact, we had actually seen the rescue squad and EMS Boston Whaler respond to its discovery out at the East End, where we happened to be snorkeling that day in Hansen Bay. Later, an ambulance boat brought the remains over to Charlotte Amalie, the capital of the US Virgin Islands on St. Thomas. That's where I work. I get a kick out of telling visitors from New York or Washington about my hellish commute. It's a ten minute jeep drive across National Park mountain ridges with majestic views on either side; then a 20 minute ferry ride to St. Thomas watching smaller mostly uninhabited islands slide by while sunning on the top deck.

I replied, "Yes, I heard a little about that, but no details. What does a deceased Marine have to do with me? Or, for that matter, a Naval Intelligence officer?"

"Sergeant Baskins was last seen alive on April 2nd on board the 'Willy T' – that floating bar in the harbor on Norman Island. Three days later his corpse was discovered in the rocks near St. John's Privateer Bay."

Ah, the Willy T! Formally known as the William Thornton, she's a 100-foot steel schooner anchored in The Bight, the sheltered harbor of Norman Island. She's served boaters' liquidity needs for decades. Willy was named for a Tortola planter, amateur architect and British citizen who improbably submitted the winning design for the United States Capitol building in 1792. George Washington himself praised the plan for its "grandeur, simplicity and convenience." For his effort, Thornton was awarded $500.

Today, we can only guess what Squire Thornton or President Washington would think of "Willy." When planning our first sailing trip from St. John to Norman Island, my wife looked up the floating bar on a travel advisory site and found a few indecorous reports. Allegedly, any woman who takes off her shirt and dives into the water from its pilot house is given a round of applause and a free T-shirt. Free drinks probably follow.

We deleted Willy from our itinerary on our first sail to Norman. In any event, rather than half-naked girls, Norman Island brings to my mind Long John Silver and his mates searching for treasure. Most consider the uninhabited British Virgin Island the model for Robert Louis Stevenson's "Treasure Island." Pirate loot was actually found there around 1800. We have snorkeled in the very sea caves where treasure was found hidden behind a false rock wall.

"OK," I said to the good Lieutenant. "I fully understand why a retired Marine would hang out at Willy's. But, surely this is a matter for BVI officials and the U.S. Virgin Islands Police Department."

"They have investigated it," Lt. Taft replied with a slight grimace contorting an otherwise well sculpted face. Had Taft been British, I'd have pegged him as an aristocrat.

"The problem is," he continued, "the Brits have no record of him entering the British Virgin Islands. We do know he flew to the US Virgin Islands. He caught a direct flight from Dulles airport in Washington, D.C. to St. Thomas on March 26th. That's ten days before he was found washed up on St. John. He has no family ties in D.C. or anywhere else that we could find. He received his pension and social security checks in a Northern Virginia post office box."

"It's not unusual for someone to 'forget' to clear B.V.I.

customs before visiting Norman," I observed. Since Norman is only a two hour sail from St John's Coral Bay, some people neglect to first make the longer trip to Tortola, the main BVI island, to clear customs and immigration. After all, the USVI and BVI are part of the same archipelago, separated only by the relatively narrow Sir Francis Drake Channel. My family, however, makes a point of clearing British customs first before venturing further in BVI waters. Penalties for customs violations can be stiff and include confiscation of your boat, if the Brits wish to make a point.

"So, some intrepid person must have sailed or motored directly to Norman Island with Sergeant Baskins aboard – they probably departed from Coral Bay," I continued.

"That's what the police believe, but no one has admitted taking him over and Virgin Islands Police Department has no budget or incentive to investigate further. The coroner ruled death by drowning with no evidence of foul play. We got involved because the Sergeant's only identification was his Vietnam War era dog tags and a fascinating tattoo on his chest: a disc-like image that looks like a flying saucer with "JFK 1971" beneath it. On his bicep was another tattoo - an anchor astride the world and 'Semper Fi'."

To say I was surprised would be an understatement. The Lieutenant handed me photos of the tattoos.

"JFK and a flying saucer? Could this guy have been a conspiracy nut and a UFO nut?"

As a conspiracy buff myself, I was enthralled by the possibilities. Fortunately, the sight of the tidy, earnest young man sitting opposite me arrested my wild speculations. There must be a plausible explanation for the Marine's pictogram.

"It *is* a very distinctive tattoo," I agreed. "And the dog tags. I assume some vets proudly wear their old tags as sort of souvenirs or good luck charms. And, we all know they like tattoos related to their service. JFK? My guess is he once served on the old aircraft carrier, the *U.S.S. John F. Kennedy.* Correct?"

"All true," confirmed Lieutenant Taft.

A wave of self-satisfaction washed over me. My Sherlock Holmesian deductions were on target and my interest in this matter was soaring.

The lieutenant continued, "Sergeant Baskins survived unscathed during two tours in Vietnam that included long range reconnaissance patrols into the highlands. They were the most dangerous missions of the war. He was then assigned to the *U.S.S. John F. Kennedy's* Marine detachment responsible for vessel security."

I had read of the horrors of long range recon patrols – vermin, poisonous snakes and centipedes, spiders, constant threat of ambush, heat exhaustion. Service on an aircraft carrier must have seemed like resort living by comparison.

"One question, lieutenant. If the dog tags were his only ID and he hadn't cleared BVI customs, how do you know Baskins was on Norman Island?"

"Elementary, my dear doctor!" He said it with good humor. "He paid his bill on the Willy T with a credit card that we easily traced. But, the card and a wallet he probably carried it in were missing when the body was found."

I was surprised Willy took credit cards.

"One other noteworthy point about the body – its pants zipper was closed. The Coast Guard tells us that many men fall off boats while in the act of relieving themselves over the side – particularly when intoxicated. But, the zipper was closed and an autopsy revealed he'd likely had only two or three beers, hardly enough to incapacitate an old Marine gunnery sergeant."

Fascinating about the zipper, I thought.

"So, what about the flying saucer, Lieutenant?" I asked

Taft actually squirmed in the straight backed, wooden chair as he looked over my desk, establishing direct eye contact for the first time.

"We're not sure. We believe it's possible that the saucer and even Sergeant Baskins' death are related in some way to his service on the *U.S.S. John F. Kennedy*, which was tattooed under the saucer as I said. During 1971, Baskins' tattooed year, the *Kennedy* was in the Caribbean and had even docked here in Charlotte Amalie at the old Navy yard. The crew enjoyed a 48 hour liberty during their week here."

"Why not just check the ship's logs and records?"

The lieutenant crossed and uncrossed his legs, seeming to be in pain as he explained.

"Part of the log for certain dates and hours during that cruise are highly classified. Worse, the only other related records I can find have been heavily redacted. Unfortunately, I am the only one assigned to this case and I don't have the clearance or rank to locate the original classified sections and unredacted docs, even if they could be found. Sadly, the Captain during that period who likely ordered the classifications – possibly after secure radiophone conversations with superiors – is deceased. Yet, reading between the lines, I conclude that something phenomenal happened to the ship in the Caribbean that year, but can't prove it."

Taft's problem was not as shocking as it might seem. In today's federal government, hundreds of millions of pages of documents have been classified. Millions more are added each year. With the deaths and retirements of senior military officers or government executives who may have witnessed "secret" events or collaborated in classifying incidents, orders or policy decisions, it's inevitable that some records evaporate from history – particularly when they date from pre-desktop computer and e-mail days.

"Let me make sure I understand this," I said. "You can't adequately investigate a retired Marine sergeant's death and resolve your suspicions about it because you, a commissioned intelligence officer in the U.S. Navy, are denied access to or can't find the Navy's own records?"

"That is correct."

"So, that brings us back to the flying saucer tattoo. You must think that is indelible evidence – so to speak – of a possible phenomenal event."

"That is correct and that's why I came to see you, Dr. Harris. Although it does appear to be a flying saucer, it could also be an unidentified submersible object. It is possible Sergeant Baskins may have witnessed or been involved in some way with a USO or UFO incident during the *U.S.S. John F. Kennedy's* 1971 Caribbean cruise."

"And, now you are interested in trying to recover that lost knowledge about the hypothetical incident. Is that it?"

"Yes. Several of us mid-level naval intelligence officers think its time we – I mean the Navy – seriously study and evaluate whatever evidence we *already* have in-house about UFOs and USOs. We might then build a case for more open reporting of these phenomena in the future. Some day we hope to bring in the broader scientific community to assist. The material could be provided to the President, as a possible prelude to public release."

A remarkable statement. And, if true, a very promising development.

"Quite laudable. But, where do I come in?"

"We liked your paper. Liked it enough for me to come down here with a proposal. It's now April 15. Your spring semester will soon be over. We'd like to give you a *sub rosa* grant to investigate Sergeant Baskins' last days, any links he and the *Kennedy* may have had to unidentified flying or submersible objects, and uncover any new or previously unreported evidence related to the phenomena."

"Interesting assignment," I replied, suppressing my excitement. "But, how do I get compensated?"

Also, would Mary give her blessing to such research?

"We believe the Annapolis Institute Press might be

persuaded to generously fund research into the role of the U.S. Navy during the Cuban Missile Crisis. Such funding would be more than sufficient for you to also investigate the more important subject at-hand."

"So, let me get this straight. I write an article on the Navy and the Missile Crisis and, at the same time, clandestinely investigate Sergeant Baskins, the *U.S.S. John F. Kennedy* and any UFO/USO connection?"

"Precisely, Dr. Harris."

My family had no definite plans for the summer break other than sailing, working on the house and avoiding hurricanes. Assuming the money was good, this sounded enticing.

"How 'generous' is the grant we are discussing?"

The grant, paid in monthly installments, was most generous – exceeding my salary – and one month would be advanced immediately.

"We would require regular progress reports sent directly to my attention and, at the end of four months, we will want a paper with your findings and conclusions. Of course, discretion is paramount."

As interesting as it sounded, I had to discuss it with Mary before accepting. And, it might be a hard sell.

"I must discuss this with my wife since it will affect our plans for the summer," I explained.

"By all means," the lieutenant replied, giving his cell phone number and the name of his hotel. I agreed to get back to him the next day.

That night, during cocktails on our deck while watching the sunset, I eased into the subject. Mary, a petite blonde with a big heart and strong mind, did voice misgivings about such research.

"What if the Dean heard you were studying UFOs? What would he or, for that matter, other faculty think?"

"This would be very confidential research for a reliably closed-mouth client," I assured her. "And, as far as anybody knows, I'm simply researching and writing an article for the Institute Press."

"Nothing is confidential on this island for long," she said. "You know what they say, 'if you don't know what you're doing, someone else does.' And, if it got out that you believe in these things, it could harm your reputation."

She had a point. Her justifiable concerns brought to mind the mixed feelings of one of the few journalists in recent years to study UFOs. In her well-regarded 2010 book, *UFO's: Generals, Pilots and Government Officials on Record*, Leslie Kean recalled that she was increasingly concerned about keeping her expanding interest in UFOs quiet:

"I began to feel as if I were covering-up something shameful and forbidden, like the use of an illegal drug . . . The subject carried a terrible stigma."[1]

I replied to Mary that my client had no interest what-so-ever in making this research public. She asked for a bourbon refill, took a sip and replied: "Well, everyone here knows you're a professor and somewhat eccentric."

"That's right, honey, and who on this island isn't eccentric?"

Finally, Mary agreed to my taking on the project, as long as I didn't talk about it outside our home and I kept her informed.

I phoned the lieutenant immediately.

"When do I start?"

"Not so fast," he intoned. "We need you to sign a non-disclosure agreement and   contract with the Institute to produce the Cuban Missile Crisis article. Fortunately, I happen to have both documents with me."

"Sounds like a done deal to me," I answered.

We met the next day over lunch at Tickles, a waterside bar and grill overlooking Crown Bay Marina and the new cruise ship docks and shopping complex. It was a highly appropriate venue. The Marina and cruise ship center had been carved out of the Navy's old docks, yards and even a submarine base.

That oversized concrete cruise ship dock, just a few hundred yards across the water from where we sat, was likely the very spot where the *U.S.S. John F. Kennedy* had once tied-up for liberty and re-supply.

The *U.S.S. John F. Kennedy* was a beautiful ship born in a poignant, family ceremony. Nine-year-old Caroline Kennedy had to swing the champagne bottle twice to break it across the bow and christen the *U.S.S. John F. Kennedy* on May 27, 1967 – two days before what should have been President Kennedy's 50th birthday.

Caroline's younger brother, John Junior; their mother, Jackie; uncles Ted and Bobby; and Aunts Joan and Ethel were all there. Even grandmother Rose attended.

As though it were the christening of an infant, the ceremony was overseen by clergy. In this case, Cardinal Richard James Cushing, Archbishop of Boston, who was no stranger to the Kennedy clan.

Aside from immediate family, John Glenn, the World War II Marine flying ace and pioneering astronaut attended the ceremony as did President Lyndon Johnson and Secretary of Defense McNamara.[2]

The largest and last U.S. aircraft carrier propelled by conventional power, the *U.S.S. John F. Kennedy* was built in Virginia by the Newport News Shipbuilding Company and officially entered service a year later in 1968 – the year Bobby Kennedy would be assassinated as his big brother had been.

The *Kennedy*, though, was just springing to life. Her eight petroleum-fueled boilers drove four propellers that pushed the ship at cruising speeds up to 34 knots. She measured 1,052 feet overall.

By comparison, with an overall length of about 652 feet, on her first and last voyage in 1912 – just 56 years before the *U.S.S. John F. Kennedy's* launch – the *R.M.S. Titanic* was driven by three propellers powered by 29 coal-fired boilers. She could only reach and maintain speeds of 21 knots.

When the *Kennedy* called at the port of Charlotte Amalie in 1971, she was virtually brand new. No doubt, Gunny Baskins and his buddies walked around joking and looking for bars and other diversions in the very waterfront neighborhood in which Lieutenant Taft and I sat talking and downing beers.

Back then, President Kennedy's roots as life-long sailor and combat Navy skipper were fresh in every seaman's mind. His comments on why the sea is so special to humans, delivered in Rhode Island in 1962 on the occasion of an America's Cup race, are hard to argue with or improve upon:

"I really don't know why it is that all of us are so committed to the sea . . . I think it is the fact that the sea changes and the light changes, and ships change; it is because we all came from the sea. And it is an interesting biological fact that all of us have in our veins the exact same percentage of salt in our blood that exists in the ocean, and, therefore, we have salt in our blood, in our sweat, in our tears. We are tied to the ocean. And when we go back to the sea, whether it is to sail or to watch it we are going back from whence we came."[3]

After long and eventful service, the *U.S.S. John F. Kennedy* was decommissioned in 2007 and now rests mothballed with the reserve fleet at the old Philadelphia Navy Yard. Many hope she will become a floating museum.

"So, Dr. Harris, just one final item," Lieutenant Taft said, interrupting my reverie. He opened his brief case and pulled out a USB device.

"Before you send me an email or open one of mine or send emails to third parties related to this case, please plug this encryption card into one of your USB ports," he explained, handing me the whirligig.

"A bit dramatic, don't you think?"

"It's standard practice in Naval Intelligence research. In fact, when you phone me, please use this number. It's a secure line. If I don't answer, feel free to leave a short message simply asking me to phone you."

I took his business card with the number written on the back and assured him I'd follow the procedure. Pure bureaucratic nonsense, I thought.

After Lieutenant Taft and I had shaken hands, I caught the ferry back to St. John. It struck me as ironic that I had to sign a non-disclosure agreement and conduct secret research to (hopefully) serve the cause of greater government transparency about UFOs in the future.

And, of course, even if I didn't honor the non-disclosure agreement, my work could still be very plausibly denied by the Navy as the product of a whacko academic. On paper, I was simply researching and writing a story on the history of the Cuban Missile Crisis. While exploring anything further, I was on my own.

Still, why not keep a log of this investigation? It might come in handy, serve as a useful record and help me sort out my thoughts as I proceeded. So, I started this narrative.

I had no idea then, just how dramatic and potentially dangerous this investigation would become.

NOTES: SANTA ANNA'S GOLD

Chapter 1: A Rebel Captain and Mexican Presidente

1. U.S. Naval History and Heritage Command, Naval History Foundation, 1968.
   http://www.history.navy.mil/research/library/online-reading-room/title-list-alphabetically/c/capt-semmes-css-alabama.html

2. http://www.wired.com/2009/05/pentagon-preps-soldier-telepathy-push/

3. "Psychic Warrior," by David Morehouse, East Sussex, U.K.: Clairview Books, paperback edition, 2004

4. U.S. Naval History and Heritage Command, op.cit.

5. "The Cruise of the Alabama and the Sumter, C.S.N.," Raphael Semmes and other Officers, assembled by Captain Raphael Semmes, published in London and New York, 1864, Chapter three, Project Gutenberg edition.

6. "The Death of Crockett," by Michael Lind, faculty member of Texas A& M University.
   http://www.tamu.edu/faculty/ccbn/dewitt/adp/archives/delapena/lind_crisp/lind.html

Chapter 2: Land Crabs Like Coffee, Captains Like Bitters

1. "Did Crabs Hide Amelia Earhart's Remains?" The Daily Mail, May 22, 2014
   http://www.dailymail.co.uk/sciencetech/article-2621610/Did-CRABS-hide-Amelia-Earharts-remains-Bizarre-experiment-prove-giant-crustaceans-scattered-aviators-body.html#ixzz3KTTJmHLv

2. "The Interesting Narrative of the Life of Olaudah Equiano Written by Himself," London, 1789. Project Gutenberg edition. Mr. Equiano later became a

freedman and a strong voice in London for abolition
of slavery.

3. http://www.cnn.com/US/Newsbriefs/9509/9-
21/am/index.htm.

4. http://www.mocavo.com/The-New-York-Times-
Volume-Xii/275817/102

5. "British Naval Policy in the Gladstone-Disraeli Era,
1866 -1880," by John F. Beeler, Stanford University
Press, 1997, page 12.

6. "William H. Seward: 1861 - 1872," by William Henry
Seward and Frederick William Seward, New York:
Derby and Miller, 1891. Internet Archive edition.

7. "Secretary Seward and Frederick Seward Continue to
Improve; Particulars of the Attempted Assassination,"
New York Times, April 20, 1865.

8. "Seward at Washington," by Frederick W. Seward,
New York: Derby and Miller, 1891. Internet Archive
edition.

9. "William H. Seward, 1861 – 1872," By William Henry
Seward and Frederick William Seward, New York,
1891, Google Books edition, page 306.

10. See Aimery Caron, "General Santa Anna in Saint
Thomas," an undated paper published in St. Thomas
at:
http://www.rootsweb.ancestry.com/~vicgl/Caron/Sa
ntaAnnaGenFinal.pdf .

11. Mike Whitelaw, faculty member, Texas A& M
University.
http://www.tamu.edu/faculty/ccbn/dewitt/adp/archi
ves/yellowrose/yellowrose.html

12. Texas State Historical Association:
https://www.tshaonline.org/handbook/online/article
s/xey01

13. "An Island of the Sea," by Charles Edwin Taylor,
MD, St. Thomas, D.W.I., 1893. Project Gutenberg
edition.

14. Aimery Caron, "General Santa Anna in Saint Thomas," op. cit.
15. "The Danish West Indies in Black and White," Enrique F. Corneiro, Triple E. Enterprise, Richmond, TX, 2012 edition, page 63.

Chapter 3: The Sea is a Harsh Mistress

1. Captain Samuel Bellamy, Geneology.com: http://www.geni.com/people/Capt-Samuel-Bellamy/6000000010763812170

Chapter 4: A Legacy of Chiclets

1. "The History of Chewing Gum and Bubble Gum, Part 2, Thomas Adams," About.com: inventors.about.com/library/inventors/bladams.htm
2. See Captain Samuel Bellamy, New England Historical Society, February 3, 2014. http://www.newenglandhistoricalsociety.com/black-sam-bellamy-pirate-fought-smart-harmed-scored-big/
3. See "El Presidente," by Clarence Wharton, 1924, as reproduced by Texas A & M University http://www.tamu.edu/faculty/ccbn/dewitt/santaanna3.htm
4. See "Santa Anna Did a Lot More Than Kill Davy Crockett," by Ramon Alcaraz, New York Press, September 10, 2002 http://nypress.com/santa-anna-did-a-lot-more-than-kill-davy-crockett/
5. "Could There be Proof We're All Psychic?" The Daily Mail, January 28, 2008. http://www.dailymail.co.uk/news/article-510762/Could-proof-theory-ALL-psychic.html
6. "Time Travel," PBS "NOVA" transcript of show aired October 12, 1999. http://www.pbs.org/wgbh/nova/transcripts/2612time.html

7. According to German physicist Serge Kernbach of the University of Stuttgart in his paper "Unconventional Research in Russia and the USSR," December 4, 2013. http://arxiv.org/pdf/1312.1148v2.pdf

8. "Voluntary Out-of-Body Experience: An fMRI Study," Journal of the Frontiers of Human Neuroscience, February, 2014 issue. http://journal.frontiersin.org/article/10.3389/fnhum.2014.00070/full]

9. The Daily Mail, op. cit. http://www.dailymail.co.uk/news/article-510762/Could-proof-theory-ALL-psychic.html

10. "Time Travel is Possible, Says Stephen Hawking," FOX News, May 3, 2010. http://www.foxnews.com/scitech/2010/05/03/time-travel-possible-says-stephen-hawking/

11. Forbes' ranking of pirates can be found at: http://www.forbes.com/2008/09/18/top-earning-pirates-biz-logistics-cx_mw_0919piracy.html

Chapter 5: First Space (Time) Shot

1. See Bridgeport Sunday Herald, August 18, 1901, page 5 http://www.gustave-whitehead.com/history/news-reports-1901-2-flights/1901-08-18-bridgeport-herald-p-5/

2. Anthony Trollope from his travelogue, "The West Indies and The Spanish Main," London: Chapman & Hall, 1859. Internet Archive edition.

3. "Reading the Enemy's Mind: Inside Stargate, America's Psychic Espionage Program," Paul H. Smith, New York: A Forge Book, 2005, Kindle edition, page 154. Mr. Smith was an accomplished remote viewer for the United States Army.

4. The store description is based in part on "Letters from the Virgin Islands: Illustrating Life and Manners in the West Indies," Anonymous, London: John Van Voorst, 1843, pages 4 - 8, Google e-book edition.

Most of Professor Harris' time travel experiences are based on 19th- century eyewitness accounts by travelers, contemporary newspaper stories and local historians.

Chapter 6: Dinner at the Commercial Hotel

1. See: "Baltimore Clipper Schooner 'Vigilant', " by Page W. Blytmann, Maritime Historical Society, 1998. http://www.blytmann.com/vigilant.htm   The much loved *Vigilant* was described by several 19th century travelers to St. Thomas.

2. Lyrics from "Mama Lisa's World," International Music and Culture, Caribbean Children's Song: http://www.mamalisa.com/?t=es&p=638&c=77 .

3. The serving techniques, foods served and dining experience is based in part on a description of dining in St. Thomas at an unnamed hotel during the 1850s by Anthony Trollope in his travelogue, "The West Indies and Spanish Main," op cit.

Chapter 7: A Bit of a Breeze

1. The *Vice Gouverneur Berg* and other descriptions of St. Thomas harbor are based in-part on "Management of the Port of Saint Thomas, Danish West Indies," by Erik Goebel, The Northern Mariner, October, 1997 http://www.cnrs-scrn.org/northern_mariner/vol07/tnm_7_4_45-63.pdf

2. See: Charles Kingsley, "At Last: Christmas in the West Indies," Macmillan & Company, London, 1872, Project Gutenberg edition, page 12, for the coal women's song and harbor scenes, and Maturin M. Ballou, "Equatorial America," Houghton Mifflin & Company, Boston and New York, 1892, Project

Gutenberg edition, chapter one, for harbor scenes and a description of the St. Thomas coal women. Many other eye-witnesses comment on their unique work.

3. The *RMS Mersey* is fictional, but based on other Royal Mail Service steamships calling at St. Thomas during the 1850s and 60s, particularly, the *RMS Paramatta* and *RMS Douro*. All other named ships described in the harbor during and after the hurricane are accurate, based on eyewitness accounts and news reports.

4. For more on the floating dock, see "Management of the Port of Saint Thomas," op. cit. On the wrecks gathered around the floating dock, see: "St. Thomas Wrecks," Harpers Weekly, December 28, 1867.

5. For history of Hassel Island, see St. Thomas Historical Trust and Virgin Islands National Park http://www.hasselisland.org/

6. http://www.hasselisland.org/sites/creque-marine-railway/

7. The term "cocktail" referencing a mixed alcoholic drink was first used in the United States in "The Farmer's Cabinet" magazine in 1803, Wikipedia informs us. Other sources tell us that gin and bitters were a favorite 19th century cocktail in the tropics.

8. "West Indies: Terrible Tornado, Hundreds of Lives Lost," New York Sun, November 5, 1867.

Chapter 8: A Poop Port in a Storm

1. "Medical Journal for *HMS Doris*, 1 January to 31 December, 1867," National Archives of the United Kingdom, http://discovery.nationalarchives.gov.uk/hbrowse?id=C4107375.

2. A New York World newspaper correspondent arrived in St. Thomas October 30, 1867 the day after the San Narciso Hurricane. He described much of the harbor destruction including the apparent "hurricane party" on King's Wharf. See: "The Scene at St. Thomas

After the Storm," The Sacramento Union, December 13, 1867, page one.

3. An authoritative description of the loss of the *RMS Wye* and *RMS Rhone* and general destruction in Road Town, Tortola and St. Thomas harbor can be found in a report by Captain Charles Vesey of the *HMS Doris*, November 3, 1867. His report can be found in several sources including:
    http://www.aquaventurebvi.com/account-vessey.html.

4. Details on destruction in the harbor and fates of specific vessels can be found in the Sacramento Union story (op. cit), and "Disaster and Disruption in 1867 in the Danish West Indies; A Collection of Accounts and Reports," compiled by Roy A. Watlington and Shirley H. Lincoln, University of the Virgin Islands, East Caribbean Center, 1997.

5. For an authoritative account of the life and death of the *RMS Rhone* and her final minutes, see: "Black Rock and Blue Water: The Wreck of the Royal Mail Ship Rhone in the San Narciso Hurricane of October, 1867," by Andrew C. Jampoler, Naval Institute Press, Annapolis, MD, 2013, Kindle Edition, Location 919.

6. See
    https://www.law.cornell.edu/uscode/text/48/1411

7. "Negro Insurrection on a Guano Island; Overseer Fatally Injured," New York Times, August 13, 1860.
    http://www.nytimes.com/1860/08/13/news/negro-insurrection-on-a-guano-island-an-oversker-eatally-injured.html

8. "The History of Underwater Exploration," by Robert F. Marx, General Publishing Company, Toronto, 1990, Chapter 5, "Diving with a Helmet."

Chapter 9: "Villainous Rascals"

1. John Richard Stephens, editor, "Captured by Pirates: 22 First Hand Accounts," Fern Canyon Press, Cambria, CA, paperback, 1996, p. 18.
2. See NOAA hurricane history: ftp://ftp.ngdc.noaa.gov/hazards/publications/Ref053 7_lander.pdf
3. "Disasters and Disruption in 1867," op. cit., page 48.
4. For more on the Crown's "Receiver of Wrecks" and British salvage law, see: https://www.gov.uk/wreck-and-salvage-law

Chapter 10: Coral Bay Birdwatching Society's Field Trip

1. Downloaded April 28, 2015 from http://www.backyardnature.net/birdlist.htm.
2. See "Quotable Sailors": http://www.ybw.com/forums/showthread.php?7202 8-Quotable-Sailors#dL7fQKYqCAHZbvDh.99
3. See declassified OSS World War 11 handbook: https://www.cia.gov/news-information/featured-story-archive/2012-featured-story-archive/CleanedUOSSSimpleSabotage_sm.pdf)

Chapter 11: Additions to Our Life Lists

1. See U.S. Naval Heritage and History Command: http://www.regulations.gov/#!documentDetail;D=U SN-2011-0016-0001 ; and, http://www.bloomberg.com/bw/articles/2014-05-05/treasure-hunters-undersea-gold-rush-threatened-by-u-dot-s-dot-navy

2. Northern Ireland revolutionary song can be found at several sources including http://www.eirefirst.com/archive/songchords.html#armalite

Chapter 12: Doing the Laundry

1. http://news.morningstar.com/classroom2/course.asp?docId=4494&page=1&CN= , downloaded April 28, 2015

Santa Anna's Gold in a Pirate Sea

ABOUT THE AUTHOR

For more than 30 years, Jeffrey R. Mc-Cord has been a free-lance journalist and public relations/public affairs consultant in Washington D.C. and New York City. Trained as an economist and historian, his by-lined work has appeared in *The Wall Street Journal*, *Barron's*, *USA-UK Magazine*, the South Jersey *Courier-Post* (a Gannett newspaper) and the online publications *Truth Out*, *Angry Bear* and *The Activist Post*. He has also published a blog, *The Investor Advocate*, promoting greater legal protections for U.S. consumers and investors.

Mr. McCord and his family now divide their time between Virginia and the United States Virgin Islands.

Photo by Alice Gebura